## ALSO BY VALERIE BOWMAN

# Kiss Me at Christmas

## VALERIE BOWMAN

St. Martin's Paperbacks

KISS ME AT CHRISTMAS

Copyright © 2018 by June Third Enterprises, LLC.

All rights reserved.

For information address St. Martin's Press, 175 Fifth Avenue, New York, NY 10010.

ISBN: 978-1-250-14752-3

Our books may be purchased in bulk for promotional, educational, or business use. Please contact your local bookseller or the Macmillan Corporate and Premium Sales Department at 1-800-221-7945, ext. 5442, or by e-mail at MacmillanSpecialMarkets@macmillan.com.

Printed in the United States of America

St. Martin's Paperbacks edition / November 2018

St. Martin's Paperbacks are published by St. Martin's Press, 175 Fifth Avenue, New York, NY 10010.

10  9  8  7  6  5  4  3  2  1

For my aunt, Constance Gale Bowman, who is wise, funny, and independent.

My aunt is a retired naval officer who loves softball, cats, and seafood. I have always loved and admired her. She's also the only person in the world who sounds and talks like my late dad, so it's always a pleasure to hear her voice.

It's an honor to be named after her . . .
Valerie Gale Bowman.

# ACKNOWLEDGMENTS

First, I'd like to thank Jenny Simon for the second and third lines in this book. I love them! Thank you to Holly Ingraham, my longtime editor at St. Martin's Press; Jennie Conway, for all of your help; and my new editor, Alex Sehulster, for making the transition smooth.

Thanks as always to Mary Behre, Virginia Boylan, and Jamie Smith Disterhaupt, the best first readers an author could have.

Finally, thank you to my agent, Kevan Lyon, for your guidance and support.

# Kiss Me at Christmas

# CHAPTER ONE
### London, December 1818

Lady Regina Haversham's thirtieth birthday was precisely one month away, which didn't leave her much time to lose her virginity. Not that she wanted it lost. She wanted to know where it went and choose to whom she gave the dratted thing.

Her coach came to a stop in front of the offices of the Bow Street Runners in central London, and she drew in a deep, unsteady breath. She pressed her hands deeper into the white fur muff that sat atop her lap and willed her pounding heart to slow its nervous beat. Christmastide was her favorite time of year. She was in high spirits, but she was also as nervous as a young lady making her debut on her way to see the queen. This particular outing had every chance to end in disaster.

She glanced out the window. She probably should have hired a hackney. It would have been less conspicuous than her uncle's resplendent coach. There were already several on-lookers staring up at the black-lacquered conveyance with

the Duke of Colchester's seal on the side. She glanced down
at her clothing. No doubt her ensemble was too elegant for
marching into the offices of the best private investigative
team in London, but she had no other clothing to wear, and
this particular message was best delivered in person. She
didn't know Daffin Oakleaf's home address, and she hardly
thought a note to him for what she had in mind would be ap-
propriate. No. Regardless of the stares, she had to see him in
person.

Regina had settled on the perfect birthday gift to herself.
She would spend the night with a man. Not just any man. The
finest candidate. One who had the face and body of a Greek
god. Thirty years old. Tall, fit, and handsome. Blond hair
and green eyes that held a twinkle she found irresistible.
She'd met him last summer at her uncle's estate. Her family
had been gathered there for the unfortunate purpose of her
cousin, the marquess's, funeral. John had been murdered,
and inappropriate or not, the man Regina had come to covet
was the Bow Street Runner who'd helped investigate his
murder.

She hadn't seen Daffin since he'd left the estate that hot
July day taking away the two murderers in shackles. Rarely
a day passed since that Regina didn't think of him. She'd
read about him in the paper, too. Lately, there'd been a se-
ries of articles in the *Times* focusing on his exploits. He'd
caught criminal after criminal and, according to her cousin
Nicole, made hefty bounties doing it. Now that Regina's
period of mourning was over and her uncle was forcing the
issue of her marriage, Regina was here to ask Daffin Oakleaf, legendary Bow Street Runner, to make mad, passionate
love to her.

Her stomach performed a somersault. Could nerves make

one physically ill? She suspected they could. Suspected hers would. She winced. It wouldn't do to cast up her accounts in front of the man. *That* certainly wouldn't attract him.

She glanced at her maid, who sat on the seat facing her, back ramrod straight. If the proper young woman knew what Regina was thinking, no doubt she'd be scandalized. Precisely why Regina had said as little as possible about their outing today. Genevieve hadn't asked many questions. Thank heavens.

The coachman opened the door and Regina took one more deep breath. "Wait here," she said to Genevieve. "I shouldn't be long."

After all, how long could an indecent proposal possibly take?

# CHAPTER TWO

Daffin Oakleaf pushed himself away from his office desk and scrubbed both hands across his face. He was tired. Bone tired. He hated Christmastide. He'd been running himself ragged chasing a particularly nasty thief across London for the last fortnight. Daffin had nearly had him, or so he thought, when a clue he'd been pursuing had turned to nothing. He was back to the start of his investigation, and severely out of sorts.

Daffin loved his work. It was perfect for him, and it had made him a wealthy man, but days like this were frustrating as hell. He much preferred to be taking down criminals and delivering them to gaol, instead of pacing his office with little to go on while they roamed free.

He was obsessed with each one of his cases, but this one kept him up at night. This case made his blood boil. A child had been injured by the bloody thief, and if there was one thing Daffin couldn't countenance, it was a grown man being violent with a child. He would track down this monster if it was the last thing he did.

Most of Daffin's investigations were done with the promise of a hefty purse at the end, but he was doing this one for free. He always took on a case or two for charity at Christmastide. It was the least he could do. Not to mention it kept his mind from the blasted season. Focusing on his cases made the holiday easier to ignore. Easier to forget.

He pulled a notebook from his inner coat pocket and scanned the words he'd written on the case so far. Perhaps he'd missed something, some detail that would finally lead him down the right path to Henry Vickery.

"Oakleaf!" came the voice of Paul, the secretary, who sat out in the offices' main room and fielded inquiries from people who came in off the street.

"I'm busy," Daffin called back, not in any mood to be taken away from his case. It was probably someone else who'd read about him in the paper and wanted to make his acquaintance. The papers hounded him of late. One reporter in particular. Mr. H. J. Hancock.

The man seemed obsessed with following Daffin's cases. Week after week, for months now Daffin had been mentioned in his articles. The stories made him sound like a bloody hero. They described how he chased down bad men in the dark of night, vaulting over walls, climbing up to rooftops, and taking more than one bullet. He'd never have answered the reporter's bloody questions if he'd known the man would go and write things like *that*. Being a hero wasn't Daffin's purpose. Never had been. He did his work to put the scum of society behind bars. To get evil people off the street. To spare their future victims.

Daffin had entertained Hancock's interrogation thinking it might help bring in tips if the public read about his work. Instead, the articles made him sound like a blasted knight in shining armor. They embarrassed the hell out of him. Ladies came traipsing into the office in search of a glimpse of him; men sought his company to ask him idiotic questions. Daffin had quickly reached the end of his patience for such things. His life's work was not a novelty, and he was not an animal in a zoological garden.

"I think ye're gonna wanna take *this* one, Oakleaf," came Paul's chipper reply from the common room.

"Damn it," Daffin muttered under his breath, flipping closed his notebook and shoving it back into his pocket. Paul found the scores of ladies coming to fawn over Daffin endlessly amusing. No doubt the younger man was merely ribbing him again.

Daffin stood, ran his hand down his red vest to straighten it, and strode out his office door and down the short corridor to the common room. He would curtly and firmly dismiss whoever it was and get back to the business of reading his notes.

He stepped into the common room, a cavernous area that smelled like a mixture of lemon polish and old papers, with high ceilings and wood beams. He scanned the space. Empty. "I'm not amused," he said to the secretary. "Interrupt me again and I'll have your hide."

He turned on his heel to return to his office when a soft female voice caught his attention. "Daffin."

He froze.

He recognized that voice.

Slowly, he turned back around, his heart thumping beneath his vest.

She stepped from behind one of the large wooden columns near Paul's desk. She wore an emerald-green velvet pelisse with white fur at the collar and wrists, and her hands were tucked into a white fur muff. Her hair was hidden beneath a green velvet hat that also had white fur trim, but he knew her hair was glossy and the color of black ink. Her eyes, blinking at him from beneath the brim of her expensive hat, were bright blue. A smile that had haunted his dreams for many a night rested on her ruby lips.

Lady Regina Haversham. The powerful Duke of Colchester's niece, and the cousin of his good friend Mark Grimaldi. A gorgeous, rich lady of the *ton*. One with whom he'd flirted outrageously when he'd met her in Surrey last summer. They'd been drawn to each other, could barely take their eyes from each other when they shared the same space, a fact that was entirely inappropriate because at the time the woman had been in mourning for her cousin.

Lady Regina had worked with Daffin and Grimaldi, along with Grimaldi's wife, Nicole, to discover the murderers and bring them to justice. Then Daffin had left. Paid handsomely by the duke for his assistance in solving his only son's murder, Daffin had gone back to his life in London chasing down criminals, and left Lady Regina Haversham to dwell in her countryside mansion with her happy, loving family, fancy servants, and gobs of money.

There may have been an instant connection between them, but Lady Regina was strictly off-limits. Not only was she far above him in class and breeding, but she was his good friend's cousin. Daffin highly doubted that Mark Grimaldi, the newly minted Marquess of Coleford and the Secretary of the Home Office, would look kindly on his blueblood cousin being courted by a Bow Street Runner. He and Grim might be friends, but their friendship didn't make up for the impossible gulf between their social ranks. It never would.

Daffin's flirting with Lady Regina had been harmless, however, and quickly over. In the months since, he had tried not to think of her, albeit unsuccessfully. Now here she was, standing in his offices on Bow Street as if he'd conjured her from his imagination. She smelled like apples. He would never forget her scent. It wafted across the space to him, and he briefly closed his eyes as he breathed it in.

Lady Regina cleared her throat and glanced self-consciously at Paul. "I mean . . . Mr. Oakleaf."

Paul turned to Daffin with eyebrows lifted.

Daffin glared at the lad before reverting his attention to the lady. He offered her a formal bow. "To what do I owe the pleasure, my lady?"

Her eyes darted about the room. She bit her lip. "I need to . . . I . . . have a proposal for you." Was it his imagination, or did her voice shake?

Daffin rubbed the back of his neck. He had an idea what her "proposal" would be. Like her cousin Nicole, who'd worked with him years ago, perhaps the lady had taken it in her head to become the next female Bow Street Runner, if unofficially. Nicole had mentioned to him a time or two that Lady Regina expressed interest in the work.

He shook his head. "My apologies, my lady, but we're not hiring at the moment."

Lady Regina cocked her head to the side. Her lips twitched. "I'm sorry to hear that, Mr. Oakleaf, but that is not why I'm here."

He frowned. "It's not?"

"No." She shook her head again, and he was captivated by the blue glimmer in her eyes. Something about the way she looked at him made him feel . . . wanted . . . admired. He remembered that feeling from Surrey, as if they were both in on the same jest.

"Then . . . why are you here?" he asked. She'd surprised him. His voice was more curt than he'd meant it to be.

"As I said, I have a proposal for you, but I'd prefer to share the details with you . . . privately."

"Privately?" Daffin echoed, rubbing the back of his neck again. It prickled with something akin to suspicion. Something about the way she spoke, the way she looked at him, told him he should be on his guard. Years of dealing with criminals and liars had taught him how to accurately read a person's movements and gestures, and Lady Regina's were telling him loudly that he should be prepared for trouble. Just what *sort* of trouble remained to be seen.

He took a deep breath and decided to invite trouble back to his office.

# CHAPTER THREE

Regina watched the look on Daffin's face go from slightly annoyed to confused to suspicious. The man had absolutely no idea what she intended to say. Good. Precisely the way she wanted it. The less he knew, the more honest a reaction she would get from him.

He looked as decadently handsome as he had the last time they'd met. His broad shoulders were encased in a crisp white shirt behind his dark red vest, his light hair was slicked back, his green eyes glimmered with intelligence. There was always a smile lurking near his lips, but she'd got the distinct impression that the ubiquitous smile was a veneer. His devil-may-care attitude hid something darker beneath. Something she wanted to discover.

"Yes . . . privately." She glanced at the young man behind the desk, who seemed entranced by her exchange with Daffin. The clerk's dark eyes darted back and forth between the two of them as he followed every word. All the more reason to speak with Daffin alone.

"By all means." Daffin waved his hand in the direction from which he'd come. Excellent. He was inviting her to his office. She hoped it had a door. A nice, big, thick one.

She preceded him down a short corridor before he guided her to a room that did indeed have a door. She entered and waited for Daffin to follow her inside, before pulling the door shut behind them. She glanced around. The office housed a large desk that occupied the center of the space with a dark brown leather chair in front of it. It smelled like him in here. A mix of soap and spice that made her want to bury her nose in his cravat. There was a map of London on the wall behind the desk and a mug filled with what looked to be black coffee on the desk next to a set of neatly stacked papers, a magnifying glass, and a . . . dear God, was that a pistol?

"May I take your coat?" Daffin offered.

"No, I cannot stay long." Regina glanced toward the door. "My maid is waiting in the coach."

"Of course. Please, sit." He waited for her to lower herself to the chair before walked around the large desk and took his own seat. He slid the pistol off the desk and into a drawer. "Hazard of the job."

"I understand," she replied with a nod.

Daffin searched her face. "I'd offer you a drink, but I'm afraid I don't have any tea."

"Do you have brandy?" she replied, her voice wavering slightly again.

His eyes widened, which made her smile. "*You'd* like a brandy?"

She sat up straight and cleared her throat. "Yes, please."

Regina didn't know whether she cared for brandy, but Nicole drank it from time to time, and Regina had decided to be bold today. She might as well be bold in every way.

Daffin stood again and made his way to the sideboard in the corner, where he splashed brandy into two glasses. "I have a feeling I may need one as well," he said as he returned and handed her one of the snifters.

She slid one of her gloved hands out of the fur muff and took the glass from him, eyeing it carefully.

He went to sit behind the desk again and took a healthy sip from his own glass. His slightly stern visage gave nothing away. "It's good to see you, my lady."

Ah, small talk. Something at which she excelled. "Yes, it's been several months. It's good to see you, too." And then, "Please call me Regina as you did in Surrey."

He grinned at her and nodded. "I've heard your uncle's health has improved."

"Slightly, yes. We're thankful for every day we have with him." Uncle Edward had suffered from a disease of the lungs for many years. The fact that he was still alive was nothing short of a miracle. One she was grateful for, even though the older man was currently making her life miserable. The duke's ultimatum was part of the reason she was here today.

"How is your grandmother?" Daffin asked next.

Regina's grandmother, Lady Harriet, was a feisty old woman who said and did outrageous things, usually while waving her ubiquitous handkerchief in the air. She knew Regina fancied Daffin. However, she had no idea the lengths her granddaughter was willing to go to get him. "She is quite well, thank you." This time, Regina cleared her throat. "I've been reading about you in the paper."

An annoyed look flashed across Daffin's face. He took another drink. He didn't care for his publicity, apparently. Interesting, but not surprising. No doubt people with secrets disliked reporters nosing around in their affairs, and Regina suspected Daffin had a great many secrets. That was why he fascinated her so thoroughly. His ridiculous good looks didn't hurt, either.

"You said you have a proposal for me," he said finally, leveling a look at her that said he'd dispensed with the chitchat.

Hmm. He didn't appear to be in a flirting mood today. That didn't bode well for his agreeing to bed her. But she'd come this far. She might as well get on with it. She took a fortifying sip of brandy, which burned down her throat and made her eyes water. Drat. She should have practiced drinking brandy before now. Nicole made it look simple. The truth was it tasted like poison. Regina much preferred wine. "Yes," she managed to choke out.

"And that proposal is?" Daffin drummed his fingertips along the top of the wooden desk. He was doing his best to appear nonchalant, but he was curious. She could tell. Excellent.

"My birthday is the thirteenth of January," she announced, her belly roiling, the glass trembling in her hand. She set the thing on the desk to keep from sloshing its contents on her lap. She'd never be able to explain to Genevieve why her pelisse smelled as if she'd taken a bath in alcohol. "Today is December thirteenth."

"Happy birthday?" he ventured, with a furrowed brow.

Regina snapped her mouth shut. Lord, she was doing a poor job of speaking in his presence. She'd practiced this countless times in her bedchamber in a whisper. She'd memorized it, experimented with her inflection, her tone. She'd changed the wording a hundred times before settling on the perfect speech. But seeing Daffin in the flesh distracted her. His height, his broad shoulders, his blond hair and sharp green eyes, and the scent of his cologne, which filled the office with its spicy clean scent and made her head spin in a very good way—these caused all of her practiced speeches to fly out of her head. She tried to remember her next line. Something about a present she wanted?

"I have decided what I would like for my birthday," she announced. Drat. That wasn't how she'd meant to say it. It made her sound demanding, possibly entitled.

Daffin's brow remained lowered. He stared at her, his head cocked to the side, a mixture of confusion and concern on his face, as if she were an inmate escaped from Bedlam and it was his task to coax her back there without causing a scene. "Do you want me to purchase it for you?" he asked, slowly.

She half laughed, half snorted, and immediately regretted the noise. Oh, lovely. She was here to offer the man her virginity, and she'd just made the most unattractive sound imaginable. This was going poorly. If she had any hope of salvaging this mission, she needed to get to her point.

"No, I, er, that is to say . . . I want *you* to be my birthday present."

Daffin's eyes widened. "Pardon?"

"I mean . . ." She sat forward on her seat, sweat trickling between her breasts. Her breathing turned shallow. She tapped her slipper against the wooden floor in a staccato rhythm. Anxiety made her blurt. "I can pay you if you'd like."

Daffin's brow dipped into a deep frown. "Pay me? For what, precisely?"

Oh. Dear. God. She had made a *complete* bungle of this. She considered jumping out the window, only she'd probably end up twisting her ankle or dirtying her gown. Besides, not only would that be cowardly, but how in the world would she face the man ever again if their paths were to cross? And they were likely to. Daffin was a friend to Mark and Nicole.

"My apologies." She took a deep breath and forced herself to start over. She swallowed hard. "Allow me to explain."

Daffin leaned back in his chair, watching her with open curiosity.

Regina pressed her gloved hand to her middle to still the nerves running amok in her belly. "For my thirtieth birthday—before it, actually—I have decided that I must . . . that I want to . . ." Her face heated. She cleared her throat. "Divest myself of my . . ." She stared at him, unable to force the word out of her dry throat.

"Of your . . ." he prompted, his eyes still narrowed on her.

"Virginity," she blurted. She grabbed her drink and sucked down an indecent amount of the stuff, which only served to spin her off into a coughing fit.

When she finally stopped coughing and returned her tortured gaze to his face, Daffin's was a mixture of surprise and . . . interest? He tugged at his cravat, sticking a finger under the neckcloth to pull at it. He opened his mouth to speak. Closed it, and opened it again. Finally words emerged from his perfect lips. "I thought that's what you meant to say, but I had to be certain."

"I understand," she said with a nod. Oh, why wouldn't he give her a hint about how he felt? His face had returned to its previous unreadable state.

Daffin cocked his head to the side and traced a finger around the edge of his glass. "I heard what you said, but I confess that I abjectly fail to understand what that has to do with *me*."

Pressing two fingers to her throat, Regina set the brandy glass back on the desk and met his gaze. Her heart felt as if it might escape via her throat. She needed to set this to rights. "When we met last summer, I felt we had a connection, and I think you did, too."

He arched a brow. "That, my lady, is a dangerous statement, and I make a habit of not commenting on dangerous statements."

She briefly closed her eyes. He was *not* making this easy for her. She blew out a tiny breath and bit the inside of her cheek, summoning every ounce of courage she possessed. Ever since her beloved cousin John died, she'd made it a priority to be courageous. Tried to, at least. Life was short, and one didn't get what one wanted by being a timid mouse. "I would like it very much, Mr. Oakleaf, er, Daffin, if you were the man to . . . ahem . . . take my virginity."

There. Now that the words were completely out in the open, they weren't so bad, were they? Only they were. She could tell by the look on his face, the expression of surprise that spread quickly across his handsome features.

"You . . . what?" The desk chair squeaked beneath his weight as he eased forward, staring at her as if she'd lost her mind. He'd heard her. She could see it in his eyes.

More courage. She straightened her spine and resisted the urge to avert her gaze from his piercing appraisal. "I am a spinster, Mr. Oakleaf." How utterly ridiculous was she for calling him "Mr. Oakleaf" when she'd just asked him to take her virginity? "I have been firmly and solidly 'on the shelf' as they say for quite some time, which has never bothered me. However, given recent events in my family, I would like to take a lover while I still have the choice to decide for myself whom I give myself to."

"You want *me* to be your lover?" he asked.

"Yes, precisely." She gulped, feeling as if she were standing in the middle of the park in only her shift, while a crowd gazed at her.

"Why me?"

"As I said, I thought we shared a connection, not to mention, Mark and Nicole think highly of you."

His eyes remained narrowed. "What do you mean, 'recent events in your family'?"

She winced. She'd been afraid he would ask that. She wasn't certain she should admit this next part, but he would find out soon enough. The announcement would be printed in the papers after Christmastide, and Mark would no doubt mention it to him. She straightened her shoulders and met Daffin's gaze. "I am soon to become engaged to the Earl of Dryden."

"Engaged?" he echoed. Was it her imagination or had disappointment flashed across his face? "To Dryden?"

"Do you know him?" she asked, perching on the edge of the chair.

"No. I can't say we've met, but I've heard of him."

She blew out a breath. "Yes, well, my uncle is dying and he's become preoccupied with ensuring that I'm settled before he goes. My grandmother is elderly. He's worried about me. I understand, but—"

"But I take it from your proposal to me, that you're not as enthusiastic about the good earl's offer as your uncle is."

Regina shook her head miserably. "Dryden offered for me years ago when I first made my debut. I turned him down. That was back when I had scores of offers, and Uncle Edward was convinced I'd choose another man. These days, however, Dryden is the only one who's offered."

"I see," Daffin replied. "Been settled on you all these years, eh?"

Regina couldn't help her unladylike eye roll. "He's much more settled on the land he stands to gain as part of my dowry, but it seems he's not one to give up easily. I've been putting him off for years, but Uncle Edward has finally told me to prepare myself to marry him."

"What do Mark and Nicole think about that?"

"They want my happiness, of course, but they also understand why Uncle Edward worries about me. He comes from a different era, one in which marriages were made based entirely on family names and dowries."

"And you don't agree with that sort of an arrangement?" Daffin asked.

"There's a reason I remained a spinster. I've yet to find the man I want to marry."

Their gazes met and an undeniable spark leaped between them, but Regina glanced away. The talk of marriage was too much. How had they got into this? She'd come to offer him her virginity, not recite the reasons she was a spinster.

Daffin cleared his throat. "May I ask why you're interested in, ahem, losing your virginity ahead of your marriage?"

Regina's face heated. She'd been expecting this question, too, but that didn't make it less awkward. "I don't want to marry Dryden and I certainly don't want to go to bed with him. But Uncle Edward is insistent. If I must marry the earl, I at least want to give my virginity to the man of *my* choice." She glanced at him sheepishly. "And that man is you."

Daffin rubbed the corners of his eyes with his thumb and forefinger. He blew out a deep breath. Tension was coiled in his shoulders. She could see it there, and it made her anxious, made her slipper tap more rapidly against the floor.

"I fully admit I felt an attraction to you when we met in Surrey. You are a beautiful, desirable woman, of that there is no doubt."

Regina swallowed. "Why do I feel as if the next word you're about to say is *however*?"

Daffin leaned forward and arched a brow. "*However*, I solve cases for bounties. I don't accept money for pleasuring my lovers."

She winced. The part about the money hadn't been in the best taste. She should have stuck to her original plan and offered that only as an incentive if he seemed hesitant, but her blasted nerves had got the better of her and she'd blurted it out. She might as well be honest with him.

"I'm sorry. I'd heard that gentlemen sometimes pay for the service when they lose their virginity; I assumed the practice *could* apply to both sexes given the right . . . circumstances." She winced again. No. Definitely not helping.

He shook his head, but the hint of a smile still played across his lips. That was encouraging. Perhaps he wouldn't order her from his office. "It seems you've confused me with a prostitute, my lady. I *should* be angry with you. But as you're obviously a novice at such exchanges, I'm willing to give you the benefit of the doubt."

Oh, dear. She'd insulted him. Of course she'd insulted him. But his words about giving her the benefit of the doubt caused hope to flare in her chest. "The offer to pay you was ill conceived, I admit. My apologies, but will you at least . . . consider it? Without money changing hands," she hastened to add.

"No." He pressed his lips together.

Hope died a quick and humiliated death. She slowly lifted the brandy glass to her mouth and drained the contents in one giant, supremely necessary gulp. At least her throat was numb. She barely felt the liquid burn its path to her belly. "Why?" She hoped her voice sounded calm and reasonable, not petulant.

Daffin crossed his arms in front of him on the desktop. "For two reasons. First, you are the cousin to two of my good friends, and I make it a practice *never* to become involved with ladies related to my friends. It's a certain way to ruin a friendship."

"But Mark doesn't—"

"Second, you've told me that you're about to become engaged, and as tempting as you are, I'm not such a blackguard that I'm willing to cuckold a future bridegroom, even if you aren't particularly keen upon marrying him. Cheating is not my style."

Regina blinked at him. "But it's not cuckolding if we're not yet married."

Daffin arched one brow. "Be that as it may, I have my standards."

Regina sighed and glanced away. He was too honorable to bed her. Drat. She'd been afraid of this. He'd turned her down with two perfectly reasonable excuses, but that didn't make it less embarrassing. She wanted to sink through the floor and be swallowed up by Bow Street. Instead, she forced herself to meet his gaze and nod slowly. She'd mustered the courage to make him the indecent proposal. She had to remain courageous during his refusal of it. She slid the empty brandy glass onto the desk. She could argue with him, but it would just make his refusal more excruciating. Wouldn't it?

"Don't you want to . . . think about it at least?" Very well. She couldn't help one last desperate attempt.

He slowly shook his head. His teeth tugged at his bottom lip in a way that made her want to cross her legs.

"Tempting, but I've made my decision." He stood and crossed to the door, opened it, and with a swipe of his arm, gestured for her to leave. "Good day, Lady Regina. Merry Christmastide and happy birthday. I wish you luck in your future marriage."

At his curt nod of dismissal, Regina bit her lip to keep her tears at bay. Then she solemnly stood, slid her hands back inside her muff, and stepped toward the open doorway.

As she passed him, he said softly, "Don't worry. I will not mention this to anyone. Your reputation is safe with me."

"Yes, but *such* a pity." She sighed before slipping out the door.

# CHAPTER FOUR

Daffin closed the door behind Lady Regina, walked back to his desk, grabbed his brandy glass, and knocked back the rest of its contents in one gulp. He groaned and pushed a hand through his hair. Damned if *that* wasn't a first. Of all the mad, absurd propositions. He'd thought the woman wanted a job. Turned out, she'd wanted to hire him for one. The hint of a grin touched his lips. A completely indecent one.

He supposed he couldn't blame her. She was an aristocrat. With their connections and money, members of the *ton* often thought they were entitled to anything and everything. He'd learned that lesson well during his childhood, hadn't he? Of all the situations he could have imagined his next encounter with Lady Regina Haversham would entail, her waltzing into his office and asking him to make love to her was the last thing . . . the absolute *last* thing he would have guessed.

He liked her. There was no denying it. Their connection in Surrey had shown him she was practical and easygoing. She hadn't put on airs or acted entitled, unlike some of the pampered ladies he'd worked for on various cases through the years. A lady of the *ton* had caused him the greatest hurt in life. He'd been wise to be skeptical of them.

But Lady Regina had been fresh and funny and willing to laugh at herself. She hadn't looked down her nose at him. She'd also been a help to their investigation. She and Nicole had truly been the ones to solve the thing. When they'd questioned the killer, they'd recognized a jilted debutante, something Daffin and Grimaldi knew nothing about.

Regardless of his undeniable attraction to her, Daffin wasn't about to bed Lady Regina Haversham. For precisely the reasons he'd told her. He didn't need to discuss it with Grimaldi to guess his friend would disapprove and he greatly valued his friendship with Grim. They'd been mates for over a decade. As newly appointed Secretary of the Home Office, Grimaldi's first order of business was to implement a police force in London. The city sorely needed it. Daffin and Grimaldi met weekly to discuss the plans.

Daffin had no intention of becoming one of the officers. The bounties he made were much higher than the wages that would be paid to the men who were given the jobs as police officers, but he recognized the need for such a force, given that poor people had little recourse to the law since they couldn't pay for their own investigations. Grim was a good man who did good work. Daffin had no intention of jeopardizing their friendship over an ill-begotten affair with Grim's betrothed cousin, no matter how beautiful and desirable she was.

The second reason Daffin refused to bed Regina was that while everyone knew the *ton* was full of liaisons and marriages based on many factors besides love, he'd been honest with her when he'd said cheating wasn't his style. Besides, starting up an affair with a soon-to-be-married woman hardly seemed prudent. What if their lovemaking resulted in a child? No. He would never put a child of his in such a situation, and it wasn't as if he and Regina could marry. They were from two different social spheres. Her uncle would never allow it.

Daffin leaned back in his chair and stared broodingly at the empty snifter she'd left on the edge of his desk. The scent of apples still lingered in the office. He had turned down her proposal, not because the idea of bedding her wasn't tempting. It was. Quite tempting. In fact, he'd spent a fair amount of time fantasizing about just such a scenario over the past months. In his baser moments, he might have pictured her spread out beneath him on his desk, his papers wiped away by a swipe of his arm, as he hiked up her skirts and freed himself from his breeches and buried himself deep inside her. He'd like nothing more than to use his handcuffs on her. Make her beg him for leniency.

That had been his fantasy, but his penchant for dominance in the bedchamber would no doubt horrify a proper lady like Regina. She'd probably want the candles snuffed and the bed sheets covering her, like any pampered virgin. Not that he'd bedded many pampered virgins, but he could imagine they'd be less than adventurous when it came to making love. He was a man who prized adventure. In bed and out of it.

Not to mention, he might be a hired hand to the aristocracy when it came to solving their crimes, but he damn sure drew the line at bedding their women *for money*. What the hell had Regina been thinking when she'd offered to pay him? Did she believe him some sort of rutting stag? A man with no morals? One who would either trace down a criminal or bed a Society miss if the purse was hefty enough? At least she seemed properly chagrined when he'd pointed out the insult.

Daffin would continue to work for those who could afford to pay him. Only he wasn't about to take up a side job as a *cicisbeo* for the lonely ladies of the *ton* while he was at it. Fine, Regina wasn't married yet, so *cicisbeo* was the wrong word for her offer; *paid lover* sounded less romantic, but it was also not going to happen.

Daffin let his head drop against the seat back, feeling strangely depleted. Damn Christmastide. Regina's visit had been another frustrating encounter during his least favorite season. He stood and crossed to the sideboard to pour himself another finger of brandy. It was near the end of the day, and if ever there was a reason to drink, this was it. He leaned back against the sideboard and crossed his booted feet at the ankles, letting the last twenty minutes play over and over in his mind.

Was this what he could expect more of after the stories in the *Times* had been printed? Regina had mentioned she'd read some of it. Clearly, something about his fame had made her think he'd be willing to do more than investigate crime for money. He regretted ever speaking to that damned reporter.

Daffin returned to his seat and flipped open his notebook again. He needed to do his best to wipe the unfortunate encounter with Regina from his memory. "Don't you at least want to think about it?" she'd asked him. If he wasn't careful,

# CHAPTER FIVE

As her uncle's coach rumbled back toward Mayfair, Regina sat silently on the seat across from Genevieve. The maid was obviously curious as to her mistress's business at Bow Street, but she had the sense not to ask about it, and Regina wasn't about to confess. She'd opened and closed her reticule half a dozen times, completely unable to recall why she'd opened the blasted thing to begin with. Her mind churned with the memory of Daffin looking at her with those mesmerizing green eyes and saying, "Tempting, but I've made my decision."

Tempting. Tempting? Had he really been tempted or had he merely said that to be polite? Polite to a woman who'd just insulted him by offering him *money* to bed her. Actual money. Currency. Coinage. He was right. She'd treated him like a prostitute. She winced just thinking about it. She'd made a complete bungle of the entire thing.

She didn't blame Daffin for refusing her. How could she? She was an imbecile. An idiot. And any other word she could think of to describe the monumental senselessness with which she'd proceeded out into the world today to make a fool of herself in front of the one man she desperately wanted to impress. Coax into bed, even. Not only had she failed spectacularly at any coaxing, she'd managed to insult and probably anger him at the same time. Now she had to figure out how she could avoid the man's presence for the entire rest of her life. A task that was certain to be difficult given Daffin's friendship with Mark and Nicole, because Regina happened to be staying with Mark and Nicole at the moment. She was a guest in their town house on Upper Brook Street.

She'd been eager to leave Colchester Manor and Surrey as soon as the Earl of Dryden, her uncle's neighbor, had begun coming around more. It turned out, Nicole was with child, due in the spring. The pregnancy was perfectly timed. Nicole had mentioned in one of her letters that she would love Regina's company if she felt she could get away from the country. Regina had immediately written back to offer her services as a companion during Nicole's confinement and made plans to leave for London with an alacrity that frightened Genevieve, who'd been awakened ridiculously early in the morning to begin packing.

Uncle Edward had allowed Regina to go because it involved Nicole's pregnancy. The baby Nicole carried was hopefully the heir to the duchy and if there was one thing Uncle Edward cared about even more than securing Regina's match, it was ensuring the heir to the duchy arrived safely. However, her uncle had made it clear that while in London, Regina should resign herself to the fact that she would marry Lord Dryden. When Nicole had written Uncle Edward to tell him that she and Mark believed Regina should be able to choose her own husband, the duke had issued an ultimatum.

Fine. Find a suitable husband in London over Christmastide or return for an engagement with Dryden.

Regina had spent the entire carriage ride to London writing a list of every single eligible man of her acquaintance. An eligible man, as far as her uncle was concerned, was one with a title, the older and more revered, the better. One by one, she crossed each name off her list. None of the prospects were particularly appealing. Not to mention, she had no idea if any of them even wanted her. Several of her former suitors had married. The few who were left were no more attractive to her than Dryden. At least if she married Dryden she could stay near her grandmother in the country.

Regina had convinced Grandmama to speak to Uncle Edward about it and Lady Harriet had certainly tried, but the duke was adamant about seeing Regina settled before he died. They all suspected Regina's marriage and the birth of the heir were the only things keeping the old man alive at the moment, and Regina loved her uncle dearly, even though he could be downright archaic when it came to things like marriage alliances.

"I've done wrong by you," Uncle Edward said with tears in his rheumy blue eyes the morning Regina left for London. "I never should have allowed you to go so long without making a match. I intend to set things to rights before I go."

Regina had tried to explain she'd made her peace with spinsterhood, but Uncle Edward wouldn't hear of it. Lord Dryden was a decent man, from a fine family, and most importantly, he'd offered. In the end, her grandmother was old-fashioned, too. She'd deferred to Uncle Edward's wishes as the head of the family and had been trying to cheer Regina by talking about how handsome and rich Lord Dryden was.

There was nothing specifically *wrong* with Lord Dryden.

The man was good-looking (he was no Daffin Oakleaf, of course, but still), indecently rich, and had always been nothing but respectful to her. But the earl didn't love her. He'd been waiting for her, not out of lovesickness, but out of a desire for the land her uncle had promised as part of her dowry. The land that connected to Dryden's. While marrying for land and money wasn't odd in their world, she still couldn't bring herself to be excited about a match with a man who was more interested in her acreage than her eyes. On the ride to London, however, she'd tried to come to terms with it. Perhaps she was being selfish, she'd told herself. Perhaps marriage to Dryden wouldn't be so bad. She'd still be able to visit London and in Surrey they'd be close to Grandmama and all her friends in town. Wasn't it the least she could do for her poor, dear, dying uncle? The man who'd taken her in when she'd been orphaned at the age of twelve? The man who'd been nothing but kind to her? Didn't she want him to be settled so he might rest in peace?

Very well. They would announce the engagement in the *Times* soon after Twelfth Night. She would marry the Earl of Dryden, but she hadn't been able to stop thinking about Daffin in all these months, and if she had to spend the rest of her life married to a man she didn't love, in bed with a man she didn't want, first, she would give her virginity to the man of her choice. That, she'd decided on the long, cold, bumpy ride to London, would be the one scrap of power she would have. The one vestige of control she could exert.

Only Daffin Oakleaf had turned her down. She sagged in defeat.

They were nearly to Mark's town house when the carriage took a sharp jarring roll to the left. Genevieve screamed. Both women tumbled to the side, knocking hard against the coach wall. The coach shook and righted itself, the wheels slamming back on the pavement with a jolt.

Breathing heavily, Regina pushed aside the curtain over the window to see what happened. Another coach raced away down the road at a breakneck speed. Her heart pounded wildly. Her parents had been killed in a carriage accident. It was one of her greatest fears.

"Are you all right?" she called to the coachman, willing her breathing back to rights.

"I was just about to ask ye the same question, me lady," the coachman called back.

"We're fine," she called. "If a bit rattled."

"Don't ye worry, me lady. We're nearly home."

As soon as the coach pulled to a stop in front of Mark's grand town house, Regina and Genevieve alighted with the help of a footman. Regina made her way to the front of the conveyance and looked up at the coachman. "What happened back there?"

"That carriage came out of nowhere, me lady," he said. "Nearly ran us off the road."

"Just like last week," Regina replied, biting her lip and staring at the ground, lost in thought.

Mark had use of his coach today, so Regina had asked to borrow her uncle's town coach for her ill-fated outing this afternoon. Last week when she and Nicole had borrowed Uncle Edward's coach to go shopping, a similar incident had occurred on their way back home. They'd shrugged it off as an accident along London's busy roads. Besides, they all had been on edge since Cousin John's murder last summer. Regina feared they'd never again feel as safe as they once had. Last week had been one thing. Today's repeat incident made the hair on the back of her neck stand up.

She and Genevieve made their way up the stone stairs to the front door of her cousin's town house and into the foyer. Genevieve quickly disappeared downstairs, while Regina handed her muff and hat to the butler and pulled her gloves from her hands.

The servant eyed her warily. "Are you quite all right, my lady?"

"No. I mean, yes. Quite." She forced herself to hold still and allowed Abbott to help her remove her pelisse. Next, she calmly handed him her gloves while she forced herself to count to ten, stilling the racing of her heart. She had to find Nicole.

"Where is her ladyship?" she asked the butler.

"She is in the study with his lordship."

Drat. Regina had hoped Nicole would be alone so she could talk to her about both the incident in the coach and her disastrous encounter with Daffin. Mark tended to be overprotective when it came to his cousin and his pregnant wife. He wouldn't like to hear that Regina had been nearly run off the road twice now. As for the incident with Daffin, she hadn't told Nicole about her plans to visit Bow Street, nor her proposal to rid herself of her virginity. She'd been afraid Nicole would talk her out of it. After the disastrous results today, she couldn't keep it to herself. Mortification called for companionship.

She straightened her shoulders and made her way to the study. Perhaps she could catch Nicole's eye and somehow indicate that she needed to talk without alerting Mark. The last thing she wanted was to allow Mark to find out what a complete fool she'd made of herself. The embarrassment of *that* might well send her to an early grave. Daffin had promised not to mention it to anyone. She had no reason to doubt him. He had never proven to be anything other than a complete gentleman, which made her shameful proposal even more humiliating.

As she approached her cousin's study door, raised voices drifted into the corridor.

"Why didn't you tell me sooner, Nicole?" Mark's tone was stern and edged with something akin to anger mixed with fear.

"I didn't think there was anything to tell, really," Nicole's bright voice returned.

"I want you to go to Uncle Edward's estate in Surrey as soon as possible and stay until after Christmas."

"But that's hiding," Nicole replied, her voice firm and resolute. "I refuse to hide."

Regina furrowed her brow. What were her cousins talking about? Not wanting to eavesdrop any further, she promptly knocked on the frame of the open door.

Mark glanced up. He had a deep scowl on his face, which softened when he recognized Regina. "Come in."

"Regina, there you are," Nicole said. Her beautiful cousin was lounging on a dark leather sofa near the wall while Mark sat behind his desk. "Will you please tell my adoring husband that we will be perfectly fine staying in London until Christmastide? You look flushed, by the by."

Mark opened his mouth obviously to retort, but Regina stopped him.

"Why wouldn't we stay in London?" she asked, purposely ignoring Nicole's remark about looking flushed. "I thought that had already been decided." They'd all agreed to stay in London until Christmastide. Was Mark being overly solicitous because of the babe? If that was the case, why hadn't he mentioned it before?

"Will you please tell my lady wife," Mark replied, still staring at Nicole, his arms folded across his chest, "that there is no possible way I will allow her to remain in London if she's in danger?"

"Danger?" Regina's wide-eyed gaze met Nicole's. "Whatever do you mean?"

Nicole rolled her eyes. "I made the mistake of telling Mark about our little carriage accident last week."

"Yes, and I'm convinced it may not have been an accident," Mark replied.

Regina bit her lip. There was no help for it. She should tell Mark about what had just happened to her. He would be angry if he found out she'd kept it from him.

Regina quickly made her way to Nicole's side and perched on the sofa beside her, her hip resting near Nicole's gently rounded belly. Regina took a deep breath. "I'm not entirely certain he's wrong. Genevieve and I had another incident on our way home just now."

"What's that?" Mark's head snapped to face her.

Regina related the incident as briefly and unemotionally as possible.

"You see?" Mark replied, slashing an arm through the air.

"Wait a moment. While it's definitely disconcerting, it's possible it's nothing more than a coincidence, darling," Nicole replied.

"That's true," Regina added, nodding, even though she didn't quite believe it herself.

"There are no two ways about it," Mark continued imperiously from behind his desk. "I must be out of town on business until Christmas Day, and I'm not about to leave you both here where I cannot keep you safe."

"Carriage accidents happen all the time," Nicole replied.

"Not with you in the carriage," Mark said gruffly, crossing his arms over his chest again.

Nicole exchanged a private look with Regina. Ever since Nicole had announced her pregnancy, her husband's solicitousness had multiplied tenfold. The two women had jested about it, but Mark seemed even more serious tonight.

"The danger of living with a spy," Nicole said with a sigh, pushing herself up from the sofa. Regina moved to assist her. "They're always so quick to jump to suspicious conclusions." She winked at Regina.

"Need I remind you that you're a spy, too?" Mark replied. He was a handsome man with dark hair and eyes. He became even more handsome when gazing at his red-haired wife, whom he obviously adored.

"Thank heavens it hasn't made me suspicious," Nicole quipped, making her way to the door.

Regina followed her friend, thankful Nicole was leaving the room without any prompting on Regina's part.

Nicole waved at her husband. "I'm going upstairs to dress for dinner. We'll talk more when you're being reasonable, darling."

"I'm being perfectly reasonable," Mark muttered, his voice still grumbly.

When Regina reached Nicole at the door, she whispered, "I need to speak to you."

"I suspected as much. Come upstairs with me," Nicole whispered back, twining her arm through Regina's.

"What's that?" Mark called after them.

"Nothing," Nicole replied in a singsong voice. "I've merely asked Regina to escort me upstairs in case a brigand jumps out from behind the staircase and attempts to accost me."

Mark scowled. "That is not humorous."

"Oh, you must admit, it's a bit humorous, Cousin Mark," Regina replied, smiling and pulling Nicole into the corridor.

As soon as they were out of earshot, Nicole whispered, "Enough about the London coachmen who cannot drive straight. I want to hear all about your meeting with Daffin today."

# CHAPTER SIX

The two ladies climbed the stairs and made their way down the corridor to Nicole's opulent lavender-and-silver bedchamber that adjoined her husband's. Regina shut the door behind them and leaned against it. She couldn't breathe. Her stays pressed into her chest, giving her the sensation that her lungs might collapse. It wasn't from the exertion of climbing the stairs. No, this was brought on by nothing other than acute embarrassment mixed with a healthy dose of shame.

She eyed her cousin carefully, waiting as Nicole walked across the rug and took a seat on the settee near the window. Her cousin knew she fancied Daffin, but how did Nicole know she'd gone to visit him today?

Nicole kicked off her slippers and lifted her feet onto the cushion of the settee. "You were so flushed when you came in, I guessed you needed to talk. Are you all right?"

"I'm not certain." Regina's face heated anew. "I've made a complete fool of myself."

"Oh, no." Nicole patted the space next to her. "In front of Daffin?"

With a miserable nod, Regina made her way to the settee and dropped down next to her cousin. "Yes, and how did you know?"

"I'm a spy, dear."

Regina had to smile at that. "I suppose I should have told you before I went, but you were napping and I thought perhaps you might try to talk me out of it."

"Talk you out of it?" Nicole's eyes widened. "Why?"

"Because of what I said to him."

Nicole arched a brow. "What did you say?"

Regina closed her eyes and took a deep breath. She might as well get this over with quickly. It would be less awful if she did it fast, like pulling a tangled pin from her hair. "I asked him to . . . to . . . take my virginity."

A long silence ensued. Regina kept her eyes squeezed closed and tried to will the settee to swallow her whole. Then, there was a rustle of fabric as Nicole shifted beside her and cleared her throat. "Oh, my. Oh, well, I see. What did he say?"

Regina opened her eyes. "You don't understand." She groaned, staring across the room at the silver vase filled with fresh white roses that sat on a table near the door. "I didn't just ask him to take my virginity. I asked him to make love to me and I . . . offered him money." She collapsed against the back of the settee in a miserable heap, burying her face in her hands.

"You didn't!" Nicole breathed.

Regina pulled her hands away and glanced at Nicole. Her cousin's countenance was aghast. Regina nodded desolately. "Yes. I did. I wish I could take it back, but I . . .

cannot. Oh, Nicole. What am I to do?" She searched Nicole's features for the wisdom and comfort she'd been looking for.

Nicole patted Regina's shoulder. Then she took a deep breath, stood, and paced toward the fireplace. She clasped her arms behind her back, much like her husband did when deep in thought. "I assume you asked him to bed you because of the Dryden debacle." Nicole had begun referring to Regina's impending engagement as "the Dryden debacle." They'd had this talk a half-dozen times since Regina had arrived in London. Nicole knew Regina was doing her best to resign herself to her future marriage, but Nicole, who'd married for love, still thought it was hideously unfair.

Regina nodded.

"I'm so sorry, dear. I really am."

Regina glanced away, fighting the tears that threatened to gather in her eyes. There was no use talking about it again.

Nicole nodded and changed the tone of her voice to one of calm authority, like a general calling orders on a battlefield. "Very well. Right, then. We must look at this logically, like an investigation. Begin by telling me precisely what Daffin's reaction was."

Regina searched her memory. Nicole's stoicism and logic made her feel better already. Perhaps together they might find a way to make her mistake with Daffin less awful . . . if they studied it.

She took a deep breath. "He told me no and stated quite clearly he is not a prostitute."

Nicole paused in her pacing and winced. "Oh, dear."

Regina pressed a sweaty palm to her aching forehead. "Yes, exactly. It was awful. I'll never be able to look at him again."

"Did you apologize?" Nicole resumed her pacing.

"Yes. But he still refused. He also said out of respect for you and Mark, he would never mention it."

Nicole nodded. "That's honorable of him."

"I know, which made me feel worse," Regina groaned. "In the midst of my horrible insult, he was nothing but decent. I didn't mean to offer him money, only I got tongue-tied. The man carries handcuffs and a truncheon, for heaven's sake. I couldn't help it. The words leaped out of my mouth. He made me anxious for some reason."

"It's because you fancy him," Nicole said, a sly smile creeping to her face.

"We are not schoolgirls," Regina replied, her nose in the air. Then she allowed a coy smile to tug at the side of her lips. "But yes, I fancy him *desperately*. Oh, why does being in his presence make me so inarticulate?"

"You didn't seem to have a problem speaking to him in Surrey. I daresay the proposal you were offering him is what caused you to become tongue-tied."

Regina pressed a hand to her throat. "You're right. I was nothing but a mess of nerves."

"It's an unfortunate turn of events, and I can certainly understand why Daffin would be offended, but surely you can make it right somehow."

Regina crossed her arms over her chest and sighed. "How?"

"Perhaps you can . . . start over?" Nicole waved a hand in the air.

Regina pulled a silken lavender pillow onto her lap and hugged it. "Start over? How is that possible? I'm quite certain I'd prefer to die before I ever see him again."

Nicole snorted. "If Mark and I could overcome what we

said to each other ten years ago and fall in love again, you can find a way to start over with Daffin."

Regina cringed. "But I'm not certain I want to start over with Daffin. At the moment, I think perhaps it's best if I never speak to or see him again. That sounds like a solid plan to me. The entire idea to lose my virginity before my wedding was ill-begotten to begin with."

"First of all, I'm not entirely settled on the notion of the Dryden debacle. I want you to have the opportunity for a love match. That's why we need to remain in London as long as possible and not allow Mark to send us off to the countryside over a couple of silly carriage incidents." Nicole nodded resolutely. "Second, hiding from Daffin is unlike a Colchester. You must be brave if you're to get what you want. Believe me, it's a lesson I've learned well in the past year. My life would be completely different if I hadn't been brave last summer, when Mark arrived on my doorstep in France and asked me to come home with him to *pretend* to be his loving wife."

"And I'm ever so pleased it worked out for the two of you, because I adore having both of you in my life. However, at the moment, I would like to die of embarrassment," Regina said with a nod. "I believe that makes my case different from yours."

Nicole hurried over to sit next to her again. She wrapped her arm around Regina's shoulders and squeezed. "You don't want to die of embarrassment. You want to have a nice affair with Daffin, preferably involving those handcuffs you admire so greatly, and I don't blame you." She winked at Regina.

Regina blushed. It was true. She'd been intrigued by the man's handcuffs since Surrey and Nicole knew it.

"I admit you'll have some groveling to do," Nicole continued. "Groveling and apologizing, but he cannot hold it against you forever. Besides, there might be a part of him that is flattered. After he has time to think about it, I mean."

Regina eyed her skeptically. "Flattered over being treated like a prostitute?"

Nicole shook her head and squeezed Regina's shoulder once more. "No, not that part, the part where a gorgeous lady wants to spend the night with him."

Regina heaved a sigh, blowing air into her cheeks to puff them out. "He did say I was beautiful and desirable. But even if he *could* find it in himself to forgive me, how would I ever have the opportunity to explain? I refuse to return to Bow Street. I'm certain he'd turn me away without seeing me."

Nicole pulled away and plunked her fists on her hips. "Why didn't you tell me he said you were beautiful and desirable? I'd say that's a fine start. Though I agree, returning to Bow Street is not the way to go about it. We'll have to think of something else." She pursed her lips and cocked her head to the side as if deep in thought.

Regina wiped a lock of hair from her brow with the back of her hand. "And I disagree with you. The carriage accidents frightened me. Especially the second one. Perhaps we should listen to Mark."

A few moments passed before a slow smile spread across Nicole's pretty face. A twinkle sparkled in her sea-foam-green eyes and she clapped her hands. "The carriage incidents, of course. Oh, Regina. You're going to love me. I just thought of the perfect plan."

corner. Christmastide. The season was supposed to be about family, and Daffin had no family. Not anymore.

He'd received a tip that Henry Vickery was staying in a house down this way. Daffin would love nothing better than to find the son of a bitch and drag him off in handcuffs today. Perhaps that would make Daffin's nagging sense of dread go away. Perhaps he could pretend Christmastide wasn't happening. Perhaps he could escape the memories this year. He couldn't sit still. Sitting still led to thoughts of the past.

He tugged the brim of his hat down over his brow. When it came to memories, there was a new one he couldn't seem to forget.

It had been four days since Regina waltzed into his office with her shocking proposal. He'd been unable to stop thinking about it since. Damn it. Her offer had been ludicrous. So why couldn't he let it go? Because it was a first? That's what he kept telling himself. Even if he didn't believe it.

Oh, he'd been propositioned by ladies before, but most of them were married and bored and looking to cuckold their unassuming husbands with a Bow Street Runner for a lark. Regina was different. She certainly was the first lady to offer him her *virginity*. She could also claim the distinction of being the first lady to offer to *pay* him for sex. He shook his head. What the hell had she been thinking?

She might be slightly older than the average Society miss, but it was ridiculous of her to believe she'd have trouble finding a lover. She didn't need to pay someone for the privilege, which was what made him uneasy. She'd said he was her choice. But why? True, they'd shared an undeniable flirtation in Surrey, but why had she chosen *him*? Because she trusted him? Because he was friendly with her cousins?

She'd looked embarrassed when she'd left his office hastily

last week. In hindsight, perhaps he'd been too harsh in his rejection. Her proposal had caught him off guard. Completely out of her element, she had bungled the thing, but the woman needed to save herself for Dryden. At the very least, she should offer herself to some chap of her same social standing. No doubt, she'd find someone from her set whom she wanted to take to her bed.

Daffin had been flattered and even slightly tempted, but he needed to stop thinking about Regina's offer and concentrate on finding Henry Vickery, the piece of rubbish who'd robbed half a dozen Mayfair mansions and brutally beaten a young newspaper delivery boy who'd witnessed him leaving one of the houses. The child would have a permanent limp thanks to Vickery. Daffin would like nothing more than to return the favor.

He came to a stop in front of the address he'd been given, number 15 Mercer. He took a deep breath, his blood rushing through his veins. This was the part of his work he liked best. He pounded on the door with his fist, then waited several seconds, leaning in to better hear. Scurrying and curse words met his ears. It took the better part of a minute before a rickety flap in the door opened and two beady, dark eyes blinked at him.

"Who be there?" a gruff male voice asked.

"Someone looking for Henry Vickery," Daffin returned dryly. "Is he here?"

The beady eyes blinked again. "Who be askin'?"

Daffin put his fists on his hips and glared. He didn't have time for games. "Why don't you open the door and I'll give you my card," he drawled.

The flap slapped shut, and the door slowly opened to reveal the beady-eyed man was short and hunched. He was also in possession of dirty, ripped clothing and questionable shoes. He smelled like a rubbish heap and his greasy dark hair stuck out in all directions from his untidy head.

Daffin bowed. "Daffin Oakleaf, Bow Street Runner, at your service. Are you Henry Vickery?"

"I ain't." The chap grimaced at him, revealing a set of rotten, yellow teeth.

Daffin watched him carefully, narrowing his eyes. Years of experience with liars had taught him how to ferret out one quickly. This man was telling the truth, at least about not being Vickery. Besides, Vickery had pulled off heists that had involved a great deal of physical acuity. Daffin doubted the man before him was capable of scaling walls and running quickly.

"Is Mr. Vickery here?" he asked, tugging at his cuff.

"No." The word came out too quickly and in a strained tone. A lie.

Daffin pushed aside his cloak, opened his overcoat, and pulled a one-pound note from an inner pocket. He held the bill between two fingers. "How about now? Does this serve to assist your memory?"

The man's eyes flicked back and forth. He was obviously weighing his desire to earn the bill against what was probably his fear of Vickery. But Daffin knew criminals. Greed always won out with their lot.

The man snatched at the bill. "'E's in the upstairs bedchamber. First door on the right at the top o' the stairs."

Daffin squinted at the man. "Is anyone else here?"

The man shrugged. "'E might 'ave a bit o' fluff wit 'im."

Daffin cautiously entered the flat, pulling his pistol from his coat pocket. He kept his back against the wall while his eyes adjusted to the darkness in the cramped, smelly space. "Which way?"

The man nodded toward an arched doorway and moved out of the way, clutching the pound note to his chest. He remained near the front door, obviously ready to run should the scene not unfold in Daffin's favor.

Daffin moved through the doorway and quickly located the narrow, cramped staircase. Still keeping his back to the wall, he made his way up the stairs in silence until he stood in front of the first door. Loud snores came from inside the room. If indeed it was Vickery in the room, Daffin had got the jump on him. He smiled to himself before taking a deep breath. Then he raised his booted foot and savagely kicked open the door.

A woman's scream was the first thing that met Daffin's ears. Beady had been right. Vickery wasn't in bed alone. The criminal startled awake and lunged from the side of the bed, but Daffin's pistol was trained on the man before he had a chance to reach for his own weapon, which sat on a table near the door. "I wouldn't do that if I were you," Daffin said, cocking his pistol and centering it between the thief's eyes.

The naked prostitute grabbed the sheet to cover herself. Her blue eyes were wild with fear as she stared at Daffin and his pistol.

Vickery growled and slowly lifted both hands, his eyes narrowing on Daffin. "Oakleaf?"

Daffin's smile widened and he took a hint of a bow. "How *did* you know?"

"Heard ye was lookin' fer me," Vickery grumbled.

"Not anymore," Daffin replied.

He briefly allowed his gaze to scan the prostitute. Her

dirty blond hair was in disarray, and bruises colored her neck and shoulders. She had men in her life who treated her poorly. Most likely a pimp. Or Vickery. Daffin hated to see women at the mercy of bad men. His throat tightened.

With his free hand, he reached into his overcoat and pulled out a guinea. He tossed it on the bed and gestured for her to get it. Ignoring her nakedness, she scrambled across the mattress and grabbed it. The coin was likely a fortune to her. Daffin clenched his jaw. "Use that to get away from whoever gave you those bruises. If you go to the almshouse on Clancy Street, Mrs. Dillon there often has positions for young women willing to work hard as maids."

The prostitute nodded and the hint of a smile touched her cracked lips. "Thank ye, guv'na."

Turning his attention back to Vickery, Daffin strolled to a pair of dirty, crumpled breeches that sat in a heap on the floor. He kicked them toward the man. "Get dressed," he commanded, keeping his pistol trained on Vickery as the thief climbed naked out of the bed and hurriedly pulled on his breeches.

Next, Vickery tossed his filthy shirt over his head and wrapped his dirty neckcloth haphazardly around his throat. Once the thief was somewhat decent, Daffin pulled his handcuffs out of his coat & slapped them over Vickery's wrists. He gestured toward the door with the pistol. "Let's go."

Vickery preceded Daffin out of the room.

"Don't try anything, Vickery. You're the worst kind of scum, a thief who hurts children. I'd love nothing better than an excuse to blow you to kingdom come."

With that, he led the scoundrel at the end of his pistol down the stairs and past the beady-eyed man who had since hidden his pound note somewhere within his questionable clothing.

Minutes later, they made it to Daffin's waiting coach and drove off in the direction of the magistrate's court. Daffin leaned back against the squabs, his pistol still trained on Vickery, who eyed him for any sign of weakness. Even in handcuffs the scum might try to grab his pistol and would kill him with it without blinking an eye, so Daffin kept his finger firmly on the trigger.

He had his man. Henry Vickery would find justice. He was going to gaol for a long, long time. Daffin was pleased to wrap up the case before the holiday. But what would he work on next to keep his mind off Christmastide?

# CHAPTER EIGHT

"No, my lord. Nothing happened. We were perfectly safe on our outing today."

Regina entered the salon. Mark stood near the sideboard, a drink in his hand. Nicole sat on the sofa, watching the interaction between her husband and one of the groomsmen while rolling her eyes. The groomsman stood near the door, clutching his hat, shaking in his boots.

"No one tried to run you off the road?" Mark intoned.

"No," the groomsman replied.

"Darling, he's told you all he can, for heaven's sake," Nicole said. "Nothing happened."

"Fine. That will be all." Mark waved away the groomsman and returned to his seat. His expression remained thunderous.

Regina made her way to Nicole and slid onto the sofa next to her. "You went out today?"

Nicole took a deep breath. "While you were in your bedchamber catching up on your correspondence, I decided to visit my mother."

"You shouldn't have gone alone," Regina insisted.

"Precisely what I've been trying to tell her," Mark replied.

"Susanna was with me," Nicole said, mentioning her maid. She stared down at her hands. "I was perfectly fine."

Regina shook her head. "Oh, Nicole, you must promise to wait for me next time. I was only catching up on my correspondence because you were napping."

Nicole pushed a lock of red hair behind her ear. "I know, but I couldn't sleep, and a visit to my mother was long overdue. I thought I'd get it over with and spare you."

Regina couldn't smile at Nicole's jest. Her heart hammered with fear. Ever since the second carriage accident after she'd left Bow Street last week, she'd been filled with worry. Her family might well be under attack.

"I think you should tell Mark what you told me last night," Nicole prompted.

Regina blinked. "Pardon?"

"You know how you said you felt as though you were . . . being watched."

Regina gulped. She *had* mentioned that to Nicole last night. She hadn't wanted to alarm her cousins, but she and Genevieve and a footman had run a few errands yesterday and she'd looked over her shoulder the entire time. She was convinced it was merely her overly active imagination at work, but she hadn't been able to help herself.

Mark turned to face Regina. "Is that true?" He searched her face, his features lined with concern.

"I'm certain it's just my nerves," Regina replied. "After the two carriage incidents, I can't help but feel as if—"

"You're in danger?" Nicole said.

Regina cleared her throat. "I'm uneasy."

"Why didn't you tell me, Regina? Did anything happen yesterday?" Mark asked.

"No. Nothing. The carriage ride home was entirely uneventful."

Mark walked to the sofa and stared down at his wife. His face softened as he looked at her. Love shone in his eyes. "I need to leave for Northumbria in two days' time. I'm not about to leave you both here alone with this uncertainty and you cannot come with me. The journey will be too difficult for you."

"You truly think someone is trying to harm one of us?" Regina asked, a lump in her throat.

Mark shook his head. "I don't know." He paced toward the fireplace. "But we've begun telling people Nicole is with child. It's possible there is still someone out there who wants the future heir to the dukedom eliminated."

Nicole placed a protective hand over her belly. "I wasn't even in the coach with Regina the second time."

"The blighter responsible may not have known that."

Nicole nodded. "I suppose that's true. Or . . . someone's after Regina." Her eyes flashed with concern and she squeezed Regina's hand.

"Also a possibility," Mark agreed. "Either way. I intend to cancel my trip."

Nicole's eyes widened and she sat forward abruptly. "No! You cannot cancel your trip. Your dream was becoming the Home Secretary and that position involves travel. I will not allow you to cancel your plans as if I cannot take care of myself. Regina won't allow you to, either."

Mark arched a brow. "I fully believe you can take care of

yourself, darling, but need I remind you that you're not exactly yourself these days?"

Nicole cracked a smile. "Is that a reference to my penchant for napping?"

Mark grinned back.

"I agree," Regina added with a firm nod. "I don't want you to change your schedule over this. It may well be nothing."

Mark set his glass on the table and came back to kneel in front of Nicole. He took her hands. "I would die if anything happened to you, my darling. No position is worth more to me than your health and safety." He turned to Regina and patted her hand. "And I refuse to allow another one of my cousins to be hurt. Not on my watch."

A loving smile transformed Nicole's beautiful face and she traced the line of her husband's dark brow with her fingertip. "Of course not, darling, but you're not the only person who can protect us. What if we stay here with proper security?"

Mark's brow furrowed. "What do you mean? I'm not about to let the coachman and groomsman be in charge of your security. Those two fools might have got you killed had things gone differently."

Nicole crossed her arms over her chest. "The coachman and the groomsman aren't trained for such things, but what if we hired someone who is?"

Mark's brow lowered further. "Who?"

Nicole shot a sly glance toward Regina. "What if we hired Daffin Oakleaf to be our bodyguard?"

# CHAPTER NINE

Regina thought she might cast up her accounts. Nicole had said she had a plan, but Regina hadn't expected *this*. Daffin, here? Dear God, could she face him? If he accepted, she'd be sorely tempted to flee back to her uncle's house in Surrey, Dryden or no, but that would only protect her for so long. Not to mention it would be cowardly of her. Nicole needed her, too.

"Daffin?" Mark's face slowly softened. "Hmm. I hadn't thought of that."

Nicole folded her hands in her lap. "I seem to recall him saying he doesn't have much family. Doesn't do much for the holiday. He could stay with us here in the town house and then accompany us to Surrey just before Christmas, where you'll meet us."

Mark stroked his chin. "I suppose the idea holds merit. I'd trust Oakleaf with my own life."

"And the life of your unborn child?" Nicole prompted.

"Indeed," Mark said solemnly, meeting his wife's gaze.

"Ahem, I'm not certain that's a good idea," Regina interjected from her perch on the edge of the sofa. Her voice had an unfortunate squeak in it.

Nicole kicked her softly just before Mark turned to her. "What? Why?"

Regina refused to look at Nicole. She cleared her throat. "I just mean . . . Mr. Oakleaf is a busy man. Do you think he'll have time to stop chasing down criminals and the like to play bodyguard?"

"It cannot hurt to *ask,*" Nicole said, nudging Regina with her foot again.

"Regina makes a good point." Mark turned back to Nicole. "Daffin may not be available."

"But if you tell him it's a special favor to you . . ." Nicole continued.

"You're right," Mark said. "It cannot hurt to ask. I'll pay him a visit first thing in the morning." He stood and made his way toward the door.

"Cousin Mark!" Regina called just before he left the room.

He paused and turned back to her. "Yes?"

"Will you be certain to tell Mr. Oakleaf that we completely understand if he's unable to help us?"

Nicole kicked her more sharply this time, and Regina squelched her yelp.

Mark frowned. "On the contrary, I intend to do everything in my power to convince him to accept."

As soon as Mark left the room, Nicole kicked Regina again. Regina jumped from her seat and leaned down to rub her sore ankle. "Stop kicking me."

"I had to kick you," Nicole retorted. "You're ruining the plan."

Regina whirled to face her. "What plan?"

Nicole rolled her eyes. "The plan in which I get you and Daffin under one roof, thereby giving you plenty of time to explain your lapse in judgment at Bow Street and charm him again."

Regina's mouth fell open. "First, I'm not certain there's enough charm left in me to overcome what I said to him at Bow Street, and second, we should hardly be concerned about my idiotic bungle with Daffin when one of us is being targeted by a madman."

Nicole crossed her arms over her chest. "First, there's only one way to find out how much charm you have left. Charm is hardly infinite. Second, *if* there is a madman after us—and I still have my doubts—we'll be perfectly safe with Daffin here."

Regina shook her head. "Do you truly think Daffin will agree to come and watch over us?" She prayed the answer was no.

"If Mark asks him to, yes," Nicole said with a firm nod. "Besides, Daffin works for bounties. Mark knows how much to offer him to make it worth his while."

"I didn't tell Daffin I was staying with you," Regina said. "It didn't come up."

"I'm certain Mark will inform him."

Regina paced along the carpet in front of the fireplace. "If it is not entirely certain someone is after us, isn't it unfair to take his time when he could be chasing down real villains?"

"We don't know for *certain* someone *isn't* after us," Nicole replied. "Besides, I think Daffin will enjoy it. He'll be with a family during Christmastide."

Regina frowned. "What do you mean?"

"I used to work closely with Daffin, and happen to know he dislikes Christmastide."

Regina couldn't stop her gasp. "Dislikes Christmastide? Why, I've never heard such a thing. Why would anyone dislike Christmastide? It's filled with laughter, and family, and food and merriment."

Nicole blew out a breath. "Yes, but Daffin has no family."

Unexpected sadness tugged at Regina's heart. "I'm sorry to hear that."

Nicole sighed. "He works himself ragged each December to keep his mind from it. This year, we'll merely be giving him something to concentrate on, not to mention he'll have our company during the holiday. If he says yes, that is. I hate to think of him all alone."

"It's terribly sad." Regina's mind raced. What had happened to Daffin's family? "I suppose when you look at it that way, our hiring him to watch over us is not such a bad thing, even if it turns out we're perfectly safe."

"Precisely," Nicole replied. "Besides, he'll be getting paid. It's a perfectly lovely plan all around. He'll be back to his real cases come Twelfth Night."

"If he says yes," Regina reminded her. "I've acted a fool to him. Perhaps I should go back to Surrey and allow him to guard you here in London alone."

Nicole's jaw dropped. "Absolutely not. That would spoil the entire plan. Besides, if you go back to Surrey, you'll have to face Dryden. Not to mention, Daffin needs to guard you, too."

"Yes, I'd thought of the Dryden debacle. It may be the only reason I'm still here." Regina's lips twitched.

"Nonsense," Nicole replied. "Besides, we're all meant to

meet together in Surrey for Christmas Eve. We'd catch up with you."

Regina shrugged. "I know, but at least there would be a delay." She grinned at Nicole.

"You're talking like a coward and you're no coward, Regina. You must face this head-on. Apologize to Daffin again and ask if you might start over."

Regina bit her lip. "I don't know if I can."

"Of course you can. Where's that Colchester spirit? At least promise me if Daffin agrees to come, you won't run away like a thief in the night."

"No. No." Regina waved both hands in the air. "I was planning to go in broad daylight."

Nicole snorted. "You know what I meant."

"Fine." Regina let her head fall back and gave a defeated sigh. "*If* Daffin agrees, I will stay."

# CHAPTER TEN

Paul, the clerk, leaned a shoulder against the wood frame doorway that led into Daffin's office. "Guess who's here to see you this time."

Damn it. Not another fame-seeking lady. Daffin couldn't take it any longer. He paused. Wait. It wasn't Regina, was it? Had she come to apologize or make him another indecent proposal? Frankly, neither would surprise him. The woman was unpredictable.

"Who?" he drawled, dreading the answer, though, if he were being honest with himself, he'd admit he wanted it to be her.

"The Marquess of Coleford."

Daffin let out a pent-up breath. "Ah, tell Grim to come back."

This would probably be just another discussion about the police force in London, but Daffin's stomach still tied itself in a knot. Had Regina mentioned her encounter with him to her cousin? Daffin, of course, had no intention of bringing it up, but if Grim did, he'd have to address it. Damned awkward, that.

Moments later, Grimaldi strolled into his office. No matter where he was, the former general always seemed to be studying a battlefield. His sharp eyes missed nothing. He commanded respect.

Daffin stood and shook the marquess's hand before taking his seat again. He searched Grimaldi's face. He wore a hard expression.

"Good to see you, Grim," Daffin said. *The Stone Man.* There were days when the moniker made sense. Since he and Nicole had reunited, however, there were fewer of those days.

"Likewise." Grimaldi lowered himself into the chair in front of Daffin's desk. "But today I'm not here to discuss the police force."

Daffin shifted in his seat. Damn. Damn. Damn. "You're not?"

"No. I'm here to discuss a personal matter. One that involves my family."

Daffin scrubbed a hand across the back of his neck. This wouldn't be easy. "Look, Grim, I told her—"

"Nicole may be in danger."

"Pardon?" they both asked in unison.

Daffin leaned forward and searched his friend's face. "The devil you say. Who is threatening Nic?"

"I don't know. But I damned sure intend to find out. The trouble is I'm scheduled to leave town tomorrow for a business trip to Northumbria. I need someone to watch her. Someone I trust. I need you, Oakleaf."

The drawn look on his friend's face told Daffin that Grim was serious. "What's happened?"

Daffin listened as the marquess recounted the two near-accidents and Regina's feeling of being watched. When Grim was finished, Daffin leaned back in his chair and scrubbed a hand through his hair. "Your cousin Regina is staying with you?"

"Yes, she's serving as Nicole's companion during her confinement. She may well be the culprit's target."

Daffin shook his head. "Who would want to hurt either of them? And why?"

Grimaldi rubbed his chin. "I don't know, but I want to find the bastard and tear him limb from limb."

"I do, too," Daffin said. Nicole was his old friend and former colleague. He couldn't stand to think of anyone hurting her, especially now that she was with child and vulnerable. And Regina, well, he didn't know how he felt about Regina, but he damned sure didn't want to see her hurt.

"I thought you'd feel the same way," Grim said. "Nicole trusts you. She asked for you personally."

"She did?"

Grim nodded.

Daffin had to wonder if Regina had confided in Nicole about her visit to him and her proposal. That could be awkward, too. "And Lady Regina? Is she agreeable to it?"

Grim blinked. "I don't see why she wouldn't be."

Daffin had his answer. If Regina had told Nicole, Nicole hadn't informed her husband. "Nicole says she thinks you might be free for Christmas," Grimaldi continued.

Daffin shifted in his seat again. This sort of talk made him uncomfortable. "Actually, I am. I just wrapped up the case that had been plaguing me for weeks."

"No plans to spend Christmastide with anyone?"

"No," Daffin answered, his tone clipped.

"Excellent. I needn't mention I'll pay you twice your regular rate for keeping them safe."

Daffin held up a palm. "My regular rate is sufficient. I'd do it for free if you asked it of me."

"Your regular rate and a half, and we won't speak of it again," Grimaldi insisted. "You must arrive tonight so you'll be there when I leave tomorrow morning. I'd expect you'd keep security measures in place in the city, accompany them anywhere they go. Nicole is adamant about not being a prisoner in her own house."

Daffin gave a wry smile. "That sounds like Nic."

"Next week, you'll be traveling to Surrey with the ladies where I'll meet you for Christmas. You'll spend the holiday with us."

Daffin nodded. "I promise I'll keep them safe. If the bastard tries anything again, I will take him down."

"I'd like nothing better," Grimaldi replied, standing.

Daffin stood too and the men shook hands. "It's settled, then."

"See you tonight." Grimaldi made his way to the door. He paused at the threshold. "One more thing. I seem to recall you and Regina flirting in Surrey last summer. Perhaps it should go without saying, but I expect you'll keep your manner entirely professional while you're under my roof."

# CHAPTER ELEVEN

Regina paced in front of the windows in her bedchamber. Daffin Oakleaf was coming to live here. Tonight. And staying with them through Christmastide. He'd be traveling with them to Surrey. She would be in proximity with him for the better part of a fortnight. It would have been a dream come true if it wasn't a complete nightmare.

She'd promised Nicole she wouldn't run off, but at the moment, the only thought in Regina's mind was grabbing her clothing, tossing it in her trunk, and jumping into a coach bound for Surrey. She couldn't do that to Nicole, however.

She must apologize again and set things to right (or as right as they could be) with Daffin. Then she would pretend it had never happened. She'd stay away from him. At least as far away as she could while they were under the same roof.

The heavy brass doorknocker down in the foyer sounded once, twice. Regina flew from her bedchamber and down the corridor to the landing near the top of the stairs. She stood with her back to the wall, listening like a guilty eavesdropper, as the butler opened the door.

"Good evening, Mr. Oakleaf," Abbott intoned.

"Good evening." The sound of Daffin's deep voice sent gooseflesh scattering along Regina's skin. She poked her head around the corner.

He stood in the foyer, a dark cloak covering his shoulders. He'd already doffed his hat and handed it to the butler. Next, he pulled his cloak from around his wide shoulders and handed that to the man too. His gloves were last. He was dressed in a red vest, black overcoat, gray breeches, and black boots. Oh, how he filled out those breeches. His blond hair was mussed from his hat, but it quickly fell back into place when he ran his long fingers through the strands. The smile on his face made her sigh. Drat. She was already half swooning over him and he'd barely made it into the house. This did not bode well for the next two weeks.

*Regain control of yourself, Regina Haversham,* she mentally scolded. The butterflies winging through her belly, however, indicated it might be a bit before she was able to do so.

Below, Mark entered the foyer and clapped Daffin on the shoulder. "Good to see you, Oakleaf. Thank you for coming on such short notice." Two footmen hurried forth to claim Daffin's trunk.

Regina pressed her back against the wall again and closed her eyes. There was little chance Daffin had mentioned her unfortunate proposal to Mark. Mark would have canceled his trip to Northumbria and not allowed Daffin through the door if he realized the designs his cousin had on the man. She trusted Daffin's promise not to tell, but the thought of Mark finding out made her nerves scatter again.

*Everything will be perfectly all right,* she scolded herself again. *You must stop being such a ninny.*

"He's just a man, for heaven's sake," she whispered. "A perfectly gorgeous, finely made man with eyes the color of spring leaves and shoulders that make one's mouth go dry." She laughed at her own silliness. Oh, poor Daffin Oakleaf had no idea what he was getting into. She had to find some way to overcome her attraction to him and act as if he were merely a plain-looking chap for the next two weeks. Yes, that would be her plan.

"Daffin!" came Nicole's bright voice from the foyer. "It's so good to see you. Thank you for coming. I cannot tell you how much we appreciate your assistance while Mark is away."

"It's my pleasure," Daffin replied.

Regina bit her lip. She wanted to hear him say those words to *her* again. Instead, the words that kept repeating in her mind were, *"It seems you've confused me with a prostitute."* They tortured her, along with the memory of the look on his face when he'd spoken them.

Sucking in a quick breath and pressing her hand to her middle, she dared another glance around the corner. This time, Daffin was staring straight up at her. She froze. Her breath caught in her throat, her heart pounding madly.

She closed her eyes tightly and winced. Oh, lovely. He'd caught her spying on him. Would she *never* stop embarrassing herself in front of this man?

Very well. No being a ninny. It was time to go down and face him. Head-on.

During the ride to Grim's house, Daffin had wondered how soon he would see her. Apparently, Regina wasn't any more eager for their awkward reunion than he was, given that she was hovering upstairs, partially hiding behind a wall.

When he caught her staring, panic flashed across her fine features. Then she closed her eyes. When she opened them again, she glanced to the side, looking as if she might turn and flee down the corridor. Then an expression of calm came over her, and she straightened her shoulders, lifted her chin, and came marching down the stairs like a queen descending to a throne.

She wore a light green gown that was tight under her breasts and flowed down her body in billowy softness. Her décolletage—highlighting the pale, silken rises of her breasts—made his throat go dry, so he concentrated on her arresting face. Her features looked crafted from alabaster. Clear skin, pink cheeks, red lips, bright blue eyes with black brows softly winged above them. She never failed to have an intelligent demeanor, as if she were sizing up everything and everyone around her. At the same time she had a fun-loving air about her, a twinkle in her eye, as if she didn't take herself too seriously. He liked that about her. Probably too much.

Daffin stood silently as Regina crossed the expansive foyer in his direction. Her dark hair was piled atop her head and she carried herself gracefully, her face perfectly calm as if she were coming to greet any other guest. He couldn't help but wonder what she would say when she reached him. The woman had arrived at his office and made him an indecent proposal. She was unpredictable. She kept him guessing. He liked that, too.

He could tell what most women, most people, were thinking before they said it. With Regina, he never had any idea what she would say next. He was on perpetual tenterhooks waiting to hear.

Daffin had accepted this position for two reasons: Nicole and Mark. The purse didn't tempt him. He didn't need it. He wanted to help his friends. The fact that Regina would be there after their awkward encounter was a fact he'd *tried* not to give much thought. Tried and failed, which was especially dangerous given that Grim had all but warned him to keep his hands to himself. Daffin had promised Regina he would not tell his friends about her proposal, and he intended to keep that promise. Would *she*?

If he were truly being honest with himself, he'd also admit taking this assignment would keep his thoughts from the ghosts that haunted him at Christmastide. That particular thought was inaccurate. He'd be spending Christmas with a happy family . . . the last thing he wanted. Nevertheless, he'd agreed to help his friends, and help them he would. He would simply make himself scarce during their holiday celebrations. That shouldn't prove too difficult.

"Ah, Regina, there you are," Nicole called as Regina joined them in the foyer. "You remember Daffin Oakleaf?"

Daffin didn't mistake Nicole's slightly dry tone.

"Yes, of course. Mr. Oakleaf, a pleasure to see you again." Regina's voice was light and airy. Her lips uttered the niceties any respectable lady would when greeting a guest in her cousins' home. She obviously intended to act as if the encounter in his office hadn't happened. Fine. He would, too. He respected her discretion.

Nicole reached out and pulled Regina closer into their circle. Was it his imagination, or did Nicole give him a knowing glance? Bloody hell. If she knew, this assignment was certain to be more uncomfortable than he suspected. Nicole wasn't the type to pretend away awkwardness. She was more likely to point it out and discuss it. He could only hope Regina had asked Nicole to keep her silence.

"Lady Regina," Daffin intoned, bowing at the waist to acknowledge her presence. "The last time we met, the circumstances were . . . unfortunate."

He'd meant their meeting in the country when they'd tracked down her cousin's murderer, but the startled look in her eye told him she thought he was referring to their encounter on Bow Street. "Your cousin's memorial," he clarified quickly.

Her face settled into calm again, and Nicole clasped her hand. "Yes, Regina's been a dear the last few months. She's come to London to stay with me during my confinement. Only, I haven't quite begun the confinement part yet," Nicole finished with a laugh.

Grimaldi cleared his throat. "Shall we retire to the study to discuss everything more comfortably?"

Daffin followed the three of them across the foyer and down the corridor to the study. He tried not to notice the graceful sway of Regina's hips as she walked in front of him. Or the mouthwatering aroma of apples coming from her hair.

Nicole ushered them into the room before turning to the butler and prettily requesting a tea tray. She shut the door behind their group. Daffin and Grimaldi waited for the ladies to take seats first, of course. Regina lowered herself into a chair next to the settee that occupied the center of the room. Nicole sat on the settee and her husband joined her, leaving Daffin to take the chair on the other side of the settee, directly facing Regina.

"We all know why you're here," Grimaldi began, giving

him a solemn stare. "I've asked the footmen to patrol the house round the clock. We aren't taking any chances." Grimaldi laid a protective hand over his wife's much smaller one.

The butler interrupted them by returning with the tea tray. "Thank you, Abbott." Nicole motioned for him to set it on the table in front of them.

Daffin waited for the servant to leave the room before he spoke. "Do the servants know what's going on?" He leaned forward and braced his forearms on his thighs, his head bent.

"Some of them do, of course," Grimaldi replied. "The coachmen and the groomsmen for certain. I suspect the gossip has spread to the other servants."

"I've mentioned it to Susanna," Nicole admitted, pouring tea for each of them.

"I haven't said anything to Genevieve," Regina offered. She took her teacup from Nicole and sipped it. What must be going through that gorgeous head of hers? Was she embarrassed? Hoping he wouldn't say anything? He couldn't help but wonder if she would renew her offer. He cleared his throat and forced himself to return his thoughts to the matter at hand.

"Good," Daffin replied. "We should keep talk to a minimum until we have a better idea what's going on."

"I agree," Grimaldi added. "I'll speak to the housekeeper and the butler about managing gossip."

"Excellent. Now . . ." Daffin's gaze scanned the ladies' faces. "Do either of you have any idea who might want to hurt you?"

Nicole handed Daffin a cup of tea. "I've been thinking about that. It seems to me that Regina may be the target. She's the one who was in the coach the second time, not me."

Daffin met Regina's gaze. "You had the feeling you were being watched as well, correct?"

Regina nodded and took another sip of tea. "Yes, but I cannot think of anyone who would want to do me harm."

"You didn't recognize the coach?" Daffin asked.

"Neither time," Regina replied.

"The coachman told me he didn't recognize it, either," Grimaldi added. "And he couldn't be certain it was the same one both times."

"If Regina is the target," Daffin said, "whoever it is must have been watching to know where the coach was coming from. He would have known who was in it."

"I don't want to discard the possibility that Nicole is the target, yet, however," Grimaldi added, his jaw turning rock hard. "We can't be certain he knew."

"That's true," Nicole conceded. "We are usually together when we go out."

"If Nicole is the target, it may well be because of the babe," Daffin said.

Grimaldi nodded. "My thoughts exactly."

"If Nicole is the target, the first place to look is with the next-in-line again. I assume it's still Mr. Cartwright." Daffin had met Mr. Cartwright last summer in Surrey. Cartwright stood to inherit the dukedom had a unique codicil not granted it to Grimaldi as a male heir on his mother's side. Grimaldi's mother had been the daughter of the former duke.

Cartwright hadn't struck either Daffin or Grimaldi as a killer, and his name had been cleared.

"Cartwright is employed at one of my residences in the north," Grimaldi said. "I intend to visit him while I'm there. I seriously doubt he has anything to do with this, but it cannot hurt to speak to him. I pay him a hefty sum, but who knows? Perhaps he's looking to make more."

"If that were the case, you'd be in danger, too," Daffin replied.

Nicole reached over and clasped her husband's hand.

"Yes," Grimaldi replied. "If the intention is to murder Colchester's heirs, it would make sense to start by taking out the future heir and setting your sights on the future duke later."

Daffin's gut told him Cartwright had nothing to do with this. "Less suspicious, perhaps, but we also shouldn't rule out another motive."

Nicole cocked her head to the side. "Such as?"

"Revenge?" Daffin met her startled gaze. "You were a Bow Street Runner and a spy, Nic. I can tell you from experience at least one of those positions generates a great deal of anger . . . from the people I've put away. No doubt you've made your share of enemies."

"And I can tell you the same is true for the other position," Grimaldi added.

Nicole nodded slowly. "And if Regina is the target?"

Daffin met Regina's gaze again. "Then I must ask, who are *your* enemies, Lady Regina?"

# CHAPTER TWELVE

Daffin awoke early the next morning to see Grimaldi off. He then proceeded to inspect every inch of the outside of the marquess's town house to check for safety. Besides the front door, there was a back door, a servant's entrance, and the coal chute. He set a team of footmen to work ensuring all of the lower-floor windows were properly secure. He intended to test them himself later.

Next, he sat down with the housekeeper and wrote out a list of every servant, tradesman, and delivery person who came in and out of the house. He wanted the names of anyone who was allowed into the residence or who might have the opportunity to sneak inside. He would inspect the locks on the ladies' bedchamber doors after they awoke.

Both Regina and Nicole were still abed when Daffin finally took a moment to get some food in the bright, airy breakfast room. An overly friendly housemaid named Louise served him his breakfast. She returned often to see if he needed anything else. As he ate, the same questions rolled over and over in his mind: Who would want to hurt Regina or Nicole? Was Nicole's baby the target? Was Grimaldi in danger, too? If Regina was the target, what possible motive was there? When he'd asked her last night, Regina had steadfastly denied having made any enemies other than perhaps the family of John's murderer.

Daffin was still contemplating it when Regina entered the room. She wore a white cotton day dress and looked as beautiful as always. This morning her cheeks were flushed. Daffin glanced up in surprise as she came to a stop in front of him.

"Nicole isn't down here, is she?" she asked.

He looked over both shoulders. "I don't see her," he replied with a grin.

Regina nodded and lowered herself into the seat directly across from him. "I think she's still abed. She's been sleeping later recently."

"Stands to reason," Daffin replied.

Regina cracked the hint of a smile. "I hope you don't mind my coming in here like this, but I wasn't certain when we'd have another chance to speak alone."

He met her gaze. "What's on your mind?"

"Daffin." Regina lowered her voice further. It was breathy and rushed and sexy as hell. "I want to sincerely apologize. Again. For my inappropriate and shameful behavior in your offices last week. I was quite overcome by your handsomeness and my own nerves, but neither is an excuse to behave in the manner I did. I do hope you can forgive me."

He tried not to smile. He did not want her to think he was laughing at her heartfelt apology. It was possibly the most endearing one he'd ever heard. "No further apology is necessary, my lady. I've all but forgotten our, ahem, meeting. I'm willing to forget it ever happened."

He couldn't hide his amusement at the look of utter relief that washed over her face. The poor woman had obviously been dragging around a great deal of guilt since their encounter. Confessing that part of the reason she'd been so rash was because she'd been flustered by his looks certainly didn't hurt. It was slightly adorable, actually. He'd already guessed she was quite green and uninformed about the ways of the world. She'd made a clumsy attempt at a pass at him. No damage done. Of course he had no intention of sleeping with her, even still. She was all but engaged and Grimaldi would kill him.

"Thank you." She smiled at him, looking young and fresh and pretty. It would be cruel to hold her mistake against her. She'd apologized, twice by his count. Now he could get about the business of protecting her. Do his job. That was all he was here for. Even if the smell of apples was making him hard.

"It will make it much easier for us to work together," she added.

"Work together?" He arched a brow.

"To keep Nicole safe," Regina replied.

"Are you certain you're not the target then?"

"I don't have the past that Nicole and Mark do. Why would anyone want to hurt me?"

"In my line of work, I've seen a great many motives. I refuse to discard the possibility until we're certain."

"Very well," she conceded. "I'm willing to do whatever I can to help you catch this man."

"Thank you." Daffin inclined his head. He liked that Regina was willing to help protect Nicole. It was brave and decent of her. He also liked that contrary to his first thought upon seeing her last night, she did not intend to act as if nothing had happened between the two of them. She took responsibility for her actions and had summoned the nerve to apologize again. That showed character.

A few moments of silence passed before she said, "Nicole tells me you don't like Christmas." Her voice sounded melancholy, as if she were disappointed to know it.

His fork arrested halfway to his mouth. How the hell did Nicole know that? Had he been that transparent?

"It's not my favorite season, no," he replied, hoping Regina inferred he didn't want to talk about it. They'd just cleared up their issue. He didn't want another one.

Thankfully, Louise came into the room, keeping Regina from asking another question. The maid stopped short when she saw Regina. "My lady," she said, looking slightly perturbed. "I didn't realize you were here."

"I'd love some tea and toast if it's not a bother," Regina replied.

"Not at all." Louise moved over to Daffin. Hovering too close, she leaned forward and displayed the tops of her breasts to him. "Can I get you anything else, Mr. Oakleaf?"

"Not at the moment, thank you," he replied, his gaze trained on Regina. This was awkward.

Louise left to fetch the tea, and Regina crossed her arms over her chest, her brows arched, the hint of a smile resting on her inviting lips. "Hmm. Seems you have an admirer."

"The maid?" He poked out his cheek with his tongue and shrugged. "Perhaps."

Regina rolled her pretty blue eyes. "Perhaps, nothing. She nearly swooned over you."

Daffin took another sip of coffee. "I must admit ever since

the stories about me came out in the paper, I've noticed an increase in . . . female attention."

Regina sat back in the chair and gave him a highly skeptical look. "Louise doesn't read the paper. She's swooning over you because you look like a Greek god descended from Olympus." She clapped her hand over her mouth. "Oh, dear. I did not mean to say that aloud," she muttered from behind her fingers.

A sly smile on his lips, Daffin poured himself another cup of coffee. "You cannot take it back now. You think I'm a Greek god."

"No. I think you *look* like a Greek god. There is a difference, and if you are a gentleman, you'll forget I said that, too."

"I'll *pretend* to forget it," he said with a wink. Damn. Was he flirting with her? He'd forgotten how easy it was. How simple it was to be in her company. She was reminding him of the sweet, funny woman he'd met in Surrey last summer. This was not good. For the next two weeks, he would be in the company of a gorgeous woman who had already offered herself to him and whom he *must not touch*. The flirting had to stop.

# CHAPTER THIRTEEN

Regina nearly danced to her bedchamber. Daffin had agreed to put the awkward encounter at Bow Street behind them. True, the Greek god comment had been unfortunate, but he couldn't possibly *not* know how handsome he was. Could he? Regardless, Greek god *faux pas* or no, it wouldn't be awkward being in the same house with him after all. They'd actually managed to return to the lighthearted banter they'd shared in Surrey. Relief swamped her. Her step was light as air.

She refused to think about the fact that that same banter was what had caused her to proposition him in the first place. She was a grown woman in charge of her faculties and in control of her urges. She could spend multiple nights under the same roof with a man who looked as if he'd been carved out of marble and not pounce upon him. She must.

"Regina? Is that you?" Nicole called from inside her bedchamber as Regina passed by.

"Yes," Regina called back. Her smile widened. Thank

goodness. Nicole was awake. Regina could tell her how she'd managed to make amends with Daffin already.

She pushed open Nicole's door and stepped inside. Her cousin was still abed and was stretching, her gorgeous red hair splayed out on the white sheets behind her.

"Good morning." Regina closed the door behind her and made her way to a lavender velvet slipper chair near Nicole's bed.

"How did you sleep?" Nicole asked.

"Terribly," Regina admitted. "But things are looking up. I had a private conversation with Daffin in the breakfast room this morning, and he's agreed to let bygones be bygones when it comes to my, ahem, unfortunate proposal."

"Oh, wonderful." Nicole rubbed her eyes. "I knew he would forgive you. He's quite reasonable."

"Yes, it is good of him." Regina took a deep breath and blew it out. "Now we can get on with the business of finding this monster who's trying to hurt us."

A sly smile crinkled Nicole's lips. "I'd much rather work on your plan to seduce Daffin."

Regina shot from her seat and put her fists on her hips. "Nicole Huntington Grimaldi, are you mad? There is absolutely no way I'm going to make a fool of myself with that man again."

Nicole waved a hand in the air. "Of course you won't. That's the entire point. This time you'll be much more subtle."

Regina leaned forward and placed her palm against Nicole's forehead. "Do you have a fever? Are you hot?"

"Not a bit." Nicole laughed and brushed away Regina's hand. "I'm perfectly fit, and I say your next course of action should be seduction." Her eyes twinkled.

"I just made up with him. I'm not about to embarrass myself again. Though I admit I *may* have told him he looks like a Greek god this morning." Regina winced.

Nicole laughed and shook her head. "I saw the way he looked at you last night when he thought you weren't watching. He's interested. Besides, I'm not suggesting you *tell* him you're seducing him. That's the entire point of seduction. It's a subtle art."

Regina rubbed her forehead and groaned. "I'm afraid I'm not particularly subtle. My artfulness is also in question. Besides, I'm done with my attempts at taking a lover."

Nicole scowled at her. "Now I must feel your forehead. Lean closer. You're usually not one to give up so easily."

"I learned my lesson quite quickly, thank you," Regina replied with a firm nod. "Soul-crushing embarrassment will do that."

"Oh, who cares about a bit of embarrassment? You said he's already forgiven you. You still want to lose your virginity, don't you?"

Regina blushed and glanced toward the door. "Keep your voice down."

"Well, do you or don't you?" Nicole asked in a loud whisper.

Regina scrunched up her nose and blinked slowly. "No."

"You're lying. You always scrunch up your nose when you're lying."

Regina scowled. "Fine, yes, I do." She spoke in a loud whisper, too. "But Daffin refused me and there don't happen to be any more likely candidates."

"Daffin is who you want and Daffin is who you shall have. Besides, I didn't go to all the trouble to get him here only to have you lose your fighting spirit, for heaven's sake."

Regina folded her arms over her chest and stared at her

cousin. "I had no idea what lengths you'd go to for my love life."

Nicole chuckled. "Anything for my favorite Colchester cousin."

Regina's chest tightened. "What if I bungle it again and Daffin resigns to get away from me?"

Nicole smoothed the bedclothes over her lap. "He won't leave us before Mark returns. Daffin's agreed to protect us. He's got too much honor to leave." Nicole leaned forward and put her hands on Regina's shoulders. "You were nervous when you went to Bow Street. You were out of your element. You hadn't seen him since summer. I say the first thing you should do is spend some time with him. Become comfortable in his presence. Talk to him. Be normal."

Regina snorted. "That's easier said than done. He makes me feel quite . . . abnormal."

Nicole pulled her hands away. She gave Regina a knowing look. "That is not a bad thing. Once you feel more comfortable with him, you can flirt with him again. It's quite simple. Just don't offer money again." She waited until Regina's horrified gaze flew to hers before Nicole burst into laughter.

A knock on the door interrupted the laughter.

"Come in," Nicole called.

Susanna pushed open the door, Nicole's breakfast tray in her hands.

Regina stood and started toward the hallway. "I'll leave you to eat."

"Come back at mid-morning after I'm dressed. Bring your fan. I'll show you how to use it to your best advantage," Nicole called after her.

Regina paused near the door. "Absolutely not. I'm going

to do something much more important than playing with a silly fan."

"What's that?"

"I'm going to ask Daffin how we may determine which one of us is the target."

# CHAPTER FOURTEEN

Daffin inspected each window on the lower two floors of the house. The footmen had done a fine job of securing them, but Daffin found a spot or two that could be shored up. He was halfway through his inspection when he encountered a window in the dining room with a broken lock. He would have to nail it shut. After procuring a hammer and some nails from the lads in the mews, Daffin had started his task when Regina came into the dining room.

She was still wearing the white day dress she'd had on earlier. She still smelled like apples, and she still made his mouth water. It wouldn't be easy to ignore her if she kept showing up like this. However, he couldn't be rude to one of the two ladies of the house he'd sworn to protect. He would just have to be professional and treat her as he would any lady of the *ton* he worked for. Respectful but reserved.

It didn't help that she distracted him by her mere presence, that her eyes were the color of the afternoon sky and her lips like ripe strawberries and— Damn it. This wasn't good. Not at all.

"How's it coming?" she asked in a bright, friendly voice.

"Quite well," he mumbled, three nails between his lips.

She gestured toward the windows. "Is it absolutely necessary to hammer them shut?"

Daffin pulled the nails from his mouth. "Only this one. The lock is broken. Though the truth is, a skilled criminal can knock out a pane of glass with his hand if he knows what he's about."

She shuddered. "Truly?"

"Yes, but the windows must be poorly made. These windows are quite fine."

Regina leaned over his shoulder. "Show me. How would you knock out the pane if you could?"

He chuckled and shook his head. He set the nails on the floor. Then he ran his hand along the top of the lower pane and pointed to the two upper corners. "Here and here," he said. "The glass is oftentimes loose. In a poorly constructed window, you could place the heel of your hand in the middle here. If you knock the wood hard enough, the pane would slide out. Of course, you must be quick enough to catch it so it doesn't shatter and send someone coming to see what the ruckus is about."

Regina peered at the window. "I never knew. It doesn't make me feel particularly safe."

Daffin chuckled again. He pounded the heel of his hand against the window frame. The glass remained intact. "See? Finely made. Nothing to worry about."

Regina shifted closer to him and the scent of apples intensified. *Ignore it. Ignore it. Ignore it.*

"Is this the first case you've taken . . . like this? Protecting someone, I mean," she asked.

He stuck the nails back in his mouth. "No," he mumbled. There. Curt, short answers might dissuade her from continuing the conversation. He'd already decided the best way to deal with his attraction to her was to spend as little time in her company as possible. He was here with a job to do and a distraction like Regina could impact his ability to do it.

"Would you like me to . . . hand those to you?" She gestured to the nails. The hint of a blush stained her cheeks. Was she still embarrassed in his presence? She had called him a Greek god after all. The truth was, she looked like a goddess, only one who blushed and bit her lip in a way that made his breeches tight.

Daffin steeled himself. He plucked the nails from his lips and carefully placed them in her outstretched hand. Their fingers brushed against each other's. It felt slightly indecent. What the hell? He'd never been sexually aroused by the mere touch of a woman's hand before.

"Thank you," he breathed, forcing his attention back to his work.

"Who else have you protected?" She arranged the nails in her hand in a precise straight line. She liked order. Duly noted.

"I protected a countess once. And a viscountess. Not at the same time." He'd tried to protect someone else. Tried and failed. He never mentioned it, and he didn't intend to begin now. Regina's questions were making him remember, however. Regret gripped him.

"Were the countess and viscountess run off the road by mysterious carriages?" Regina asked, the hint of a smile on her inviting lips.

Daffin hammered one of the nails into place before glancing at her. "No. One was fearful of her father, and the other wanted protection for her jewels."

The smile remained at the corner of her mouth. "You were hired to protect *jewels*?"

He nodded. He couldn't help but smile, too. It sounded ridiculous when said aloud. He reached for another nail and Regina handed it to him. Their hands brushed again. He blew air into his cheeks.

"And you took the assignment?" she continued.

"I did. That particular bit of employment was when I was much younger and would do just about anything involving security for money." He arched a brow. "I take it you don't worry that your jewels will be stolen, my lady?"

She laughed. "Never. I don't have many jewels, and the ones I inherited from my mother are much less important to me than, say, my friends and family. I would give away every jewel I've ever owned to have John back."

Daffin nodded. "Of course." Their banter made it easy to forget the circumstances under which they'd met. She must miss her cousin terribly.

"Have you ever had anyone close to you die?" she asked next.

He stared, unseeing, at the windowpane for a few moments. "Yes . . . my mother." He shook his head and gestured to Regina to hand him another nail. When their hands brushed again, a current rushed through him and settled in his groin. He turned away from her to study the windowpane. He needed to change the subject. "I'm happy to say that I no longer take on cases involving jewel protection."

"Thank you for taking our case," she said softly.

Daffin hammered the nail into the window frame. "I'm not

about to sit by and allow my friends to be hurt if I can prevent it."

Regina nodded. "I hope you consider me a friend, too."

"I'd like that." He turned to her and grinned. "Do you think you can be friends with a Greek god?"

A smile tugged at her lips. "It shall be a challenge, but I do believe I can manage it." She gave him the final nail, then rubbed her arms as if she were cold. The fireplace was lit, but it was across the room. "What about the other case?" she continued. "The one where the lady was afraid of her father."

"Yes," Daffin replied. "He'd married her off to a wealthy viscount, hoping to get back some of the purse. His daughter refused to give him any money, however, and he threatened her."

Regina sucked in her breath. It was barely perceptible, but he heard it. "I cannot imagine a father being so awful to his own child."

Daffin made use of the final nail. He couldn't imagine a father being good to his child. "I've seen my share of fathers be nothing but hideous to their children."

"That's a shame," she murmured. "I'm sorry to hear that." To his amazement, her eyes were misty. "Was your father hideous to you?" She searched his profile.

Daffin clenched his jaw. Why were her tears affecting him? He shouldn't have been so blunt with her. "In his own way." Damn it. Why did he say that?

"He didn't . . . beat you, did he?" Regina asked, her eyes wide.

"No. But if there's one thing I cannot countenance, it's a grown man harming a child. I recently put a bloke in the bowels of Newgate for just such an offense."

Regina's arms fell to her sides. She stepped toward him. "You're noble, aren't you?"

His brow furrowed. "I wouldn't say that."

"Yes, you are. You're a good man, Daffin. I could tell it the moment I met you."

Daffin shrugged as if to divest himself of her words. No one had told him he was a good man before. No one had ever told him he was noble.

"My father was a good man, too," Regina continued, glancing out the window. "But he died young. Is your father still alive?"

"No." Daffin's throat tightened at the sadness in her voice, but it was better for her to talk about her family than ask about his. "Your mother was the duke's sister. Is that right?" He hammered the final nail into the window frame.

She nodded, meeting his gaze again. "Yes. My mother, Uncle Edward, and Mark's mother, Aunt Mary, were siblings. They each had one child, me, John, and Mark."

Daffin whistled. "Not a prolific family, were they?"

"No." Regina shook her head sadly. "Now John's dead. We have only Mark to rely on to carry on the family line."

Daffin tested the window frame to ensure it wouldn't give. The hammer still in his hand, he turned to face her. "What about you and Dryden?"

"I suppose that's a possibility." She sighed and glanced away, rubbing her arms again. "I'd rather not think about it."

"Why haven't you married before now?" he asked.

She took a deep breath, folding her arms across her breasts. "I never found anyone I cared for enough to marry. Much to Grandmama's chagrin. My parents were happy together. I was hoping for a match like theirs."

He turned the hammer over in his hands. "And no love match ever came along?"

She tilted her head to the side, a wistful smile touched her lips. "No love match ever came along." She shook herself and rubbed her arms again. "Nicole still holds out hope for me, however. It's one of the reasons she wants to remain in town."

Daffin cocked his head to the side. "What do you mean?"

"Uncle Edward told me I may have until Christmas to find a husband of my own choosing."

Daffin whistled. "Is that so?"

She still looked melancholy. "Nicole and I plan to go to a Christmas ball at the Hillards' tomorrow night."

Daffin lifted his brows. "Husband hunting?"

She swiped a lock of hair from her forehead. "I suppose you can call it that, though I don't hold out much hope. I've had over a decade to find a love match. I doubt I'll find one in a sennight's time."

"I wish you luck, my lady. Rest assured, I'll accompany you to protect you, so you may go about the business of finding a husband without a care." Why did the thought of her dancing with some blue blood at a ball make his stomach clench?

Regina shook herself and moved toward the door. "That reminds me. I actually came in to ask you something about the investigation. Is there some way to discover whether this madman is targeting me or Nicole? Without putting Nicole in danger."

Daffin put his fists on his hips. "Putting *you* in danger, instead?"

Regina put her hands on her hips, too. "I'm not worried about myself."

"That's brave of you." Daffin rubbed his chin. "Actually,

I've been thinking about something. Both times you were targeted, you were in your uncle's coach. Is that correct?"

"Yes." Regina nodded. "Do you think it's a coincidence?"

Daffin slowly shook his head. "In my line of work, I don't believe in coincidences. I think *you* may well be the target."

Regina met his gaze. "Very well, then. I want to offer myself as bait."

# CHAPTER FIFTEEN

Regina walked slowly up the stairs toward Nicole's bedchamber. Her cousin wanted her to flirt with Daffin. She didn't want Regina to give up on her original goal of coaxing him into bed. But Regina didn't feel right about it any longer. Daffin wasn't just handsome. He was a good man. He was a noble man. The kind of man who wanted to protect his friends. The kind of man who would go after a criminal who'd hurt a child. She'd treated him like an object. She'd called him a Greek god. But he was a person. A human being with thoughts and feelings . . . and a past. A past she suspected was a difficult one.

He was easy to talk to, she'd discovered. She'd told him what she hadn't told anyone else, that she'd held out hope for a love match. She supposed the idea of a love match had always been silly. If a love match hadn't happened for her by the ripe age of thirty, did it stand a chance of happening now?

But Daffin didn't seem to judge her, the way people in her own social sphere did.

Had his parents been a love match? He didn't seem inclined to talk about them and his father had been hideous according to Daffin. How so? And how had his mother died? Regina felt it had cost him to say as much as he had. In the dining room just now, she felt as if she and Daffin had shared a connection, however fleeting. He hadn't wanted to talk about his past, but she'd got the impression he wanted to tell someone about it. Perhaps they were a burden, the things he found painful. She wouldn't tell Nicole. She didn't want to betray the confidence Daffin had placed in her.

She knocked on Nicole's door.

"Come in," came her cousin's bright voice.

Nicole was sitting at her writing desk, daydreaming. She tossed down her quill and turned to Regina. "What did Daffin say about how to discover which one of us is being targeted?"

Regina walked slowly toward her, rubbing her arms. "He said he didn't think it was a coincidence that both attacks were on Uncle Edward's coach."

"Hmm. What does he make of it?" Nicole asked, blinking.

"He thinks it's likely I am the target."

Nicole nodded sagely. "I hate to believe that but it may well be true. I just don't know who would want to hurt you."

"Neither do I. It makes no sense." Regina sighed. "Daffin didn't like my suggestion offering myself as bait."

Nicole rolled her eyes. "Of course he didn't. He doesn't want to place you in danger, but we cannot stay prisoners in this house."

"I agree. He said if we would like to go out, I'm to let him know and he'll make preparations. I already told him about the Hillards' ball tomorrow night."

Nicole leaned an arm on the back of the chair. "Is it silly of me to hold out hope that the two accidents were mere coincidences? Perhaps no one is after either of us."

"I do hope you're right. I suppose we'll find out sooner or later. Now." Regina nodded toward the letter sitting in front of Nicole. "Who are you writing to?"

"I was attempting to write my friend Daphne Cavendish. But you know how much I hate writing."

"Daphne Cavendish? She's married to the Viscount Spy, is she not?"

"That's right, her husband, Rafe, is good friends with Mark. So is Rafe's twin brother, Cade. The last I heard from her, she was having trouble with her young cousin's parrot."

"Her *what*?" Regina asked, slightly shocked. "Did you say parrot?"

"Yes," Nicole replied. "It's quite a long story, but after her thirteen-year-old cousin Delilah discovered she had a pirate in her family—she insists Cade is a pirate, but I promise you, he's truly a privateer—the girl was obsessed with procuring a parrot. Rafe indulged her and now she's got the thing and apparently it's been nothing but a nuisance."

"How so?" Regina asked, still smiling.

Nicole's eyes sparkled. "According to Daphne's last letter, he repeats everything he hears, and if that's not annoying enough, he *bites*."

"Everyone?" Regina asked.

"No. Only certain people. Delilah insists he's jealous." Nicole laughed.

"She sounds like quite the character, that one," Regina said, shaking her head.

"She is," Nicole agreed, nodding. "You should meet her one day soon. She'd love to help you find a husband. She adores matchmaking. Though she admits she's a hideous matchmaker at present, she argues that she needs opportunities to practice."

"I do look forward to meeting Delilah," Regina said, "but I'd need the most experienced matchmaker in the country if I'm to find a better husband than Dryden in a week's time."

"Hmm." Nicole stared at the wall, as if lost in thought. "The most skilled matchmaker in the land, eh?"

"Who?" Regina prompted.

"Delilah's mentor. Do you know the Duchess of Claringdon? Lucy Hunt?"

Regina was sitting in the front salon that evening after dinner, reading periodicals, when a slight knock sounded at the door. It had grown dark and the maids had lit the lamps. She glanced up to see Daffin enter. She self-consciously pushed a lock of hair behind her ear, cleared her throat and sat up straight. Then slumped a bit so as not to look as if she were trying too hard.

"Lady Regina," he said.

"Yes?" She did her best to seem nonchalant. She might have decided that they would merely be friends, but he was still good-looking. And smart. And funny. And brave. And . . . oh, she could go on.

"May I . . . have a word?"

"Of course."

He closed the door behind him and came to sit near her on the settee. "I've thought about what you said."

She'd said a great many things earlier today. "About?"

"About determining who the target is."

Her back went ramrod straight and her eyes widened. "You've changed your mind? You're willing to use me as bait?"

"Bait, no, but I do think it's important that we isolate you from Nicole the next time we leave the house."

Regina closed the periodical and nodded. "I can always find errands to attend to, and there's the ball tomorrow night."

Daffin leaned forward in his seat. "Yes, I think the ball will be perfect, and I will be there with you to ensure you remain safe."

Regina nodded. A thrill shot through her belly. She still feared another carriage accident, but the idea of helping Daffin bring down the madman—if any—targeting her family made her feel useful, just as she had in Surrey when she'd helped find John's murderer. "What do you suggest?"

"Is there someone besides Nicole who can attend the ball with you tomorrow night to act as your chaperone?"

Regina absently ran a hand over the cover of the periodical. "It's funny you should mention it because Nicole wrote to the Duchess of Claringdon earlier to ask her to accompany us."

"Excellent. If we can convince Nicole to stay here, we may be able to coax this blackguard into making a move. And if nothing happens . . . perhaps Nicole is the target after all."

A smile tugged at Regina's lips. "I'm game if you are."

# CHAPTER SIXTEEN

The next evening, Lucy Hunt arrived at Mark's town house and readily agreed to send her coach back home so they could use Uncle Edward's coach instead. It had been a chore to convince Nicole to stay behind, but in the end, she understood Daffin's reasoning.

Regina liked Lucy immediately. The duchess was bright and funny with black hair and two different-colored eyes (one blue, the other hazel). She was quick to laugh and had a nearly encyclopedic memory of the aristocracy, including who was and was not eligible. She took the news of Daffin's necessary presence with equanimity, while informing Regina she hoped very much she did not, in fact, have a madman after her. She agreed to keep the matter secret and remained quite calm about the possibility their coach might be waylaid.

Regina, Daffin, and Lucy piled into the coach.

"I daresay it'll be an adventure," Lucy said as soon as she was settled on the velvet-squabbed seat. "Not to mention I've never been under the protection of *a Bow Street Runner* before. Jane Upton will be sorry she missed this. She adores experiencing things she could write about in a book."

"I've had quite enough written about me of late," Daffin said with a half smile.

Lucy tapped her cheek. "Ah, yes, I've been reading about you in the *Times*. H. J. Hancock seems to be endlessly fascinated with your exploits." She pushed a dark curl behind her ear. "I can't say I blame him. My life seems quite humdrum compared to yours, Mr. Oakleaf."

The remainder of the ride to the ball was filled with chatter as Lucy rattled off the names of eligible gentlemen while Regina gave a perfectly logical excuse for every one of them as to why they were not necessarily preferable to the Earl of Dryden. Daffin sat across from the ladies, his back to the coachman, his expression stonelike, his eyes trained out the window for any sign of trouble. He didn't appear to take note of their conversation.

The three of them hadn't been at the ball an entire hour when Lucy pulled Regina aside. They moved behind a potted palm on the outskirts of the dancing. Lucy nodded toward the ballroom.

"Do you see anyone you fancy, dear?" Lucy asked. "I know nearly everyone here."

"Some of them I recall from my debut," Regina replied with a sigh.

"I was thinking Viscount Barclay might be good, though admittedly he's less handsome than Dryden and less rich."

"That's the problem," Regina replied. "There's nothing specifically *wrong* with Dryden. I simply don't love him and he doesn't love me."

"I completely understand, dear. I was wasting away on the

shelf when my husband, Derek, came into my life, but I knew he was special immediately."

Regina searched the duchess's face. "How? How did you know?"

"Every time I was in his company, I felt a bit sick in the middle. But in a decidedly good way."

Regina gulped. She'd had that same feeling . . . every time she was in the company of a certain Bow Street Runner.

"You know what I mean, don't you?" An excited smile lit Lucy's face. "You've felt it too. Tell me. For whom?"

Regina shook her head. The last person her uncle and grandmother would allow her to marry was a Bow Street Runner, or any man with no title. It had been drilled into her since she was a child. Her husband must be a member of the aristocracy. She'd be an outcast otherwise. Not to mention the fact that Daffin had rejected her advances and the question of marriage had never come up between them. She wasn't about to embarrass herself further in front of him by asking if he'd like to propose. No. Daffin wasn't suitable. He'd made it clear that he refused to get involved with a relative of a friend, and Mark was his friend. The idea of marrying Daffin was ludicrous. That's all there was to it.

"No one," Regina lied. "It's just that . . . the way you describe it, that's exactly what I want. I want to light up every time my husband enters the room. I'm afraid I'll never feel that way toward Dryden."

"I understand, dear. Sometimes the suitors who seem as if they should be the most acceptable just aren't, for a completely indefinable reason. My parents had all but despaired of me ever making a match." The duchess pulled her fan from her reticule and waved it rapidly in front of her face. "As for

Dryden, I've heard Lady Rosalind Millingham has been after him since her come-out five years ago. Poor woman should have made another match long ago."

Regina sighed again. "She can have him as far as I'm concerned."

"What about Lord Treadwell?" Lucy offered, her eyes scanning the ballroom.

Regina glanced over to the refreshment table where she'd seen Lord Treadwell minutes before. "Yes. He seems . . . nice."

"Oh, dear, *nice*." Lucy pulled a face. "The worst word in the world when it comes to husband hunting. Ranks up there with *pleasant* and *decent*."

Regina gave Lucy a wan smile and shrugged.

"Too bad the Duke of Huntley is a bit young yet." Lucy snapped her fan shut. "He'd be perfect, though I daresay, I already have a match picked out for him one day." Her eyes twinkled.

Regina was barely listening. She was supposed to be paying attention to the duchess and looking for a husband, but her gaze scanned the crowd for Daffin. He'd allowed the ladies to enter the crush ahead of him while he kept his distance. Regina had had a quick, discreet talk with Lady Hillard to briefly explain the situation. Thank goodness Lady Hillard wasn't a gossip. She'd readily agreed to act as if Daffin were just another guest at the party. She seemed thrilled, actually, to have the famous Bow Street Runner from the paper as a guest in her home.

For his part, Daffin didn't seem particularly amused with the party. He faded into the background so seamlessly that, at times, Regina had to look twice to find him. Once in a while, she'd catch him talking to someone, but his gaze remained focused on her. He was doing his job, she knew, but she couldn't help but catch her breath every time she found those green eyes intently watching her from across the crowded ballroom. Her belly felt a bit sick. But in a good way. Just as Lucy described. Drat.

"Oh, there's the Marquess of Morvenwood," Lucy said, a catlike smile on her face. "I've been looking for him all evening. Widowed over a year ago. Recently back in the marriage mart. *Highly* eligible. I'll just pop over and greet him and bring him over for a visit."

Regina watched Lucy go with halfhearted interest. She was being the worst sort of matchmakee, she knew, but she couldn't help herself. Her fantasies just happened to be filled with Daffin.

Moments later, Lucy came strolling back with the Marquess of Morvenwood in tow. Regina narrowed her eyes on the man. She didn't recall him from her former days on the marriage mart. He'd been married by the time she'd made her debut. The marquess was nearly forty years of age, tall, with dark brown eyes and dark brown hair with a bit of silver at the temples. He was certainly a decent-looking chap. There was something about his eyes that looked hard, however, perhaps tired. No doubt losing your wife did that to you. She felt a tug of sympathy toward him.

"Regina, there you are," Lucy exclaimed as if she hadn't left her side moments ago. "I was just telling the marquess what a wonderful dancer you are."

Regina nearly choked on the champagne she was sipping. She was *not* a wonderful dancer. Never had been. She was more likely to step on the marquess's feet than impress him.

Lucy made the introductions and the marquess bowed to Regina. "My lady," he intoned. "A pleasure."

"You absolutely must dance to the next waltz," Lucy declared, and as if her words conjured the music, a waltz began to play.

The hint of a smile touched the marquess's lips. "It would be my honor." He presented his arm to Regina, who swiftly handed her glass to Lucy and placed her gloved hand on the marquess's sleeve.

Regina managed to dance the entire waltz without injuring the marquess. She was feeling quite pleased with herself, when he surprised her by saying, "Would you care to see the conservatory?"

"The conservatory?" She blinked at him. Had she heard him correctly?

"Lady Hillard was telling me earlier about her prized roses," he continued. "I've been hoping to get away to look at them. I thought perhaps you would like to join me."

It might have been years since Regina had been actively searching for a husband, but she keenly remembered that gentlemen did not ask ladies to go away with them privately at events such as this. Perhaps the marquess was taking a liberty due to her advanced age. She was about to refuse him when he added, "My apologies. I can see the request has made you uncomfortable. I forget myself. My wife would have loved to see the roses and I must remember she's no longer here. I shall go by myself."

Suddenly Regina felt petty for refusing to look at some flowers. The man was obviously still in love with his deceased wife. He wasn't trying to make an unwanted pass at her. "I'll meet you there," she said to him. "I, too, love roses."

The marquess smiled at her and took his leave and Regina turned around and nearly ran straight into Lucy. "Well?" the duchess asked, tapping a slipper on the parquet floor. "How was the dance? Any sparks?" She waggled her dark eyebrows.

"I'm afraid not," Regina replied. "He seems like quite a nice man who misses his wife terribly."

Lucy shuddered. "Oh, dear, there's that word again, *nice*."

"I'm not certain which would be worse, being married to Dryden who's certain to ignore me, or being married to a marquess who wishes I'm his dead wife."

Lucy scrunched up her nose. "Neither seem appealing, dear. I hoped you might feel a spark."

A spark? At the mention of a spark, Regina lifted her head to scan the ballroom for Daffin again. She didn't see him.

"I'll be back in a few minutes," Regina told Lucy. No use courting scandal by telling Lucy where she was going. Besides, she would only stay briefly. No one would be the wiser. She should tell Daffin. But Daffin, for the first time all evening, was nowhere to be found. She bit her lip and glanced toward the door. The marquess would be waiting for her. She wouldn't be gone long.

She slowly made her way to the doorway and waited until a new waltz began to play, before turning, lifting her skirts, and slipping from the ballroom, headed in the direction of the Hillards' conservatory. She remembered the way from a long-ago tour of the home with Lady Hillard. Down the corridor, a right and then a left, the conservatory sat at the end of a long portrait gallery.

The moment she opened the glass doors that led into the humid room, the smell of roses overwhelmed her. She closed her eyes and breathed it in, enjoying the scent. What a lovely place. The conservatory at Colchester Manor had always been one of her favorite places, too.

"Lady Regina," came the marquess's voice from beside her, startling her. "Thank you for coming."

Regina opened her eyes. The rose arbors were lit with twinkling candles and the entire setting was entirely romantic. She wished Daffin were there, which was ridiculous, of course, because she and Daffin would not, could not be romantic.

"Come this way," the marquess said, taking her hand and leading her down a narrow mulched path through the flowers.

He pulled her deep into the middle of the room where they were quite obscured from view of the door. A skitter of apprehension traced down Regina's spine. "Wh . . . where are the roses you wanted to show me? Which ones?"

"These." The marquess pointed to some lovely pink ones on the other side of a round stone bench in the center of the space.

"Oh, those *are* lovely." Regina stepped closer. She intended to sniff them, exclaim upon their loveliness once more, and then make her excuses and return to the ballroom. She was quickly regretting her decision to come in the first place. She should have at least waited to find Daffin and inform him where she was going.

She lifted her skirts to make her way around the stone bench when the marquess's hand shot out and grabbed her arm. He pulled her into his tight embrace and his mouth came down to crush hers. The scent of alcohol on his breath was overwhelming.

She struggled in his embrace and managed to pull her mouth away from his. "My lord, you forget yourself."

His lips moved to her neck and he rained kisses along her bare skin. "No, I don't. You knew what I wanted when you agreed to meet me. A woman doesn't get to your age without

knowing about these sorts of things. You shouldn't be looking for a husband. You should be looking for a protector. I
could be such a man for you."

Tears sprang to Regina's eyes. She tried to push him away
but he was far too heavy. "You're mad," she muttered. "No!"
Her mind raced. If she screamed, someone might come
running, but she would also be caught in a compromising position and either become an outcast or forced to marry this
blackguard. The Earl of Dryden's apathy would be better than
spending the rest of her life with the lecherous Marquess of
Morvenwood.

The next thing she knew, the marquess's heavy body was
pulled away from her and he went sailing through the air,
where he landed in a heap on the far side of the bench.

"The lady said no." Daffin stood next to Regina, his hands
on his hips, his eyes flashing fire. A muscle appeared in his
jaw as he stared at the prostrate marquess with daggers for
eyes.

The marquess's eyes flared. Fear was etched in his features.

"If I catch you touching her ever again, you'll be a eunuch
within moments, do I make myself clear?" Daffin ground out.

It was only then that Regina glanced down to note that
Daffin had a dagger in his hand. The blade flashed in the
candlelight. The marquess nodded shakily, jumped up, and
ran past them as quickly as his legs could carry him, his
coattails flapping behind him.

Daffin turned to Regina. Her hair was mussed and her gown
askew, but she still looked as gorgeous as ever. How dare that
piece of rubbish touch her? He wanted to punch the marquess.
"Are you all right?"

Regina nodded shakily. She tugged at her décolletage to set it to rights. "Yes. Thank you."

Daffin pulled his handkerchief from his coat pocket and handed it to her. "That bastard better be happy I didn't slice off his hands."

Regina dabbed at her eyes. She was still shaking uncontrollably. "I shouldn't have come out here with him. Only his wife died and he seemed so sad." What would she have done if Daffin hadn't saved her? She shuddered. She didn't want to think about it.

"The bastard had no right to do what he did. Your meeting him here did not give him license to accost you like that."

"You're right," Regina replied with a nod. She handed him his handkerchief.

"If that bloke is the type of man Lucy Hunt is trying to match you with, I'd say she's doing a poor job."

Regina swallowed hard. "I daresay Lucy had no idea he was capable of that." Regina walked away and scrubbed her hands up and down her arms. "I never should have come here tonight. You cannot force a love match, especially not under a time limit."

Daffin pulled off his coat, stepped forward, and wrapped it around her shoulders.

"Thank you, I was cold," she murmured.

"I could tell." He cleared his throat. "Why is your uncle unwilling to give you more time to find a husband?"

Regina shook her head. "He says I've had twelve years already. He's not wrong."

Daffin kicked at the mulch with the tip of his boot. "I'm sorry."

"You've nothing to be sorry for." Regina wrapped his coat more tightly around her.

Daffin put his hands on his hips. "I never realized the amount of pressure put on ladies of your social set to make a good match."

"It begins at birth, I'm afraid, but I can't help but wonder if it would all have been different had my parents remained alive."

"What happened to your parents?" Daffin asked. He couldn't help himself. She looked so vulnerable and pretty. He told himself he should stay away from her, but seeing her attacked by that damned marquess had brought out not only his protective side, but apparently his sensitive streak, too. He truly wanted to hear about her parents. Truly wanted to learn more about her.

"They died in a carriage accident when I was twelve," Regina replied. "Grandmama raised me after that."

He studied her profile for a moment, his gaze tracing the curve of her cheek, her tender mouth, her stubborn chin. Then he inwardly shook himself, stepped closer, and said in a low voice, "My mother was dead by the time I was twelve, too."

"Really?" She lifted her face and peered up at him with those bright blue, assessing eyes.

"Yes." Why was he telling her this? He'd never told anyone. Why had he told her any of the things he'd already shared with her? Something about her made him feel as if he could trust her. Made him feel as if she wanted to know about him, too. Made him feel noble.

"What happened to your mother?" Regina asked.

He paused for a moment, only a moment. Tonight apparently, here in the rose arbor, was a time for confessions. "She was murdered."

Regina gasped. "No!" She lifted her hand and grabbed at

his wrist. A spark shot down his arm. "I'm sorry, Daffin. That is awful."

He briefly closed his eyes. He'd never admitted that to anyone, either. His life. His past. His family. They were subjects he kept tightly guarded. He moved away from her and took a seat on the stone bench.

"Did your father raise you then?" Regina asked, tiptoeing toward him.

"No," Daffin said, "I barely knew my father." She might have been enamored of him for a moment, thinking he was dashing and charming and handsome, but once she learned the truth about his family, she'd realize her mistake. Perhaps that's why he was reluctant to tell her.

Her eyes bright with unshed tears, Regina leaned toward him and placed a warm hand on his arm, just above his elbow. Her touch simultaneously burned him and comforted him. "Is that why you're a Bow Street Runner?" she asked. "Because your mother was murdered?"

Just like that, she'd cut to the heart of who he was, why he did what he did. But she didn't know the truth. She didn't know why his mother had died or who his mother had been. If she knew that, she'd recoil from him. She'd make her excuses and return to the ballroom as quickly as possible. Instead, she was watching him with real sympathy in her eyes. Real tears. He'd seen enough fake ones over the years from criminals who were only sorry they'd been caught to know real from fake. And she'd *touched* him. Even now, her hand rested on his. His instinct was to move away. He did not do well with sympathy. It made him want to shrug out of his own skin.

She finally drew her hand away and stared up at him quietly. She was obviously waiting for him to answer the question she'd posed. A question that burned in his gut. Yes, that was why he was a Bow Street Runner. Because he'd found his mother dead at the bottom of the stairs in their elegant town house, and even at the tender age of eleven, he'd known immediately it hadn't been an accident. But he damned sure didn't want to talk about it.

His answer was a curt nod. He moved to the side of the bench, giving her space to sit next to him.

"Do you have any brothers or sisters?" she asked, squeezing into the tight space. Her hip brushed against his.

"No." It was the best and only answer he would give. None who would claim him. None he would claim.

"We have that in common then," Regina replied, "growing up without parents. Without siblings. Were you lonely?"

Daffin stared unseeing at the canopy of bright pink roses that adorned the nearby white trellis. He'd meant to escort Regina back to the ballroom by now. Why was he still here? Why had he sought her out to begin with? He'd assumed her life had been perfect. She came from one of the best families in the country. He assumed she had been raised by loving parents in a loving household rife with servants and money and cousins and friends and happiness. All things he knew nothing about. He'd been mistaken about her—she'd known sorrow—and he wasn't used to being mistaken about anything. His instincts were usually dead-on.

She'd asked if he was lonely. Why did that cause a lump to form in his throat?

"I suppose so," he replied quietly.

"I was, too," she admitted softly.

Daffin turned to her. He'd made a mistake, sitting this close to her where he could smell her scent. All he had to do was reach out and touch her, and oh, how he wanted to.

His mouth lowered toward hers slowly, so slowly, giving her plenty of time to move away. But she didn't move away. She stared up at him with those big blue eyes and when his lips touched hers, she melted against him. Her arms moved up, pushing his coat off her shoulders, twining around his neck.

His lips pushed hers apart and his tongue invaded her mouth. She clung to him, making moaning sounds in the back of her throat, while he went rock hard in his breeches. She was responsive and delicious and all the things that made kissing someone good. He kept up his lips' gentle assault. He couldn't stop. He was mindless. His hands moved up to cup her face, to keep her mouth melded to his. His lips shaped and molded hers, as if he could never get enough. Minutes later, he finally dragged his mouth from hers. Breathing heavily, he pulled her arms from his neck, clasped her hands, and touched his forehead to hers.

"What was that?" she breathed.

"That . . . was a mistake."

# CHAPTER SEVENTEEN

Regina sat silently on the coach ride home. She'd decided not to tell Lucy what had happened with the marquess in the conservatory. It would only worry the duchess and make her ask questions. Questions that might end with her wondering why Regina had been absent from the ballroom for so long. Lucy chattered happily until they reached her house to drop her off.

"I probably should be worried about your reputation, dear," Lucy said, eyeing Daffin as she alighted from the coach. "But I suppose you couldn't be in any safer hands than a bodyguard's, now could you?"

Daffin shifted in his seat, while Regina merely forced herself to laugh and thanked the duchess for the attempts to find her a husband, however unsuccessful.

After Lucy left the coach, silence reigned. Regina stared out the window, trying to make sense of the evening's activities. She'd been a fool to go into the conservatory in the first place. On the other hand, it had ended in an extremely enjoyable kiss from Daffin. She couldn't regret that. Only he'd called it a mistake. He'd called it a mistake and quickly escorted her back to the ballroom, where he'd encouraged her to enter one door while he went around to another so they wouldn't be seen returning together.

She'd quickly found Lucy and made some inane excuse about where she'd been that she was certain the duchess didn't believe. They'd left within the hour after it was apparent that Regina was quite through with her husband hunt for the evening.

She glanced across the seat at Daffin. The side of his face was illuminated in the soft candlelight from the lamp on the coach wall. He looked angry . . . or determined. His gaze was fastened out the window, no doubt searching for a runaway coach. Did he truly think their kiss had been a mistake? Did he have a sick feeling (in a good way) in his belly when he saw her? Or did that kiss mean nothing to him? *Mistake. Mistake. Mistake.* The word rang in her head. Sick feeling or no, Daffin Oakleaf obviously didn't want her.

The coach pulled to a stop in front of Mark's town house and Daffin's shoulders relaxed.

"No trouble tonight," Regina breathed.

Daffin nodded. "Not the kind I expected at least."

The next morning, Daffin sat behind the desk in Grimaldi's study. His friend had told him to use the room for any business he needed to conduct while staying at the house. Daffin was hunched over a set of papers, reading notes from another case in which a noblewoman had been targeted. In that case, it had involved ransom. Regina's and Nicole's circumstances were different. The intent clearly seemed to be to harm or to frighten . . . but perhaps he could learn something from the investigative techniques used in the similar case. The last thing he wanted was to put either lady in harm's way, but how else was he to determine which of them was the target? After last night, he was beginning to wonder if either of them was. Perhaps the time of day mattered. He needed to take Regina out alone, during daylight hours.

Regina. His concentration was constantly interrupted by thoughts of her. A week ago, if he had been told he had something in common with Lady Regina Haversham, he would have denied it. Now he realized they had more in common than he guessed. She'd been a lonely only child in a house full of adults. She'd been an orphan. She'd surprised him with one revelation after another, culminating in the biggest revelation of all, the fact that she was an excellent kisser. He hadn't been able to keep his hands off her last night, and that made him the worst sort of cad. The woman had just been accosted in the same room minutes earlier. He'd shown up as her protector, only to prove himself no better than the marquess. She'd been strangely quiet on the ride home. He hadn't known what to say to her. But he knew now. He owed the lady an apology.

A light knock interrupted his thoughts. He glanced up to see Regina in the doorway. Today she wore a light pink gown that matched the color in her cheeks. She was gorgeous. He shook off his body's immediate reaction to her.

She cleared her throat. "Excuse me. Nicole sent me."

Daffin furrowed his brow. "Is everything all right?"

Regina took a tentative step into the room. "Yes, everything's fine. She asked me to let you know she needs to go out this afternoon . . . to the dressmaker's."

"The dressmaker's?" Daffin echoed.

"For a fitting," Regina explained.

A fitting wasn't something Nicole could send Regina to do in her stead. They would both have to go. So be it.

"Yes, Madame Duval," Regina continued. "Her shop is on Curzon Street."

Daffin nodded. "Ah, yes, I know the place. When would Nicole like to go?" He did his best to keep his tone entirely professional.

"She's dressing now."

"I'm ready, actually," came Nicole's bright voice from behind Regina.

The marchioness swept into the room with a smile on her face. "Good morning, Daffin. I know Mark wants me to stay home as much as possible, but I need new gowns for my confinement. I'm barely able to fit into my current ones." She patted her belly. "Besides, there have been no carriage incidents for days. I'm beginning to think this entire thing is much ado about nothing."

"I'll call for the coach." Daffin stood and brushed past the two women. This outing would give him something to concentrate on. Something besides his inconvenient attraction to Regina.

Less than an hour later, they stood outside Madame Duval's quaint shop. Boughs of holly and fir were strung along the shop fronts on Curzon Street and groups of carolers sang on the corners. Daffin brushed past it all, alert for any sign of someone following them.

He'd kept a vigil the entire way to the dressmaker's, glancing out both sides of the coach and scanning the street for any conveyance that seemed to purposely get too close. Somewhat to his disappointment, the coach ride had yet again been entirely uneventful. He'd like nothing better than to track down the bastard who'd tried to hurt his friends, beat him to a bloody pulp, and send him off to gaol before Christmastide. Then the Colchesters would have peace of mind, and Daffin wouldn't have to spend the holiday with them, intruding where he didn't belong.

The three of them entered the shop where the smell of fabric and lavender surrounded them. The proprietress hurried forth to greet the marchioness and her cousin.

Nicole smoothed a hand over her middle. "I must go in the back for my fitting. Madame and I won't be long." She followed the dressmaker toward the rear of the shop. Regina made to join them, but Nicole shooed her away. "Stay out here, Regina. Keep Daffin company."

Regina's eyes darted to the side. She looked anything but convinced that keeping him company was her best option, but she allowed Nicole and Madame Duval to whisk behind the burgundy velvet curtains in the back of the shop without her.

Daffin busied himself by standing guard near the front door to look for any sign of someone watching them. Regina folded her hands behind her back and strolled toward the window that faced the street. She sighed. "Nicole is attempting to play matchmaker, but I want you to know I've done all I can to discourage her."

Daffin smiled. "Did you . . . tell her about your trip to Bow Street?" he asked, not entirely certain he wanted to know the answer. Damn. Why couldn't he stop thinking about that proposition? He'd told himself a hundred times to let it go. Obviously, he couldn't.

"I did," Regina admitted, biting her lip in that adorable way of hers. "After the fact."

He winced. "I guessed as much."

The hint of a smile tugged at Regina's lips. "She had to

talk me out of hiding in my bedchamber for the rest of my days."

Daffin chuckled. "It wasn't that awful, was it?"

Regina folded her hands behind her back and took a few steps away. "I quite thought so at the time."

Daffin kept his gaze trained out the window, still looking for any signs of trouble. It was best to concentrate on his duty instead of Regina's pretty face. "My apologies. You took me by surprise."

"I took myself by surprise, too." She took a deep breath. "Daffin . . . I . . . about last night."

He winced again. "Did you tell Nicole about that, too?"

Regina shook her head. "No. I didn't. And I don't intend to."

He turned toward her. "I want to apologize to you, for what happened last night."

"I should have told you I was going to the conservatory to meet Lord Morvenwood."

"No, not that." Daffin stepped closer to her. "I meant I'm sorry for kissing you."

Regina straightened and turned away to look out the window. "Yes. You made it quite clear last night that you thought it was a mistake."

"It was a mistake." Was she . . . angry with him for calling it a mistake? She must realize it had been one. "It's not that I didn't want to, it's that I had no right." Damn it. He was making this worse. Why *had* he kissed her last night? He asked himself the question for the hundredth time. They'd just got off on the right foot, and then . . . he'd gone and kissed her. They should only be friends. Like he and Nicole were friends. But Nicole had never flirted with him. Nicole had never propositioned him. Nicole didn't have ink-black hair he wanted to sink his fingers into. She didn't have dark blue eyes he wanted to get lost in. Damn it. Not helping.

Regina turned to him and her face softened. "It's all right, Daffin. I'm glad to know you wanted to. I thought perhaps by *mistake* you meant that you wished you hadn't."

"I wish I didn't want to," he replied, biting at his lip. "I would hate for Grimaldi to come back and murder me."

She turned to face him. "He wouldn't do that. He adores you."

Daffin arched a brow. "Would he still adore me after knowing I kissed his engaged cousin?"

"Not-yet-engaged cousin," she corrected, smiling.

"Almost-engaged cousin," he replied.

Daffin scanned the bustling street again. No one seemed out of the ordinary. No one appeared to be lurking or watching. Who would want to hurt either of these women? The thought raced through his mind for the thousandth time. He glanced over to see Regina stroking a bolt of deep purple velvet. She had crossed her arms over her chest and rubbed them as if she were cold again. She did that often, he'd noticed. It made him want to take off his coat and wrap it around her again, but he couldn't do that here.

"You know, before Cousin John was murdered, I never thought any sort of crime would ever happen to any of us," Regina said, her voice strained. "Certainly not something as ghastly as *murder*." She shuddered and glanced down at the floor. "Now . . . I cannot help but feel as if anything could happen."

Daffin nodded. It was true, but she shouldn't have to worry about such things. "I'm sorry to say you're right, and when it comes to the safety of both you and Nicole, we should take every precaution until we know what is happening."

She nodded. He'd never noticed how long and gorgeous her eyelashes were.

"My fitting is finished," Nicole announced, coming out of the back of the shop with Madame Duval in tow. "We can go now."

Regina whirled around. "That didn't take long."

Nicole pulled the strings of her reticule tight. "I only had to try on one gown. The rest will be fitted the same way."

"Excellent," Daffin replied. He scanned the street one last time, preparing to escort the ladies to the coach that waited in front of the shop.

"We could stop at Gunter's and get an ice," Nicole said, rocking to and fro on her heels.

Daffin frowned. "It's the middle of December."

"Ice still tastes good when it's cold out," Nicole retorted. "It's better in the winter, actually. It doesn't melt as quickly."

"I'm not certain it's prudent." Daffin cleared his throat. "Given the circumstances."

Madame Duval glanced between them and lifted her brows, obviously interested in what the "circumstances" might be, but too polite to ask.

"I refuse to act as if I'm under siege." Nicole lifted her chin. "You want an ice, don't you, Regina?"

Regina glanced between Daffin and Nicole. "Ices are lovely, of course. I particularly enjoy the burnt filbert, but I want you to be safe, Nicole."

Nicole rolled her eyes. "I want you to be safe too, but I refuse to cower. Now, we're going for ices. I insist."

Less than twenty minutes later, the coach rolled to a stop in front of Gunter's on Berkeley Square. Daffin jumped from the coach first, scanned the area, and pulled down the stairs to help the ladies alight.

"Now that we're here, I'm feeling awfully sleepy," Nicole announced, stifling a yawn.

"Stay in the coach," Regina replied. "We'll get the ices."

"Indeed," Daffin agreed. He helped Regina down the steps.

He and Regina turned away from the coach. They waited for a few conveyances to pass before crossing the road toward the confectioner's shop.

A crack went off.

Daffin dove to the ground, taking Regina with him. He covered her with his body. "Keep your head down," he whispered fiercely.

He glanced up at the crowd that was forming. A man broke away and ran across the square.

"He had a pistol!" one woman yelled, pointing after the man. "He shot toward the lady," she informed Daffin, nodding at Regina.

Daffin jumped up and pulled Regina into his arms. He ripped open the door to the coach and handed her inside to a wide-eyed Nicole. "Stay down," he warned them.

He yelled to the coachman to take them home, then he sprang to give chase to the culprit. If he could catch the bastard, he could put an end to the speculation as to who was after them and why.

By the time Daffin ran the length of Berkeley Square and turned the first corner onto Bruton Street, where he'd seen the shooter run, there was no sign of the man. Daffin scanned the area. His gaze swept every inch of the place, his eyes narrowed and alert. The culprit had been of medium build and height, in working-class dress, including a hat that had been pulled down to obscure his face, but Daffin didn't know if he was young or old. He didn't know his hair color or any of his features.

Damn. Damn. Damn. He turned in a circle. The bloody bounder could be anywhere. In any of the store fronts. Hiding somewhere. Or perhaps he'd run down an alley. Or lurked in one of the many sets of mews behind the buildings. For all Daffin knew, the chap lived near here and was already home. Damn again. It would be nothing short of a wild-goose chase to singlehandedly search the area. He needed to get back to Regina and protect her.

Frustrated, Daffin set out back in the direction of Gunter's. He could only hope the coachman had kept them safe. Sweating from his run, he pulled off his coat and tossed it over his arm. He'd just turned the corner back onto Curzon Street when the duke's coach pulled to a stop in front of him. Damn it. They hadn't gone home.

The door to the conveyance opened, and he was greeted with looks of horror from both ladies.

"Dear God, Daffin," Regina cried. "You've been shot!"

# CHAPTER EIGHTEEN

Daffin glanced down to see blood seeping from his white shirt. How the hell had he failed to notice the wound to his shoulder? He had felt no pain, and apparently, his dark coat had obscured it. The two ladies quickly helped him into the carriage, and Regina shouted for the coachman to drive as quickly as possible.

As they raced home, Regina examined the wound. It appeared the bullet had merely grazed him, but that didn't stop the ladies from behaving as if he were in mortal danger. Regina pulled off her scarf and used it to stanch the blood. She pressed the soft fabric tightly against his bare flesh. She was so close her apple scent made his head swim. Or perhaps it was the blood loss. He grinned to himself.

"What are you smiling about?" Regina demanded. Her face was drawn and pale. She looked frightened half to death.

"Don't worry. This isn't the first time I've been shot," Daffin whispered to her. "But it's certainly the first time I've had a scarf that's probably more expensive than my entire set of clothing stanch the blood."

"You've been shot before?" Regina turned a shade paler.

"Twice," Daffin replied.

"What's that?" Nicole asked from her perch on the other side of him.

"Daffin says this is the *third* time he's been shot at," Regina replied.

Nicole nodded. "In his line of work, it comes with the territory."

"No. No." Daffin shook his head. "This is the third time I've been *hit*. I've been shot *at* more times than I care to count."

Regina didn't say a word. She continued to press her scarf to the wound as the coach pulled to a stop in front of Mark's house.

"Don't leave this coach until I'm certain the street is clear," Daffin warned, wincing as he reached for the door handle.

"Mr. Hedley, please scan the road for shooters before we take Mr. Oakleaf into the house. It's no worry. He's only been shot. Take your time," Regina said, irony dripping from her voice.

"The point is I don't want you to be shot, either," Daffin said, shaking his head.

Moments later, both the coachman and the footman indicated the street appeared to be empty. Regina and Nicole escorted Daffin into the foyer like mother ducks keeping an eye on their egg. The ladies insisted he go into the first drawing room and lie on the settee while Nicole ordered Louise, the housemaid, to prepare hot, soapy water and bring clean rags to treat the wound. Apparently, the ladies were intent upon setting up a makeshift hospital in the salon.

When Louise returned, Regina took the basin of soapy water and rags and dismissed her. The maid left with a sour look on her face.

"Why's she so unhappy?" Nicole asked.

Regina set the basin on the table in front of the settee and began wringing out the clean rags. She lifted one shoulder, a sly smile on her face. "My guess . . . she wanted to see Daffin with his shirt off."

Despite the pain in his arm, Daffin couldn't help his snort. "Doubtful."

"Mark my words. We'll find her peeking in the keyhole if we bother to check," Regina replied.

Nicole immediately put her hand to her forehead. "Oh, dear. I find the scent of blood makes me queasy in my condition. Regina, there's no help for it. You're going to have to treat the wound."

Daffin met Regina's gaze. She visibly swallowed.

"I'm fine," he insisted. "I don't need a nursemaid."

"No you're not. You've been shot, and I'm shaking," Nicole insisted weakly.

Daffin's nostrils flared. "I'm only angry the scoundrel got away."

"Nevertheless," Nicole continued, "I refuse to allow you to stay in my home with an untreated pistol wound you incurred on our behalf. Regina will treat it. Carry on." With that, Nicole hurried from the room.

Daffin's gaze met Regina's over the steam rising from the water basin.

"Do you mind?" she asked quietly, gesturing to his shoulder.

"Please." He watched her move closer. Her lips were parted and as she bent over him, her chest rose and fell. Sweat beaded between her breasts. He knew he shouldn't be looking there but couldn't help himself. He swallowed, hard.

Louise had also brought a set of shears and Daffin pushed himself away from the back of the settee to allow Regina to cut his shirt from his wounded shoulder. He winced a time or two, but her touch was sure and gentle. He appreciated that. She wasn't trying to baby him.

"Does it hurt terribly?" she asked.

"Not much," he replied, gritting his teeth. *Like the devil.*

"Would you like some brandy?"

"Would love some."

Regina made her way to the sideboard and returned with an entire bottle. "Drink as much as you wish. I won't judge you."

He smiled at that. "A nursemaid after my own heart." He uncorked the bottle and took a swig. Then another, longer swig. "Don't tell Grimaldi I drank his best brandy from the bottle."

"I won't tell if you won't. Besides, I'm certain Mark will understand, given that you took a bullet meant for his cousin."

Daffin flashed her a grin. "You may be right about that."

Regina turned her attention back to his wound. Her face was pale.

"Are you certain you want to do this?" he asked.

She nodded. "I used to help the groomsmen and the stable boys when the horses gave birth. I'm quite used to blood."

"Horse blood?" He gritted his teeth again as she dabbed at the wound with one of the soapy cloths. He took another long swig of brandy and concentrated on the liquid burning a path to his belly.

"Blood is blood," Regina said, her bright blue eyes focused

on his wound. "We should probably remove your shirt entirely. Regardless of how pleased that shall make Louise."

"And what about you?" he asked. "How pleased will it make you if we remove my shirt entirely?" Why the devil had he said that? He hadn't had *that* much brandy. Yet.

"Depends on what I see when the shirt comes off," Regina replied saucily.

Using the shears again to make it less painful, Regina tenderly helped him off with his shirt. When his chest was completely bared to her, she sucked in her breath. Good. It was the exact reaction he'd hoped for. Why, he didn't want to examine at the moment, but apparently, Regina liked what she saw. Pride filled him. Why did he care so much what this woman thought of him? At least this time he could blame the brandy. He took another swig of the delicious stuff.

Regina fought her blush. Her gasp had been telling enough, she didn't need to make a scene. But the man's chest was in keeping with his Greek-godlike appearance. She was certain Michelangelo himself couldn't have done a better job if he'd carved it out of stone. Hard and ripped with muscles, it was lightly dusted with hair and rippled when she touched it with the hot wet rag. She swallowed again.

"My apologies." She fastened her eyes back on his shoulder. "It's just that I've . . ."

"Never seen a man's chest before?" Daffin finished for her.

"Is it that obvious?" She dared another surreptitious glance at his perfect torso. The man obviously kept himself in good shape. "Chasing down criminals clearly keeps you quite . . . fit," she murmured.

"I also lift heavy objects and dabble in boxing," he replied with a roguish grin.

"That explains it." She leaned forward, refocusing her attention on his wound, carefully examining it. "It's a deep furrow," she announced after a few moments. She didn't meet his eyes, tenderly dabbing at the wound. "No doubt it will leave a scar."

"Won't be the first, and hopefully won't be the last." He raised the bottle in the air in salute.

She blinked at him. "Hopefully? You mean you look forward to being injured?"

"It means I'm alive," he murmured, swiping the back of his hand across his wet lips.

"Where are your other scars?" Regina ventured before realizing what a loaded question it was.

His grin turned positively roguish. "Care to see them?"

He was flirting again. She liked it. His words made her bold. "Depends on where they are."

"One is on my back." He slowly leaned forward and Regina glanced behind him to see a ragged round scar just below his opposite shoulder. "Another is on my calf." He leaned down and pulled his breeches from his boot, lifting the garment high enough to reveal his leg covered in blond hair and another large roundish scar on the side of his calf.

"Is that all of them?" Regina ventured.

"No. But the last one is somewhere . . . private."

A thrill shot through Regina's core. "Where?" she couldn't help but ask.

"My upper thigh." His hot gaze didn't let go of hers.

"I suppose it would be entirely indecent of you to show me that one."

"I suppose so," he said with a sigh. "Pity."

She lifted her chin in the air. "It's bad of you to even mention it. Especially knowing I fancy you a bit."

The hint of a smile tugged at Daffin's bottom lip. "Only a bit?"

Regina laughed. This time she boldly glanced down his chest and back up again. She met his eyes, and her breath caught in her throat. "That's right."

"I thought we weren't going to talk about that." Daffin set the brandy bottle on the floor next to them.

"I promised not to talk about my indecent proposal." Regina dipped the cloth back in the bowl of hot water and wrung it out. The water in the bowl turned pink. "I never said I promised to stop thinking you're handsome."

He leaned back against the settee pillows, his eyes half closed. "So you admit you think I'm handsome?"

"Even more so without your shirt on, I'm afraid." She shook her head. "But I'm quite through feeding your vanity when I'm supposed to be seeing to your shoulder, and as to that, the good news is it looks as if you've only been grazed."

Daffin turned his head sharply to the side to look at his shoulder. "I'm fortunate." He grabbed the brandy bottle again.

"I'll have to sew it, but first . . . this." Regina pulled the brandy bottle from his hand, placed a fresh rag over the lip of the bottle, and turned it upside down to apply the liquid to the rag. Daffin braced himself as she touched the alcohol-laden rag to his shoulder.

The sting made him wince, but just as quickly he forgot about the pain as Regina's hand clamped his inner thigh. She squeezed the area just above his knee. He'd never felt anything so erotic. His gaze met hers as she drew the cloth away. "That should do it," she breathed.

*Give me a cockstand? Yes.*

By God, she'd done it to distract him from the pain. "Thank you," he whispered, his lips inches from hers.

"Now for the sewing part," she replied. She grabbed up the needle and thread Louise had provided and held the needle over the nearest candle for a few moments.

He took another long swig of brandy. "Are you good at sewing?"

"Better than Nicole," she replied with a smile.

Sweat beaded on his brow and he kept his jaw tightly clenched as Regina made quick work of her task. She sewed the jagged flesh with four quick stitches and used the shears to clip off the end. "There, that should do it."

"Thank you." Daffin poured more brandy down his throat.

She moved away from him and gathered the rags and shears. "You'll be right as rain in no time."

"I never saw that chap coming." He shook his head.

Regina lifted the bowl of water in her arms. "Don't blame yourself. It was a crowded street. None of us saw him."

He clenched his fist. "Until I catch this man, it's not safe for you to be in crowds."

She nodded. "I suppose it's clear that he's after me now, isn't it?"

"I'm afraid so," Daffin replied.

Regina straightened and met his gaze. "Whoever it is knows when we leave the house. That frightens me."

"Yes." His gaze drifted to the window, while his thoughts chased themselves in circles. "He is watching."

Balancing the water basin on one hip, Regina handed Daffin a blanket from a nearby basket. He draped it over his shoulders to cover himself.

He captured her hand. "Thank you for your tender ministrations, my lady," he said. "I am in your debt."

"Nonsense, you saved my life today. I am in your debt." She pulled her hand from his and turned toward the door to leave.

Daffin's voice followed her. "If you'd like to see my other scar sometime, all you need do is ask."

Regina paused but didn't turn around. "Careful. I just might take you up on that offer."

# CHAPTER NINETEEN

Regina couldn't sleep. She'd tossed and turned for hours and finally gave up. Her mind raced with thoughts of an unknown man pointing a pistol at her as he emerged from a crowd. She threw off the covers, slid from her bed, tossed on a dressing gown, and sneaked down the stairs to the library. She would find a book. One that would either entertain her or bore her to sleep.

The library was chilly, its miles of books emitting the pleasant, faintly musty promise of a good read. The Persian rug was velvety beneath her bare feet as she lit a candle and wandered from shelf to shelf, her eyes skimming but not really seeing the titles on the spines, as thoughts of Daffin raced through her mind.

The past twenty-four hours with him had been unbelievable. Not only had he nearly been killed, but when she'd treated the man for a pistol wound, of all things, she'd been lusting after him like a common street doxy. At the very least, she should have been able to keep her lascivious thoughts to herself while he'd been *bleeding*. But no, she'd gone and told him how alluring he was with his shirt off.

Dear God. The man had muscles that went on for lengths. His shoulders were broad and smooth and strong, and the six muscles that stood out in sharp relief on his chiseled abdomen made her mouth water. It was hardly decent to mention it while he was in pain from a shot he'd taken while protecting her. What in heaven's name was wrong with her? Adding to her egregiousness, she'd touched his *thigh*. She may have done it to distract him from the pain of applying alcohol to his wound, but his *thigh*? His *inner* thigh. She could have grabbed his knee or even his hip. Ooh, she'd like to grab his hip, too.

She didn't just lust after him. She liked him, too. The man was noble and kind and funny and flirtatious and a bit arrogant. Just enough to be attractive, not irritating. He was decent and strong and protective, too.

She knew she shouldn't focus on her attraction to Daffin. She needed to focus on the danger she was in. And she *was* in danger. There was no doubt now. It would be entirely foolhardy of her to allow her attraction and flirtation with Daffin to make her forget about the madman who was intent on causing her harm.

Daffin was handsome. Fine. The man was muscled. All right. The man smelled like soap and spice and something else she wanted to bury her nose in. Very well. None of that mattered. She needed to end her flirtation with him immediately so the two of them could concentrate on finding the man who wanted to hurt her.

She cuddled up on the sofa with a copy of *As You Like It* near a brace of candles. She'd been there less than a quarter hour, when the door opened softly and Daffin stepped in. Despite everything she'd just told herself, her belly did a somersault. Bellies could be downright obstinate.

"Can't sleep?" He rubbed one hand through his slightly disheveled hair.

He wore a burgundy silk robe over trousers and what looked to be nothing else. A hint of his broad, bare chest showed beneath the robe. Not the best start to their supposed friendship, her staring at his chest again.

Regina sat up straight and pulled her own dressing gown tightly over her chest. He shouldn't see her like this. Her hair was down. She was not properly dressed but couldn't summon the will to care. They'd already had such a strange relationship, it didn't seem to matter that they were in the same room alone with each other, wearing night clothes. "I . . . no, I cannot sleep."

"Neither can I," he admitted. He shut the door with a gentle click and wandered toward her, the wood floor creaking beneath his steps.

"I'm worried," Regina admitted. It was a relief to be honest about it. She'd felt as if she might burst with worry until she'd just said the words aloud. She let out a long breath.

Daffin nodded. "I'm worried, too."

She tipped her head to the side and contemplated him. "Bow Street Runners worry?"

"Yes, it's a secret. Don't tell anyone." He reached the sofa and sat down next to her. The scent of his light cologne—a mixture of rosewood and fig—wafted toward her. She closed her eyes.

"I promise not to tell." She crossed her fingers over her heart. "I suppose someone in your profession has a great many things to worry about."

Daffin nodded. He sank down in his seat, his beautiful bare feet pushing out ahead of him, digging into the rug. "I want to keep you safe. You and Nicole."

Regina glanced away. His feet were beautiful. The thought was troubling, to be sure. "It's quite a large responsibility, what you do."

"I don't know how to do anything else," he murmured.

It was so quiet in the house, the low timbre of his voice vibrated through her. It felt like they were the only two people awake in the whole world.

"Have you ever lost a case?" Regina turned to face him. They were only an arm's length apart.

Daffin cocked his head to the side. He lifted his hand and scratched at the day's growth of beard on his chin. "A time or two." He grinned. "But *only* a time or two."

She studied his profile in the flickering candlelight. He had smiled, but there was an undercurrent of anger there. Or was it tightly leashed resolve? She'd thought he had secrets. She was certain of it now. "It bothers you, doesn't it?" she asked.

Daffin stared into the banked fireplace and crossed his arms over his chest. "Every day I'm haunted by the cases I didn't solve." His voice was rough, but honest. His honesty. That was something else to admire in him.

Regina nodded slowly. She fidgeted with the hem of her dressing gown, trying to work up the courage to ask the question that rested on the tip of her tongue. She took a deep breath. "Did they ever solve your mother's murder?"

Daffin's jaw clenched. She shouldn't have asked. He clearly didn't like to talk about his childhood or his parents, but that only served to make her wonder about them more.

"*They* didn't," he replied, his face a mask of stone. "I did."

Regina closed her book and stared at him reverently. "You did?"

He nodded slowly, his gaze still focused on the fireplace. "Many years after the fact but yes, I did."

Regina took a long, deep breath. She pushed the book aside and leaned toward him. "What happened to her, Daffin?"

He slowly turned to meet her eyes. "A man came into our house and murdered her. On Christmas Eve."

Tears filled Regina's eyes. "Christmas Eve?"

"Yes." A muscle ticked in his jaw.

Regina searched his face. "Who was it? Why did he do it?"

"His name was Knowles. He was a paid murderer."

"That's horrifying," Regina breathed, trying to comprehend such a tragedy.

Daffin sat back against the sofa. "Yes, well. It's the reason I sometimes find it difficult to sleep during the Christmas season."

Regina lifted her chin. There were more questions she wanted to ask, but she sensed it had cost him something to tell her that much. "When I can't sleep, I usually read."

"When I can't sleep, I usually have a drink," Daffin replied. "But I think I've had enough today, what with the bottle of brandy."

Regina winced. "How's your shoulder?"

Daffin gave it a sideways glance and lifted his arm as if testing it. "Sore, but fine. Thank you again for bandaging it."

"I think you're terribly brave to put yourself in harm's way on a regular basis," she whispered.

Daffin gave her a humorless smile. He shifted in his seat, moving closer to her. He leaned toward her. "Brave? Or mad?"

She twirled a dark curl around her fingertip, her heart beating like a hare's foot in her chest. "Perhaps a bit of both."

They fell silent and stared at each other, Daffin's eyes so steady on hers, she had to fight the urge to avert her gaze. Then his attention moved . . . slid, really, up and over her hair, her brow, skipped down her nose, and landed resolutely on her lips. She wet them with her tongue, an involuntary reaction, and noticed the way the candlelight seemed to flare in his appraisal as his own lips parted.

He leaned closer, the brush of his exhale soft on her skin.

She closed her eyes.

His lips were firm, but moved across hers with gentle tenderness. He pulled her into his arms, cradling her against him as they kissed. Her fingers inched up his chest and his neck to twine through his hair and hold his head in place. His arms enveloped her, holding her close while his mouth slashed across hers. Then his left hand moved down to touch her hip and Regina thought she would go up in flames. His hand stayed there, riding her hip, not moving, while they kissed as if they could never get enough of each other.

His mouth moved to her ear and her body bucked. His hand on her hip helped to settle her back down. Then his lips moved to her neck and she arched into his kiss. He trailed his mouth down to her décolletage, and began to push her dressing gown aside.

"There you two are," came Nicole's voice from the doorway, jolting Regina and Daffin apart like guilty children. "Oh, dear. I haven't interrupted at an inopportune time, have I? I could kick myself."

Regina and Daffin quickly moved away from each other. Daffin retreated to the spot he'd occupied moments earlier, a good arm's length away.

Regina cleared her throat. "We, er, couldn't sleep. We both came down here and met quite coincidentally."

"I can't sleep, either." Nicole slowly wandered into the room, her hand on her belly. "I'm a bundle of nerves." She, too, wore a dressing gown, and, shivering, quickly snuggled under the blanket with Regina. Daffin stood and moved to the fireplace to stoke the fire.

Nicole sighed and laid her head back against the cushions. "I know I should write Mark and tell him what's happened, but I cannot seem to bring myself to do so. I'm so worried for you, Regina. Mark will be, too."

"I can write him if you like," Daffin offered.

"Oh, that would be lovely, Daffin. Thank you. I must admit I'm frightened. A pistol shot is no laughing matter," Nicole added in a tremulous voice.

"I agree," Daffin replied. "I think we should leave for the duke's estate in Surrey immediately. You'll both be much safer in the country, where I can keep Regina away from crowds."

Nicole nodded. "If the man who is trying to hurt Regina follows us, he'll be out in the open."

"Precisely." Daffin jabbed the logs with a poker, sending sparks flying up the flue. "Pack your trunks, ladies. We're going to Surrey tomorrow."

# CHAPTER TWENTY

Daffin woke with the sun the next morning. There were dozens of details to see to before their party could leave for the countryside. He'd already decided the fewer people who knew about their trip, the better. After he left the ladies in the library last night, he'd returned to his bedchamber to write a quick missive to Grimaldi, informing him of the incident on Berkeley Square and telling him of their plans to leave for Surrey. He assured the marquess his wife and cousin were safe and promised to keep them that way. Regina would not be harmed on his watch. Neither would Nicole.

Daffin spoke to the housekeeper and butler, instructing them to tell any visitors only that the family was not in London, and not to provide any details as to where they had gone or when they would return. He also asked them not to share the details with any of the other servants.

Next, he went out to the mews to speak to the coachman and groomsmen. Those servants would be traveling with them to

Surrey, but Daffin needed a bigger entourage in case they were waylaid on the road. "I'd like to bring two footmen with me. Whom do you suggest?"

"Matthew and Timothy," the coachman said. "They're the best footmen Lord Coleford has."

Daffin returned to the house and worked with the butler to make arrangements for the two footmen to accompany them. He asked the housekeeper to write a note to the duke and his household to let them know they'd be arriving earlier than expected, and he had requested Regina and Nicole be ready as early as possible. He wanted to arrive in Surrey before nightfall. They'd be safer traveling during the day.

The two ladies were clearly still sleepy when they made their way down the stairs to the foyer. Yawning, they meandered outside to the coach. The footmen marched behind them with their trunks. The maids had been up early packing.

"Ready?" Daffin asked Regina as he helped her into the coach, trying to ignore the scent of apples as he helped her up.

"Ready," Regina replied with a nod.

"Nicole?" Daffin asked.

"I cannot wait to leave," she replied. "I only want Regina to be safe."

"Yes," Daffin replied. "Staying in London would be madness after what happened yesterday."

Their entourage set out in two coaches, one carrying the servants, including the two footmen and the ladies' maids. The other contained Daffin and the two ladies.

The first hour of the ride passed mostly in silence. Nicole and Regina sat quietly, wrapped in a pile of fur blankets. Daffin kept the curtains drawn until they made it out of the city. Once they were well on the way to Surrey, he opened the curtains to scan the countryside and see if they were being followed. He also regularly checked with the coachman to ask if any other conveyances were behind them. The way had been mostly clear except for the odd wagon or mail coach headed toward the city.

Two hours into their journey, Nicole fell deeply asleep against the side of the coach. Regina pulled a blanket up to her cousin's neck and patted it softly. "She says she can barely keep her eyes open now that she's with child."

"Another reason we must ensure she doesn't get too upset about all of this," Daffin said.

"I know. The shot frightened her terribly, but she's already told me she wants to investigate it herself."

Daffin couldn't help his smile. It was so like Nicole to want to investigate her own family's case. "If she wasn't with child, no doubt she'd have run the blighter down in the street herself. But I understand why she's more cautious." Daffin gazed out the window at the rolling fields. "It must be an awesome responsibility, being a parent."

Regina pulled the blanket up under her chin and met his gaze. "Do you want children, Daffin?"

His gaze shot back to hers. "I can't say I've thought about it much."

"What about marriage?" she prodded.

Daffin turned back to face her and rubbed his forehead. "In my line of work, it would be asking a great deal of a wife not to constantly worry about me."

Regina settled back against the corner of the coach. "Are none of the men who work for Bow Street married, then?"

"Not many of them." He gazed at her, snuggled into the furs. She looked incredibly vulnerable and incredibly beautiful. "What about you? Do you want children?" The question shot out before he even had a chance to examine why he wanted to know.

She turned her head to stare out the window. "I never thought I did. But I suppose with the right husband—"

"Dryden?"

She rubbed her forehead as if she had a headache. "I suppose Dryden will want children."

"Why didn't you want them, before?" Daffin prodded.

"It's difficult to explain, really."

He leaned back in his seat, making himself comfortable and crossing his booted feet at the ankles. "Try explaining it to me."

Regina took a deep breath. She traced a fingertip along the edge of the blanket. "I . . . I never wanted my children to go through what I went through."

Daffin froze. The answer was so close to his own thoughts about children, it unnerved him. He'd never met another person who'd articulated it to him before. "You don't want to raise children who might possibly become orphans," he finally said.

"Precisely," Regina replied. "I know that must sound mad."

"On the contrary." He pressed his lips together. "I know exactly what you mean. I never wanted to sire a child only to have him go through what I went through."

Regina leaned her head back against the seat. "Your hideous father?"

He nodded. "Among other things."

Regina touched her foot to his. "But Daffin, *you're* not hideous."

His breath caught. He wanted to shrug off those words, too. "Regardless, it's always been my fear."

She pulled her foot away. "Mine, too."

Daffin leaned to the side and braced himself against the seat on one elbow. "Do you think that fear might have also been what kept you from making a match?"

Regina poked at a curl that had escaped her coiffure. "I've never considered it before, but I suppose that may be true."

"It might explain why you've been 'on the shelf,' as you said, all these years. You're the niece of one of the most powerful dukes in the kingdom. You must have had your share of offers."

She rolled her eyes. "Yes, and when you're the niece of one of the most powerful dukes in the kingdom, many fortune hunters come looking for you."

Daffin studied her face. "Isn't that to be expected?"

Regina lifted one shoulder, then looked back at him and sighed. "I suppose so. Everyone in the *ton* knows my parents left me a great deal of money, and with my grandmother's fortune and my dowry, I'm worth quite a purse."

"Better than being a pauper, one would think."

Regina snuggled the blanket up higher. "Perhaps, but at least a pauper knows her husband truly loves her. I'm afraid I'm always suspicious of any man who attempts to court me."

Daffin studied her face. He'd misjudged her. She might not be used to the kind of crime he saw on a regular basis, but she was savvy. She could see the truth about people. She had a spine of steel. After losing her parents, she'd obviously become toughened to the world to keep from falling prey to fortune hunters. She had reasons to keep men at arm's length.

"In all these years, you haven't found one man who wasn't interested in only your dowry?" He tilted his head to the side. "Given your beauty, I find that difficult to believe, my lady."

"My beauty?" She flushed.

"You must know how beautiful you are." He watched her carefully. Her eyelids lowered. "I suppose it's as you said," she admitted. "It wasn't just the fear of falling prey to a fortune hunter. It's also been the fear of becoming a mother. Though I've told myself all these years that love was my goal."

*"Love?"* he asked, his voice incredulous.

She laughed out loud, causing Nicole to twist in her sleep. Regina clapped a hand over her mouth. "I mustn't wake Nicole," she said in a loud whisper. "But the way you said the word *love* was so comical. It was as if it were the verbal equivalent of a cockroach on your lips."

Daffin scratched at his chin and chuckled softly. "I suppose I'm not the biggest believer in love."

"Perhaps I'm not, either," Regina said, focusing her gaze out the window once again. "That may be why I've yet to find it."

He lowered his brow. "How did you expect to find a husband in London before Christmas then?"

"Oh, that was just pure desperation. Nicole can be convincing when she wants to be. I already know there's no one in the *ton* I want to marry."

"Dryden's just as good as any other."

"I suppose so."

"Then why did you wait for love all these years?"

She sighed. "When I was a child, I asked my mother whom I should marry one day."

"Did she give you a name?" he asked, suddenly a bit too interested to hear the answer. Perhaps Regina's love had been unrequited. Perhaps there was a man she'd fancied who'd married someone else. The thought made him uneasy.

She stared unseeing out the window, obviously lost in

memory. "'My girl,' she said, 'it's quite simple. You must marry the man you cannot live without.'"

Daffin slowly expelled his breath. Now *that* was some excellent advice about marriage. "And you've never found that man?"

"Not yet," she replied. She shook her head, returned her gaze to his, and pinned a smile to her lips. "Now it seems I've run out of time."

Daffin nodded.

"I know what you're thinking," she said after a few moments passed.

He arched a brow. "You do?"

She glanced at Nicole. The marchioness was making tiny little sighing noises, but didn't wake. Nevertheless, Regina lowered her voice to a whisper. "You're wondering why I so cavalierly offered you my virginity."

Daffin tugged at his cravat. "Perhaps," he said in a low voice, pasting what he hoped was a lazy smile on his face.

She lifted her chin. "Because I wanted to know what it felt like to do exactly as I pleased."

He cocked his head to the side. "Pardon?"

She pushed the blanket down to her lap. "I don't expect you to understand. You're a man. You couldn't possibly know what it feels like to have little recourse in life. That's why I wanted to know why you became a runner."

He shook his head. "I don't follow."

Regina stretched her arms high above her head. "I've never been able to choose what I do in life. I've had my whole existence planned for me since the moment I was born. It fascinates me to know some people can actually do as they please. Like you. You wanted to become a lawman, so you did. I suppose I enjoy hearing about it. Wondering what it would be like to have that sort of freedom."

He narrowed his eyes on her. "What was planned for your life?"

She shrugged. "Be a dutiful innocent, marry, produce little heirs. All of that."

"But you haven't done it."

"Not yet. But it's still expected of me. I cannot even marry the man of my own choosing. No. He *has* to have a title."

Daffin traced a knuckle along the windowpane, still watching her. He'd never considered how trapped someone like Regina must feel. "I always thought being a pampered lady would be the easiest life imaginable."

She sighed. "Easy in some ways, perhaps, but also incredibly unfulfilling. What use am I? What good do I do? That's why I was so eager to help you determine if I was the target. That's why Nicole wanted to be a Bow Street Runner and a spy."

Daffin rubbed his chin. "I never thought of it that way."

She glanced at her sleeping friend. She kept her voice low. "And that's why I wanted to spend the night with you. I wanted it to be *my* choice. My decision. I wanted to know what it would be like to spend the night with a handsome man without having to marry him for the privilege."

"Privilege?" Daffin's eyes widened.

Regina met his gaze head-on. "I'm quite attracted to you, Daffin. That's been no secret."

"I'm attracted to you, too," he admitted. "And I am flattered, my lady, believe me. But I should not be the one—"

Regina waved a hand in the air. "All my life my family has told me what I should and shouldn't do. What rules I must follow. And I've lived by them. Mostly. Where's it got me?

Lonely. I thought if I could pick the man I'd give my virginity to, if I could choose you—you who made me feel special for a little while—the night would live in my memory forever."

His pulse picked up. He cleared his throat. "You should give your innocence to someone who . . ."

"Loves me? Is that what you were going to say?" She gave a humorless laugh.

Daffin didn't know what he'd been about to say, exactly. "Someone special. Not me." He glanced away, suddenly wishing they'd never begun this conversation.

"You're special to me, Daffin. You were since the moment I first saw you."

He stole another glance at her, as something warm and sweet crept into his chest.

No one had ever told him he was special before.

# CHAPTER TWENTY-ONE

When the coaches pulled to a stop in front of the grand estate house that was Colchester Manor, Lady Harriet, Regina's grandmother, came hurrying down the steps, wrapped in a giant gray cloak and a set of colorful woolen scarves.

Daffin stuck out his head and scanned the area before nodding to the ladies that it was safe to alight.

"Grandmama," Regina called, allowing Daffin to help her down the coach steps. "You shouldn't be out in this cold. Go back inside. We're coming in."

"Nonsense," Lady Harriet replied, her voice muffled under all the scarves. "I want to see you and Nicole safe and sound. I've been worried sick about you both."

Daffin helped Nicole down next and hurried the three women into the house, shouting commands to the coachmen, and scouring the area for any sign of someone who'd followed them or was watching.

Their small party entered the foyer where Uncle Edward

sat in his wheeled chair, waiting for them. The butler took everyone's coats, hats, and gloves, while the duke and Lady Harriet greeted them all.

"We're so glad you're here and safe," Grandmama said, fluttering her handkerchief in front of her face. "I've been pacing this house for days. Haven't I, Edward?"

The duke nodded, and Regina crossed her arms over her chest. "Who told you there was anything to worry about?" she asked the older woman, her eyebrow arched.

"I did," the duke admitted. "I've been getting regular letters from Mark and Mr. Oakleaf here. You didn't think I'd allow my remaining family to be in danger and not keep a close eye on the situation, did you?"

"Yes, and then there was the story in the paper," Lady Harriet said.

"What paper?" Daffin asked.

The duke pulled a folded bit of newspaper from his side. "This morning's copy of the *Times*."

Daffin grabbed the newspaper and scanned the headline. "FAMOUS BOW STREET RUNNER SAVES LADY REGINA HAVERSHAM" it read. A quick perusal of the story, written by one Mr. H. J. Hancock, proved that they'd got most of the facts right.

Daffin swore under his breath. "How does that man know everything I do?"

"Who knows," Uncle Edward replied, "but I'm certainly glad you were there, Mr. Oakleaf. It might have been a much different story if you hadn't been."

Regina leaned down to kiss the old man on his papery cheek. "Don't worry, Uncle Edward, we're here now, and we're safe."

"And the babe?" the duke asked, eyeing Nicole carefully.

"Also safe," Nicole replied with a wide smile, patting her belly.

"Shall we all go into the salon for tea?" Lady Harriet nodded toward the green salon. "I have so many questions about how you've escaped a lunatic, not once but three times!"

After they'd settled into the salon, Grandmama rang for tea. Regina launched into a much-tamed version of the story of the two near-accidents in the coach and the incident with the pistol. Nevertheless, Grandmama and the duke were quite vexed. Their eyes widened with worry, and they exchanged a fraught glance when they heard Daffin had been grazed with the bullet.

"Thank you, Mr. Oakleaf, for taking such good care of my nieces. I owe you a great deal," the duke said, lifting his chin and addressing Daffin directly.

"On the contrary, your grace." Daffin stood near the mantel, his unhurt forearm braced against it. "You owe me nothing. I was merely doing my job. I promised Grimaldi I'd take care of them."

Seated on the settee beside Nicole, Regina leaned forward and said, "Don't let him fool you, Uncle Edward. Daffin needed stitches for his trouble."

"Egad!" Grandmama exclaimed, her ubiquitous handkerchief fluttering near her cheek.

"A flesh wound, I assure you." Daffin side-eyed Regina.

She pressed her lips together to withhold a smile.

"You're here now and you're safe." Lady Harriet reached out and patted Regina on the knee. "Thank goodness. Now, let's talk about something more pleasant."

"Ah, yes," the duke said, the hint of a smile lighting his rheumy blue eyes. "I have a surprise for you, Regina."

"Ooh, I love surprises," Regina replied with a bright smile. "What is it?"

"I've invited the Earl of Dryden to Christmas dinner."

An hour later, Daffin was walking around the perimeter of the house, checking all of the entrances and windows. He couldn't shake the memory of Regina telling him he was special in the coach earlier. She thought he was special? She was wrong. He was hardly the type of man who should put his soiled hands on her. She didn't know the truth about him. If she did, she wouldn't want him to touch her.

Bright laughter floated on the cold air. He glanced up to see Regina on the snow-covered lawn behind the manor house. She was alone and she appeared to be . . . building a snowman. She was bundled up in a red wool coat, white scarf, and black boots, a jaunty red wool cap on her head and white fur mittens on her hands. She looked bright and happy. She made him smile, though he couldn't help but worry about her being outside alone.

Daffin had strictly forbidden both ladies from going outside, but Regina had insisted upon getting some fresh air. Meanwhile, he was scouring the grounds for any sign of an intruder. So far, he'd found nothing. Hopefully they'd escaped London without the attacker being any the wiser, but Daffin refused to let down his guard until he knew for certain.

He changed course and headed in Regina's direction. "What are you doing?" he called to her.

She turned to look at him and her smile widened. "What does it look like?"

He pursed his lips and came to a stop next to her and her creation. "Building a snowman?"

"On the contrary. She is a snowwoman. Can you not tell from her eyelashes?" She batted her own.

Daffin peered at the short, black, vertical stripes above the snowperson's eyes. He poked at them with a gloved finger. "Eyelashes? What are they made from?"

"Licorice," Regina replied, her eyes sparkling with delight. "I got it from Cook. She always has black licorice at Christmastide."

He crossed his arms over his chest and watched her. She was obviously pleased with her task. She'd seemed happier since they'd arrived. "You grew up here, didn't you?"

She kept her gaze focused on her work. "Yes. After my parents died, my uncle became my guardian. Grandmama came back here and moved into the dower house to watch over me."

Daffin turned back to look at the enormous manor house. "It must have been quite a life, living in an estate like this."

She stuck a carrot in the center of the snowwoman's round white head to make her nose. "It's the only home I know. I barely remember my life before my parents' accident."

Daffin understood that sentiment. Sometimes his life before his mother's death seemed more like a dream than reality. He tugged on his gloves. The wind was getting colder. The protective part of him wanted to usher Regina inside where she would be safe and warm.

"As for the snowwoman," Regina continued. "It's a tradition for me at Christmastide. I've been doing it since the first year I came to live here." She glanced around. "I must admit I've been looking over my shoulder this year. I feel safe with you here, however." She gave him a tentative smile.

"I'm glad to hear that," Daffin replied. Keeping her safe was his first priority, but he'd begun to look forward to their talks, too. He nodded to her creation. "Snowwomen are your tradition. Do you have any others?"

"Our family has a tradition of trading small gifts on Christmas Eve. Nothing extravagant."

Daffin stared off into the copse of trees several yards away. "My mother and I gave each other gifts at Christmastide, too." He'd never admitted that to anyone before. It was getting easier and easier to share things with Regina, but the memory still made his throat ache. He shook his head. "What sorts of gifts do you give each other?"

She stepped back to squint at the snowwoman's nose, adjusted the carrot a bit to the left, and sighed. "One of my favorites was a tiny frosted gingerbread man Uncle Edward gave me when I was still a girl. I ate it so quickly no one else had a chance to see it. Grandmama laughed for hours." Regina tilted her head to the side and blinked at him. "What was your favorite gift?"

A lump formed in Daffin's throat. He scrubbed the back of his glove against his forehead. "A dagger. My mother gave me one. That Christmas Eve before she died. It was the last gift I received."

Regina swallowed. "From anyone? Ever?"

Daffin nodded once. His chest felt tight.

Regina stepped toward him and put a mitten on his shoulder. "Oh, Daffin. I'm so sorry."

He shook his head and forced joviality back into his voice. "Tell me, what do *you* want for Christmas this year, Regina?"

She cocked her head to the side. "What if I told you I wanted to learn more about you?"

He shook his head. "I suppose that's an easy enough gift to give. What would you like to know?"

"Where did you grow up?" she asked.

"In London."

She laughed and shook her head again. "Yes, I'd gathered that, but what part?"

He dug his boot into the packed snow and took a deep breath. "Belgravia."

A slight flash of surprise flared in Regina's eyes when she glanced at him. Belgravia was an affluent part of the city. Perhaps not as affluent as Mayfair, but a close second.

"Belgravia?" she echoed. "How did we not know each other?"

"I was only in Belgravia until my mother died. She wasn't a part of Society." Officially.

"Why not?"

No. There was no way he was going to explain his mother's place on the fringes of Society, no matter how curious Regina was. "It's a long story and I have a personal question for *you* now."

"Very well, I suppose it's only fair. What's your question?"

"Do you truly intend to marry Lord Dryden?"

Her smile faded. "What choice do I have? There is a considerable shortage of eligible bachelors in Surrey at Christmastide." She was trying to be funny, but Daffin didn't laugh.

He watched her closely. Her attention remained intent on the snowwoman. "So that's it? You intend to give up? No more looking for love?"

She snatched a green velvet bonnet from her pile of supplies nearby, placed it on the snowwoman's head, and tied the ribbons under its chin. "I don't think of it as giving up. I think of it more as succumbing to my fate."

"That doesn't sound like you." He couldn't keep the hint of anger from his voice. To see this beautiful, special woman give herself away in marriage to a man who didn't appreciate her . . . Daffin couldn't stomach it.

She glanced at him, surprise in her eyes. "That's what Nicole says."

"Nicole's right," he clipped.

Regina plunked two pieces of coal into the snowwoman's face to give her eyes and wiped her mittens together, apparently finished with her task. "Have you ever met the Earl of Dryden?"

"I don't believe I have," Daffin answered.

Regina tugged her red cap down over her ears. "Well, I have, on many occasions, and he's perfectly . . . *nice.*"

"Sounds like a stunning recommendation."

"Maybe nice is good enough. Maybe nice is all there is. Marrying the Earl of Dryden is what's expected of me. I've put it off long enough. It's been selfish of me to believe I'm special."

He stepped forward and cupped his hands under both her elbows. He stared into her eyes. "Regina, you've no idea just how special you are."

# CHAPTER TWENTY-TWO

Regina slowly climbed the stairs to her bedchamber. Daffin had called her special. He understood her reasons for not wanting to marry Dryden. He even understood what it was like to be fearful that your children would experience the same hurt you did. So fearful you didn't even want to have children. She'd never realized anyone else felt that same way. What had happened to Daffin after his mother died? Had he stayed with his hideous father? How must that have been for a young boy? He was opening up to her, but slowly. She'd wanted to ask him why a paid murderer had been after his mother, but that was a question for another time. So was the question about where he'd ended up after his mother's death.

He'd seemed a bit angry with her for seemingly giving up on her quest to find love, which made no sense because he himself had said he didn't believe in love. The perfect man did not exist. The one who made your stomach flutter was not the one with a title and neighboring lands. It was a lesson she was learning all too well.

She entered her bedchamber, closed the door, and climbed atop the bed. She sat in silence, staring into the fireplace, until a knock sounded at the door.

"Regina? May I come in?" Nicole called.

"Of course."

Nicole opened the door and stepped inside. She walked over to the bed and sat on the side of it, her hip turned to face Regina. "Are you all right, dear?"

Regina expelled her breath. "Honestly, I don't know."

"What's happened?"

Regina calmly folded her hands over her middle and stared at the canopy above her. "I've kissed Daffin. Twice."

A sly smile crept to Nicole's lips. "I *thought* I'd interrupted something in the library the other night, but I didn't want to pry."

"It's all right. We needed to be interrupted. It's all so confusing. I don't know what to think. He makes me feel so . . . oh, I cannot describe it. All I know is that I want to kiss him again."

Nicole patted her knee. "I know, dear. I know."

"Did he ever tell you anything . . . about what happened to his family?"

"Not much." Nicole shook her head. "I only know his mother died when he was a boy. He went to boarding school after that."

"Oh." Regina considered that for a moment. So he hadn't had to live with his hideous father.

"I get the impression his childhood was far from happy," Nicole added.

"I do, too." Regina grabbed a pillow and hugged it to her chest. "I did what you suggested. I've talked to him. Tried to get to know him, and I've decided I like him. I *really* like him. But I'm not certain if he's truly not interested in me or just thinks he shouldn't be."

"Yes. Those are two quite different things. However, if he's kissed you twice, I tend to think it's the latter, dear."

Regina expelled a breath. "I'm going to ask him."

"I think that's an excellent idea." Nicole winked at her.

Regina signed. "Why can't life be easier?"

"If it were easier, dear, I think it would also be terribly boring."

The two women exchanged smiles.

"Now," Nicole continued. "Let's focus on Christmastide. Mark will be here soon and we should be merry and bright."

"I do adore Christmas," Regina replied, before wrinkling her nose. "If only Lord Dryden weren't coming for dinner."

Nicole crossed her arms over her chest and drummed her fingertips on the opposite elbows. "It is unfortunate. I do wish Uncle Edward had consulted with me before inviting the man, but Uncle worries about you. You cannot blame him."

"I don't," Regina replied. "Truly. Perhaps I'll learn to . . . love . . . Dryden one day."

"I'm not certain that's how love works," Nicole said softly. "Not true love, at least."

Regina pressed her palms against her eyes. "Oh, enough about the Earl of Dryden. I'll deal with him when I must. I'd much rather discuss how I can kiss Daffin again." Her bright humor returned.

"Oh, my dear." Nicole gleefully clapped her hands. "That is what mistletoe is for."

# CHAPTER TWENTY-THREE

The day before Christmas Eve, Regina made the rounds, visiting friends in the countryside and her uncle's tenants. She went shopping for gifts in the village. She caught up with the servants. She shared nice, long talks with her grandmother, and managed to scour the grounds for a fresh bough of mistletoe, which, as evening set in, she promptly handed to Nicole, who promised to handle everything.

Regina sat in the front salon, ostensibly reading letters from friends, but her mind was elsewhere. Her heart ached at the thought of an eleven-year-old boy learning his mother had been murdered. At Christmas of all times.

She remembered that day, so long ago, when her grandmother had come into her bedchamber to tell her that her parents were never coming home. She'd been playing with her dolls. After Grandmama left the room in tears, she'd put away the dolls and never played with them again.

At least she'd had her grandmother and her uncle to rely

on. It sounded as if Daffin had had no one. He hadn't mentioned any other family and he'd said his father hadn't been part of his life. What exactly did that mean? What had happened to Daffin? She desperately wanted to know the answers to these questions. He needed love and support.

She hadn't seen much of him in the last few days. There had been no opportunity to catch him under the mistletoe. He'd been busy each morning making his rounds around the estate grounds. He watched her like a hawk watched its hatchling. Regina stayed in the house playing the pianoforte and talking to Uncle Edward and Grandmama. Nicole remained inside as well, attempting to do things she hated, like writing letters and embroidering pillows. In the afternoons, Nicole stared out the window toward the north. Regina could nearly feel her cousin's longing. Nicole missed Mark desperately. He would be here tomorrow night, in time for Christmas with the family.

"Regina," Nicole called from her perch near the window in the front salon.

"Yes." Regina moved into the room. Through the window, she saw Daffin marching through the snow toward the back door. "Do you need something, Nicole?"

"Will you see if I left my embroidery near the servants' entrance? I went there earlier to peek out."

Regina shook her head. It was killing her cousin to have to remain cooped up in the house. She could picture Nicole peering out the back door. No doubt she'd left her embroidery there on purpose.

Regina trailed her way toward the back of the house. When she got to the servants' entrance, she looked right and left. There were cupboards on both sides of her, but no sign of Nicole's embroidery.

A slip of paper on the cupboard caught her eye. Her name was written on it. She frowned and picked it up. She glanced out the window. Daffin was headed toward her, about to enter through the door in front of her. Unfolding the paper, she saw the words, *Look Up,* just as Daffin opened the door and stepped inside.

Regina lifted her gaze to the bough of mistletoe strung above her head. Daffin looked up too, then back down at her, suspicion etched on his features.

He obviously thought she had planned this moment. Regardless, she wasn't about to let it pass. She took a deep breath, locked gazes with him, and said, "Kiss me. It's Christmas."

Daffin pursed his lips. There was indeed a bough of mistletoe hanging above their heads. And Regina, who was standing directly under it, was tempting. Each time they shared each other's company he came away liking her more. She was sweet and funny and thoughtful and kind. She thought about others more than herself. Hell, she was even willing to marry a man she didn't want because she wanted her uncle to die in peace.

The thoughts she'd shared with Daffin about wanting to control her own destiny made him realize how brave she really was. Being a young lady in her position and refusing to take a husband for so many years hadn't been easy. She risked being ostracized by the people who made up her world, but she was willing to take that chance to make her own decisions in life. He admired her for it.

She appeared to be at the end of her rope, however. Her implied duty was catching up with her and she seemed resigned to her fate. Daffin had already decided he would meet the Earl of Dryden before determining whether the man deserved Regina. Daffin was looking forward to it.

Daffin glanced down at Regina's pretty face. She was looking up at him with a mixture of vulnerability and longing in her eyes. He should not kiss her for a third time. The first two had been lunacy. But he *wanted* to kiss her. Besides, what harm would a small kiss do?

He glanced around to ensure they wouldn't be seen, then he pulled her into his arms and lowered his mouth to hers. She sighed against his mouth and leaned into him, while Daffin held her for a few precious moments. When their mouths broke apart, he kissed her cheek, too.

"Merry Christmas, Regina," he murmured, before summoning his strength and walking away.

# CHAPTER TWENTY-FOUR

"But Daffin, it's been days and there's been no sign of anyone," Nicole insisted the next morning. She was lying on the sofa in the middle of the green salon, her hand resting on her forehead, one foot rocking back & forth. "I cannot stay inside a moment longer or I'll go mad. I merely want to have a short jaunt around the meadow on my horse. I need some fresh air. Desperately. *Please,* it's Christmas Eve."

Regina sat across from Daffin, nodding vigorously. "Yes, I agree. Please, may we go for a ride?"

"Should you be riding in your condition?" Daffin countered, addressing Nicole. His booted foot was crossed over his knee and he was eyeing her with a mixture of suspicion and tolerance.

"Racing, no," Nicole replied, her voice still pleading. "But a quick jaunt will hardly hurt me, and Atalanta is a perfectly trained horse."

"Grimaldi wouldn't want either of you to go," Daffin replied.

Regina paused and set the embroidery in her lap. She contemplated the question for a moment. "Yes, but in all these days, you've found no evidence we were followed here. I say it's safe to believe the man who tried to hurt me is still in London."

Daffin groaned and rubbed a hand across his face. His gaze bounced between the two ladies. "I have a feeling I'm going to regret this, but very well. I insist upon accompanying you, however."

"I never doubted it," Nicole said with a smug smile. She hoisted herself from the sofa and headed toward the door. "I'm off to dress in my riding habit."

Less than an hour later, outfitted in his own riding gear, Daffin accompanied Regina and Nicole out the back of the manor house. As they set out on the path to the stables, Daffin glanced around uneasily. He didn't like the idea of Regina being out in the open. It was true that he had seen no evidence of an intruder since they'd been here, but he didn't like to take chances.

Nicole spun in a circle and sucked in lungsful of air. "It's so good to be outside. I don't even care that it's so cold."

Regina laughed. "I agree. It's been positively stifling in that house."

He was barely listening. He was focused on keeping his eyes and ears sharp, attuned to any noise or movement. The usual servants bustled about. He'd got to know them all over the last several days. Nothing appeared out of the ordinary.

"Honestly, Daffin, you cannot think the shooter could be

here of all places. We'd see him coming a field's length away," Nicole said.

Daffin continued to scan the countryside. The meadow was clear and packed with untouched snow. Beyond it, a copse of trees. Nicole was right. No one could approach the house without being seen, and he'd had the footmen and groomsmen on watch round the clock. He stood watch daily himself. "Until we have a better idea who he is, I don't know what he's capable of, which means if you're outside, you're potentially in danger."

They entered the stables and the smell of fresh hay, leather, and horses met their nostrils. Nicole waved to one of the groomsmen. "Good morning, Jacob. Did you saddle Atalanta?" They'd sent a footman to ask the groomsman to saddle the horses.

"Yes, my lady," the groomsman replied. "She's right there in the stall."

"And Excalibur?" Regina added.

Daffin's head snapped to the side to face her. He arched a brow. "Your horse is named Excalibur?"

"And she's a girl," Regina said with a nod. "I was a bit grandiose as a child."

Daffin shook his head and grinned at her.

"Let me go greet my girl," Regina said, on her way toward the stall. "I've missed her so much."

Now that they were in the confines of the stable, Daffin relaxed a bit, but his guard remained up. They were about to ride through open fields, and that would be dangerous. Jacob should come with them for added protection. It couldn't hurt to have another set of eyes. He turned to speak to the groomsman.

A gasp from Regina made him swivel. She stood by her horse's stall, her hand over her mouth.

"What is it?" Daffin asked, quickly making his way to join her.

Regina pointed toward the saddle. Daffin turned his gaze in the direction she'd indicated. He narrowed his eyes. There was a small card sticking up between the saddle and the horse's back.

He leaned closer and snatched up the card. Only five words were scrawled on it in a messy hand.

*I'm watching you, Lady Regina.*

# CHAPTER TWENTY-FIVE

The front door slammed and Regina jumped. She and Nicole had been waiting in the green salon for what felt like hours. Nicole paced in front of the grand fireplace while Regina stood near the door, waiting for Daffin's return. Two footmen had been posted at the doors to the salon to ensure no one other than the duke, Lady Harriet, or an approved servant came in or out. After seeing the ladies safely back to the house, Daffin had returned to the stables and the meadow to search for tracks in the snow, any sign of the intruder. He'd just returned.

Regina had never been more afraid. She'd been so certain she was safe here. There'd been no sign of anyone following them from London but it wouldn't be difficult to guess where she had gone, and the location of the Duke of Colchester's manor house was hardly a secret. Knowing that the madman had followed them to her country home made

Regina's stomach twist in knots. It still made no sense. Who wanted to hurt her? And why?

When Daffin entered the room, Nicole whirled to face him, her eyes flashing. "I don't care if I am with child, Daffin. I want to help you search. I cannot stand to think of someone skulking about our property. I am angry beyond words."

Daffin began to pace in front of the fireplace. "I understand, Nic, but you must think of the babe. Sit. Rest. Please."

"I don't want to sit. I don't want to rest." Nicole had nearly ripped her handkerchief in two. "I want to go find whoever this is and beat him."

Daffin gestured to the settee. He waited for her to sit before he spoke. "I know you're not used to letting other people do things for you, Nic, but in this case, you must trust me. I cannot allow you to help search when you could be hurt. You know you'd give the same advice to someone in your position."

Nicole groaned. "Fine. I agree with you, but I don't have to like it."

"Did you find anything?" Regina came to stand next to Daffin. She searched his face. It was somber. He scrubbed a hand across the back of his neck.

"There are several sets of tracks around the stables. They all lead to and from the house . . . except one."

"Where did those tracks lead?" Nicole asked, leaning forward.

"To a copse of trees beyond the stables," he replied. "From there, they disappear. I questioned every servant in the stables thoroughly. They all claim to have seen and heard nothing."

Regina crossed her arms over her chest and paced away,

biting the tip of her finger. "How can that be? If Jacob had just saddled the horse, he had to have seen something."

"I agree," Daffin replied. "He claims there was no note when he finished preparing Excalibur, however. That was about a quarter hour before we came out, according to his memory."

"So we're dealing with someone who sneaked in and out of the stables in less than a quarter hour, silently and possibly invisibly." Nicole tugged on her handkerchief. "Sounds like we're dealing with a professional."

Daffin nodded. "That's what I'm afraid of."

Regina and Nicole spent the rest of the afternoon in Nicole's bedchamber, waiting for Mark to arrive. Regina felt safer upstairs. Knowing the man who'd tried to harm her had been so close made gooseflesh rush along her skin. Daffin Oakleaf was the best of the Bow Street Runners. He would find the culprit. But he needed a better lead.

"Who could it possibly be?" Regina asked. The weather had turned colder as the sun set, and she pulled a shawl over her shoulders. She stood in front of the fireplace, rubbing her hands together.

"I don't know," Nicole replied, "but whoever he is, he'd better pray to the god of criminals that Daffin finds him before Mark does."

The front door slammed and bootsteps thundered on the stairs just before Nicole's door flew open. Mark rushed to the bed and pulled Nicole into his arms. "Darling, I'm sorry I wasn't there when that bastard took a shot at you."

Nicole's eyes filled with tears and she clutched her husband's coat, which he hadn't bothered doffing. She closed her eyes and pressed herself against him. They hugged for several moments before Mark pulled away and stared lovingly at his wife's face. "I love you so much, Nicole."

"I love you, too, Mark," she said as they kissed passionately.

When the couple pulled apart, Mark scanned the room. "Regina. I'm sorry I wasn't there to protect you, too. I was so convinced Nicole was the target. Are you all right?"

"Yes," Regina replied. "I am."

"Where's Daffin?" Mark touched his wife's face with the back of his hand. "Are you all right? You were pale when I first walked in."

Nicole hugged him fiercely again, then patted the spot next to her on the bed. "Mark, darling, sit down. There's something I must tell you."

His eyes flared. "God. No. The babe?"

"The babe is fine," Nicole replied. "And so am I, but . . ."

He searched her face. "Tell me."

"We convinced Daffin to allow us to go riding earlier," Nicole began. "Neither of us could stand being trapped in this house another moment."

"That sounds like you," Mark said with an exasperated smile.

Nicole exchanged an uneasy look with Regina. "When we got to the stables, we found a note on Regina's saddle."

"What?" Mark's face drained of all color. "What did it say?"

"'I'm watching you, Lady Regina.'" She winced.

"Damn it." Mark stood and paced around the bedchamber like a caged tiger. He scrubbed his hand through his hair.

"There's more," Nicole added.

Mark continued to pace, but his shoulders relaxed a bit. "What?"

Nicole took a deep breath. "Daffin said there was only one set of tracks leading away from the stables. They disappeared into a copse of trees."

Mark clenched his fists. "One of the servants had to have seen him. We must line them up and question them."

"Daffin has already questioned the stable servants thoroughly. None of them saw anything," Regina said. "Susanna and Mrs. Bell, the housekeeper, are the only servants Daffin is allowing near me at present. None of the tracks in the snow were women's boots except ours."

"Darling." Mark crossed back to his wife and hugged her again. "What do you want me to do?"

"Just hold me, and let's try to have a nice Christmas Eve."

"I can do that." He glanced at Regina. "Don't worry, Regina. We will find whoever this lunatic is. You're safe."

"Thank you, Mark. I know I am. I trust you and Daffin completely. Though I cannot help but wish, given the circumstances, that Uncle Edward will rescind his dinner invitation to a certain earl."

"What do you mean?" Mark asked.

"Oh, we have another unwelcome bit of news," Nicole said with a sigh. "Lord Dryden is coming to Christmas dinner tomorrow . . . to court Regina."

# CHAPTER TWENTY-SIX

"Do you think the culprit stayed in the stables? He didn't sneak into the house, did he?" Grimaldi asked Daffin over a glass of brandy in the duke's study.

"I doubt it," Daffin replied. "I can't imagine he would have been that bold or been able to do so without being seen. Whoever he is, he's toying with us now. He wanted us to know he's here."

"But why? What would he have to gain from tipping his hand?" Grimaldi took a swig of brandy.

"That is a good question."

After bringing Grim up to speed, the two men agreed to put aside the investigation for the night and the next day for Nicole's sake, but neither man intended to let down his guard. The footmen were told not to let Regina out of their sight. They stood guard at her bedchamber door even as Grimaldi and Daffin were talking.

As night fell, the tension eased a little for everyone but

Daffin. He watched the homey scene in the green salon from his perch at the doorway, his shoulder resting against the frame. The duke sat in his wheeled chair near the fireplace. Lady Harriet had just finished serving everyone mulled wine out of a punch bowl. She took a seat on the velvet sofa near the duke. Regina was perched at her side. Nicole and Mark sat across from them on the settee.

Daffin glanced down at his boots. This time next year, there would be a baby here. The family was growing. They were talking and laughing and singing. A perfect Christmas Eve scene. The way Christmas Eve should be. Regina had asked him once if he wanted children. He'd never allowed himself to contemplate it. He didn't know how a happy family worked.

He glanced at her and the breath caught in his throat. The firelight played against her hair, making it look like blue silk. Her eyes danced and her uninhibited laughter struck a note of joy in his heart. Their kiss under the mistletoe had made him realize how dangerous it was to get close to her. Even a little bit. If he kissed her again, he might not be able to stop. Being so near her, breathing in her applelike scent, even the touch of her soft lips against his, had made him realize he didn't want just a little bit of her. He wanted more. And that was a fruitless, foolish desire. Even if she thought she wanted him, what she didn't know about him would send her away from him forever.

When the family began passing around the gifts they'd purchased for each other, Daffin knew it was time to leave. He moved back into the shadows and slipped away from the door. They wouldn't notice he was gone. He didn't have any gifts for any of them, and of course they wouldn't have any for him. He didn't belong here.

He turned and stalked off, in search of the library and the brandy he knew rested on a sideboard within. The cavernous room was cold and dark. A fire burned low in an enormous fireplace. An utter contrast to the warmth and love in the green salon. Daffin lit a brace of candles and made his way to the sideboard. He'd just finished pouring himself a glass of brandy when the door opened behind him.

"There you are," came Regina's bright voice.

He turned to watch her as she crossed the floor to meet him. She wore a ruby gown with a bright white bow around the bodice and a matching one in her dark hair. She carried a wrapped gift in one hand. It was a small box wrapped in silver paper with an emerald bow atop it. In her other hand was her glass of mulled wine.

"I didn't want to interrupt your family holiday," Daffin said inanely.

She stopped before him and the scent of apples hit his nostrils. His cock hardened. He glanced away. How inappropriate could he be? It was Christmas and he was on an assignment.

"You weren't interrupting a thing," she said, softly. "You should have joined us."

"I don't like Christmas," he said.

"I know. But I do hope you'll accept this . . . from me." She held out the gift to him.

He swallowed. "That's . . . for me?" He didn't take it. He stared at it as if it were a coiled snake.

"Yes. It's for you." She gave him a smile that made his thoughts scatter. He wanted to kiss her again.

"I didn't get you anything," he replied, his throat unexpectedly dry.

Regina's smile turned mischievous. "We can discuss your present for me after you open this."

He arched a brow.

She didn't wait for a reply. "Come on, then." She tugged his hand, pulling him toward the leather sofa in the center of the room. She sat first and placed the present next to her, then patted the empty space beside her. "Sit."

Daffin followed and shifted his brandy glass to his other hand. He lowered himself to the sofa, took a swig for mental fortitude, and placed the glass on the table in front of them. Then he drew in a deep breath, grasped the gift with both hands, and moved it onto his lap.

He took his time, carefully untying the bow, pulling the edges so it would unravel. For some reason, he wanted to savor the moment. A strange emotion roiled in his chest.

He slowly lifted the top of the box and looked inside. It was full of shredded newspaper. A vision of the last time he'd opened a present flashed through his mind. He savagely quashed the memory and forced himself to paw through the papers until his hand touched something hard. He grasped it and pulled out a . . . dagger. A beautiful silver dagger with what looked like real sapphires on the handle.

His breath caught in his throat. His chest was tight. He swallowed again. "Where . . . where did you get this?"

"In town. At a little shop in the village. After you told me about your first one, I saw this one and I couldn't help myself. I hope you like it."

"Like it?" He stared at the little knife, unseeing. "Yes. I like it. Very much." It was the kindest and most thoughtful thing anyone had ever done for him. She'd listened . . . and remembered.

"I'm glad. I thought perhaps you might think it too forward of me." She glanced at him shyly, her cheeks flushed. "But I decided we've already been completely inappropriate with each other. Why stop now?"

A lump lodged in his throat. He tried to smile but couldn't. Instead he searched her sparkling gaze. "This was kind of you, Regina. I appreciate it."

A smile tugged at his lips. "What would you like for Christmas from me?" he asked, tilting his head to the side and watching her. He was half hoping she'd repeat her demand for a kiss.

"So you usually don't do anything for Christmas?" she asked, pointedly ignoring his question.

Daffin turned the dagger in his lap. "Oh, Fielding invites me to his house, but I never accept."

"You'd rather be alone?"

He expelled a breath. "The day brings up a lot of bad memories for me."

"I understand." She reached out and squeezed his hand. "I'm usually quiet and withdrawn on the anniversary of my parents' deaths."

He didn't need to say anything. They both knew. It was a day burned in your memory forever, whether you wanted it there or not.

After several moments of silence, Regina shook her head. "I've found replacing a bad memory with a good one is much more satisfying than hiding in the shadows from the bad one forever."

Daffin studied her face. Despite her pain, she was bright and hopeful. She hadn't lived a perfectly happy life as he'd first suspected, and they had more in common than he'd thought . . . no parents, no siblings, lonely childhoods spent wishing things were different from how they were. But no amount of commonalities could bridge the gap between their stations in life. He was a paid investigator and she was the niece of a duke. He was something she never could accept. They might be friends, but they could be nothing more.

"Thank you for this." He placed the dagger back inside the box and lifted it. What was the proper protocol when a duke's niece gifted you with a fine dagger? What did one say to a woman who has seen past your defenses and into your heart?

A sly smile appeared on her tempting lips. "I'm ready to tell you what I'd like for my gift now."

"What?" But Daffin already knew what she wanted from him. A gift he *shouldn't* give, but one he couldn't help but desire.

"I want more than a kiss from you this time. I want you to tell me how you truly feel about me."

# CHAPTER TWENTY-SEVEN

Daffin moved closer to her and she breathed in his spicy cologne. He smelled like the wood in the fireplace, like balsam. She breathed him in, his heat and nearness. That alone was nearly enough to make her toes curl. She hadn't been nervous before, but now her belly was jittery.

He bridged the space between them, he took her hands in his and stroked her palms, rubbing the centers with his thumbs in tiny circles. Gooseflesh spread quickly up her spine. He leaned forward and breathed deeply near her ear. "You smell like apples. Do you know that?"

She blinked. "Apples?"

"Yes. Delicious, red apples."

"Please don't tell me you think of me like an apple."

"No, I think much more highly of you than a common fruit."

"I'm glad to hear that, I suppose, but I'm waiting, how do you feel about me?"

His lips hovered at her ear, his voice a husky whisper. "What if I told you I've thought about kissing you again all day?"

Her breath came in short pants. "You . . . you have?"

"Yes."

"Why?"

"Because you look like a goddess descended from Olympus?"

She couldn't help but smile. "That's not a very original thing to say."

"My apologies. Seems your nearness makes me unoriginal." His lips brushed against the soft skin beneath her ear. She shuddered and closed her eyes. Heat raced through her body and pooled in the private space between her legs. "Ooh, I . . ."

"What?" he whispered, his lips moving up her neck. His hands dropped away from hers and came up to cradle her cheeks. His mouth moved along the tender skin of her throat. He kissed the underside of her jaw, then moved to the corner of her lips. He slowly bit her bottom lip, sucking in its plump fullness while her eyes remained closed.

Then his tongue slowly parted her lips and moved deftly inside. His mouth boldly slanted across hers as his strong hands moved up to hold her head in place. It was an endless, drugging kiss, designed to seduce. When he finally dropped his hands from her cheeks and pulled his lips away, he was breathing heavily and so was she.

"Well?" he said, a triumphant smile on his lips.

"Well what?" she breathed, unable to process what he was asking her after *that*.

"Does that answer your question?"

"Not in the least!"

"Pardon?" This time he blinked.

"I want to know whether you're *not* interested in me or if you simply think you shouldn't be interested?"

Daffin scratched his cheek. "How much have you had to drink tonight?"

"Only a glass and a half of mulled wine. I've drunk more than that at boring dinner parties in London. Don't worry, I'm entirely in my right mind." She lifted her glass. "But you are trying to change the subject again, and I—"

"No. I promise I'm not."

"Go ahead then. Answer the question."

He leaned close to her and placed his hands on her hips. "The truth is I'm interested. Too interested. I thought perhaps my kissing you all these times may have given that away." He grinned at her. "But you're right. I think I shouldn't."

She tilted up her chin, a defiant look in her eye. "But why do you think you shouldn't?"

He scrubbed a hand across his forehead. "Let's see, your impending engagement, my friendship with your cousin, and—" He took a deep breath. "Suffice it to say I'm not who you think I am."

She reached up and cupped his cheek. "I know who you are, Daffin. And I *want* you. Tell me you don't want me too and I'll never bring it up again."

He tipped up her chin with his thumb and forefinger. "Love, you could tempt a saint. Of course I want you."

A slow satisfied smile spread across her face. "What would you say if I said I wanted more?"

He pressed his forehead to hers. His common sense warned him, but his emotions ignored the warning. "I'd say meet me in my bedchamber after midnight."

\* \* \*

Daffin walked Regina back to the salon where her family was no doubt looking for her. Then he took himself off to his bedchamber where he was hard-pressed to make his cockstand subside. No doubt he'd made a mistake inviting her to his bedchamber, but she wanted more and so did he. He could finally admit that to himself. He had no intention of taking her virginity. That would be too much, but he could touch her. He could make her body sing with pleasure. He wanted to give her that. He sat staring out into the darkness, sipping his brandy, remembering the feel of Regina's body against his, her soft mouth, the tiny moans she made in the back of her throat. God, he wanted her. He didn't care anymore if it was wrong.

Sometime well after midnight, a soft knock on his door jolted him from his thoughts. He'd begun to think she'd changed her mind. He'd begun to think she *should* have changed her mind. He knew damned well he shouldn't open the door. Even as he told himself that, he found himself heading straight for it. With a deep breath he swung it open.

Regina stood in the corridor in her night rail, a dressing gown slung over her shoulders, her glass of wine still in her hand. Her gorgeous dark hair was down, streaming down her back. His mouth went dry.

"May I come in?" she whispered.

He glanced both ways down the corridor to ensure it was clear, then pulled her into the room. For her to be caught in her state of undress even speaking to him would ruin her.

The moment he shut the door behind her, his lips descended to hers. She tasted like mulled wine and innocence. Her night rail hugged her curves. The diaphanous material made his mouth water. He wanted to run his hands all over her. He wanted to carry her to his bed and never leave it.

He forced himself to pull away and put her at arm's distance. "You didn't change your mind?"

"Of course not." She strolled toward the bed and let the dressing gown drop from her shoulders, leaving her clad only in her night rail. "Kiss me again." She wagged a finger at him. "A toe-curling kiss, if you please."

He chuckled and made his way to stand next to her by the bed. "Fine."

"And I—"

"Shut up. You've won. I'm going to kiss you now." Daffin was on fire for her. He pulled her into his arms and his lips descended to hers, silencing further words. The taste of mulled wine was going to make him hard forever.

She wrapped her arms around his neck and pushed herself up on her tiptoes to meet his kiss. Their last kiss had been hot. This one was scorching. She didn't just part her lips for him. She boldly stroked her tongue into his mouth. Her hands came to wrap around the back of his neck, holding him in place as if she never wanted it to end. Her leg slid up the side of his, her knee rubbing up and down his thigh. He was certain he'd go up in flames.

When he finally pulled away from her, his heart hammered. He looked at her as if a unicorn had appeared in his bedchamber. Who was this gorgeous woman, and what had he done to deserve even a moment of her company?

She pulled away from him and climbed up on the bed.

"Jesus Christ," he breathed. He glanced down at the floor, his hands on his hips. He was not going to survive this. When he looked back at her, she'd pulled the shoulder of her night rail down and exposed one creamy shoulder.

"What are you doing?" His voice shook.

"Didn't you say you never back down from a challenge?"

"What's the challenge?" he asked.

"Touch me."

"With pleasure." He didn't want to let her go. He wanted her with every bit of his soul.

Daffin had long ago pulled off his boots and cravat. He wore only his breeches and shirt when he climbed onto the bed to face her. They were both on their knees, staring at each other. He wanted to rip the gown from her body and bury himself inside of her. Instead, he pulled her against him and slowly lowered himself atop her, cradling her head in his hands. He kissed her again, an endless kiss that did nothing to diminish his raging cockstand. When he finally pulled his lips from hers, Regina pressed her forehead to his.

His hands moved to her shoulders. He buried his face in her neck, breathing in her maddening scent. Then he lowered his head to the spot just above her breasts, licking at the smooth skin exposed by her night rail. He pulled down the bodice. His lips found the nipple of one perfect breast and closed around it and sucked, gently biting and tugging.

Regina gasped. Her fingers tangled in his hair, holding him to her. Her back arched and her hair fell in a dark, silky wave behind her.

He lowered her onto her back again and moved atop her, letting his gaze sweep her breasts. God, he'd dreamed of these breasts. He lavished attention on first one, then the other, while she moaned in the back of her throat, driving him mad. She lifted her knee and curled a leg around his hips, her gown falling down to her thigh. He didn't want to stop. At least not yet. "Regina," he breathed. "Are you all right?"

"Yes, please don't stop."

His hand made its way down her body, skimming her hip

and flat belly before he pulled up her gown to find the perfect spot between her legs.

He skimmed his fingers along the seam of her sex and parted her lips to slowly dip a finger inside her. Regina. Sweet Regina. She was tight, and hot, and wet.

He withdrew his finger and slid it back in again, mimicking a motion his hips were desperate for. Her eyes widened. Her head thrashed against the sheets. He leaned over her to watch her face while his finger moved inside of her.

"Daffin," she moaned. "I want you."

He leaned down to cover her mouth with his.

"Tell me, Regina," he whispered. "Tell me what you want."

There was something else he could offer her, something unbearably intimate and delightful. Shifting to his knees, he tossed her gown over her thighs and slid down to position his head between her legs. Then, meeting her wide gaze a final time, and finding arousal instead of trepidation, he slowly lowered his mouth to her. The first taste of her was like heaven. He licked her deeply, while she gasped. "Oh."

Instead of clamping her legs together and pushing him away like he'd guessed she might, she spread her legs wide and grasped his head. "More," she called in a throaty voice. He smiled against her flesh, and kissed the silken skin of her inner thigh, before drawing his tongue languidly over the heart of her. Even in the midst of lovemaking, she surprised him. Damn it. He was so hard he ached. He ground a little against the mattress, knowing this time wasn't for him and trying to keep the sweet, primal drive at bay.

Driven by the taste of her, desperate to claim her and knowing only one way to leave her fulfilled and yet whole, he plied her with his tongue, explored her tight warmth with the slow, inexorable thrust of his finger, until her hips rose to drive against his every caress. Then he found the little nub at the top of her sex and lightly sucked it into his mouth.

Regina cried out. Her fingers tightened in his hair, her thighs quaked. Her spine arched off the mattress with the force of her release. Daffin didn't relent until she breathed his name and fell back against the pillows.

He straightened, breathing hard, as his gaze anxiously searched her face. Tears leaked from the corners of her eyes, but they were tears of wonder, not dismay. Daffin uttered a breathless laugh of relief, of joy. He had given her the greatest pleasure. Doing so—despite the unanswered ache of his own body—had granted himself the same.

Daffin pushed himself up to lie at her side and drew her night rail down to cover her. He remained silent while her breathing evened out. He lay on his back and stared at the canopy overhead, willing his own desire back to a manageable place.

Finally he pulled her tightly against him and kissed her ear. "What do you think?" He would give anything to bury himself inside of her, but this would be as far as they ever went. Perhaps he shouldn't have waited so long to do this. He'd been able to pleasure her without ruining her. The perfect compromise between her wish and his unworthiness.

Regina blinked once, twice. Then she closed her eyes, shifted to face him, and stretched like a satisfied cat. "That was the most extraordinary thing that has ever happened to my body."

He grinned, brought her hand to his mouth, and kissed the back of it. "My pleasure, my lady."

"It was *my* pleasure."

He laughed and brushed a dark curl away from her cheek. "Was it what you expected?" Curiosity spurred him to ask.

"No." She shook her head. "It was better than what I expected. Much better."

He rubbed a knuckle across her cheekbone. "Don't make me arrogant."

"You should be arrogant after *that*."

He leaned up on an elbow and searched her face, becoming entirely serious. "Regina, you must agree, we cannot do more than that and we must not allow it to happen ever again."

She rose on her elbow too and stared right back at him. "I agree to no such thing."

# CHAPTER TWENTY-EIGHT

Sunlight streaked through the windows of her bedchamber. Regina rolled over and threw her arm across her eyes. Her head pounded. She groaned. The memory of what had happened last night galloped into her brain. She pulled her arm away from her face and shot upright, then groaned again when the bright sunlight hit her eyes.

Oh, dear God, what she'd done with Daffin last night! A slight smile curled her lips.

She'd had a wonderful time. Better than wonderful, actually. The word *magnificent* came to mind but she still wanted more. She couldn't help herself. Daffin had wanted her last night, too. She could feel it. She'd wanted to touch him, but he'd refused.

After he'd given her the most satisfying physical experience of her life, he'd lifted her from the bed, stood her up, smoothed her night rail back down her legs and up over her shoulders, and belted her firmly into her dressing gown. Then he'd stuck his head out the door, checked the corridor, and asked her in a loud whisper, "How far is your bedchamber?"

"Only four doors to the right." She braced her hand against the wall, still feeling woozy from the wine and the lovemaking.

He grasped her hand and pulled her quickly into the corridor and down to her room. He nodded to the door for her approval and she nodded back. He opened the door and spun her inside. "Good night, Regina," he said, kissing her outstretched hand. "Merry Christmas. Sleep well." Then the door closed in her face, and he was gone.

She had turned to face her bed, spread her arms into the air, and whispered, "Merry Christmas to me," before sliding between the soft cool linens. She blinked into the darkness for a moment or two, feeling as if she were floating on a cloud, and quickly fell into a deep sleep, in which she dreamed about Daffin and his magical mouth and hands. She didn't want to wake up. Not after all that.

Now she stared at the ceiling of her bedchamber, a blush heating her cheeks. She'd have to face him today after they'd done all *that* together and his mouth had been on places she wasn't certain she'd ever even *seen*.

If that wasn't enough, there was another reason not to get out of bed today. Christmas dinner . . . with the Earl of Dryden.

The encounter would be nothing but awkward, especially when her mind kept playing scenes from her time in Daffin's bed.

She sighed and pushed herself up on her palms. Might as well get this day over with. She tossed back the covers and rang for Genevieve. The clock on the mantel showed she was already late for Christmas breakfast.

Less than half an hour later, she strolled calmly into the

breakfast room, dressed in a white satin gown with a red sash around the waist. Nicole and Mark were there, and so was Daffin.

She pressed her lips together and silently slid into a seat next to Nicole.

"Good morning and Merry Christmas," Nicole said.

"Good morning. Merry Christmas," Regina replied, hoping her greeting would suffice for the entire table. She asked a maid for a cup of tea before she dared a glance at Daffin. He was digging into his eggs, a smile riding his lips as if he hadn't a care in the world.

For a moment she wondered if she'd dreamed the entire episode last night. But then his gaze caught hers, and he gave her an unmistakable wink. She took a sip of tea.

"Did you enjoy your Christmas gifts?" Mark asked her, causing Regina to choke on her beverage and Daffin's private smile to widen.

Nicole glanced back and forth between the two of them, her gaze narrowing.

"Yes . . . er, I did enjoy them. Very much," Regina managed to choke out.

"What was your favorite gift?" Mark prodded.

"Yes, *Lady* Regina," Daffin asked, taking another large bite of eggs. "What was your favorite gift?"

Regina took a sip of tea. Then another. He was obviously enjoying this. "I don't think I could pick just one," she finally managed.

"I hope you enjoyed your Christmas Eve," Nicole added. "Because I spoke with Uncle Edward this morning, and he's still expecting Lord Dryden's visit."

"Lovely," Regina replied, rolling her eyes.

\* \* \*

The Earl of Dryden arrived just after noon and was shown into the green salon, where he was promptly joined by the duke, Lady Harriet, and Mark.

Regina stood at the bottom of the stairs with Nicole, doing what she could to delay having to spend time with the man. She hadn't been able to speak with Daffin all morning. Directly after breakfast, he'd left for the stables, saying something about how he intended to scour the grounds again to look for any sign of the intruder. Not that Regina had known what she would say to Daffin if she *had* had a chance to speak with him. What precisely did one say to someone after a night like that? "Thank you" seemed inadequate. "Let's do it again" seemed needy. She decided to worry about it later. First, she had to survive the afternoon with Lord Dryden.

"Go ahead," Nicole prompted, nodding to the door of the green salon. "You might as well get it over with."

"Easy for you to say," Regina replied, her lip curled.

"Don't worry." Nicole patted her arm. "Mark and I shall help you keep up the conversation. It will all be over soon."

Regina nodded. "I know. I'm being a complete ninny, but he's just . . ." She let the sentence fade away but the words *not Daffin* came to mind.

"Just be your normal charming self and pretend you've no idea why he's come. That's worked for you in the past, hasn't it?"

Regina glanced at Nicole out of the sides of her eyes. "Obviously not well enough or he wouldn't be back."

Nicole laughed. "Be charming, but not too charming. You don't want to encourage him."

Regina tugged her gloves to her elbows. "I think I could snarl at him and gnash my teeth and it wouldn't discourage him."

Nicole rubbed her hands together. "Ooh. That's not a half-bad idea. You could pick up a bad habit. Laughing like a donkey, perhaps?"

"Or slurping my soup?" Regina added.

"No, dear. I'm not certain *I* could take that," her cousin replied with another laugh. She paced away from her for a moment, then turned back. "I have an idea. I'll ask him what he dislikes, and then you can begin doing it."

"Ooh, that is clever," Regina agreed. "Good plan. Let's go."

As soon as they entered the room, Lord Dryden stood. He was tall and passably handsome with light brown hair and hazel eyes. He wore a green vest and a black overcoat and looked perfectly tidy and presentable. Her stomach most certainly did not flip when she saw him, however.

"Ah, Lady Regina. There you are." He bowed to her. "I'm pleased to see you again. Merry Christmas."

"Merry Christmas, my lord." Regina curtsied and did her best to smile. Then she greeted the others in the room.

Where was Daffin? She hadn't seen him since breakfast. Did he intend to stay away from this madness today? She wouldn't blame him.

"My lord." Nicole curtsied to Dryden, as well.

"Regina," Uncle Edward intoned from his wheeled chair. "Come sit next to Lord Dryden."

Regina smiled with gritted teeth. "Yes, of course." She made her way to the settee near the earl. It had been less than five minutes and she already wanted to run far away. She sighed. This was certain to be a long, long afternoon.

"So, Lord Dryden," Nicole began. "What brings you here this fine Christmas Day?"

"Yes," Regina continued. "Where are your mother and sister?"

Lord Dryden grasped at his lapels with both hands. "They've gone to Plymouth to have Christmas with my uncle. I promised to meet them there later this week. I didn't want to miss a chance to see you again, Lady Regina."

The smile remained plastered on her face. "You flatter me, my lord."

"I'm hoping to do more than flatter you, my lady." He inclined his head toward her.

Nicole cleared her throat. "The weather has been quite fine lately. Don't you agree, my lord? Aside from the cold, that is."

"I don't mind the cold, it makes for pleasant coach rides under blankets. Would you like to go out riding with me later this afternoon, Lady Regina? We can take a tour of our properties. Together they would make a fine bit of land, wouldn't you agree?"

"I do believe I might be coming down with a cold," Regina replied, faking a cough.

"Nonsense," the duke interjected. "You've been right as rain since you've been here. I daresay a ride with the earl later will do you good."

Lady Harriet's handkerchief fluttered through the air like a fidgety bird. "Tea?" she offered in a strained voice, her gaze darting between her obviously unhappy granddaughter and the tenacious Lord Dryden.

"Please." Dryden did his best to smile at Regina, but she could tell he was pretending.

"Erm. You say you don't mind cold," Nicole doggedly continued. "What is it that you dislike, my lord?"

Lord Dryden tugged on his lapels again. "I cannot say there's much. I'm a fortunate chap."

"Certainly," Nicole replied. "But surely there is *something* you dislike. I, for one, cannot countenance anyone slurping soup."

Lord Dryden laughed. "I cannot say I'd enjoy soup slurped in my presence, either. I suppose I'm not particularly fond of dogs. Dirty things. Always shedding."

Regina nearly choked on her tea. "Is that so? Why, I adore dogs. Always have."

He managed another tight smile. "Opposites can attract."

Regina turned back to Nicole with a pleading look. Their plan was not working.

"Tell me, my lord," Nicole jumped in again. "Why haven't you taken a bride yet? What precisely are you looking for in such a lady?"

Nicole was a dear.

"I daresay I'm looking for someone very much like Lady Regina."

Regina whimpered. Meanwhile, her uncle stared at Dryden approvingly, while her grandmother looked as if she might stuff her handkerchief down her own throat. Regina had never known Grandmama to remain silent this long. It worried her.

Thankfully, Regina was spared having to respond to Dryden's loaded remark when Daffin strolled through the door. She fought the urge to jump from her seat and run to him. Daffin offered his greetings to everyone. Regina's belly did a somersault.

Grandmama jumped from her seat, finally able to say something of use. "Lord Dryden, this is Mr. Oakleaf, the Bow Street Runner."

Lord Dryden squinted for a moment. He did not stand. Instead, he eyed Daffin up and down. "Oakleaf? Where have I heard that name?"

"He's the best of the runners," Regina offered with a smile.

"I know!" Lord Dryden snapped his fingers. "I read about you in the *Times*. More than once, I believe. You do excellent work."

"Thank you, my lord," Daffin replied, bowing. He glanced at Regina, giving her a sympathetic look.

"Excellent work," Lord Dryden continued, nodding to himself and the room at large as if he'd been the one to discover Daffin's merits.

The butler entered the room to announce dinner was ready.

"Shall we all go in?" the duke asked.

"I'll excuse myself," Daffin said. "I plan to eat with the servants today."

"Nonsense." The duke slapped his hand against the arm of his wheeled chair. "You'll eat with us as an honored guest."

"As you wish, your grace." It would be rude of Daffin to turn down the offer. Regina couldn't be more pleased. It didn't rid them of the Earl of Dryden, but at least Daffin would be with her.

The earl stuck his nose in the air. "I thought *I* was the honored guest today, your grace."

"Of course," Uncle Edward began, looking flustered.

"No matter." Lord Dryden waved his hand dismissively. "I'm certain there is room for *two* honored guests at your table, your grace."

"It *is* a terribly long table," Regina interjected.

Nicole snorted.

"Shall we?" Grandmama said before Dryden could add anything else.

As the party made their way from the salon to the dining room, Mark made a show of occupying the earl. He pointed out to him some of the portraits along the walls, and they spoke while they walked. Nicole rushed forward and grasped Regina's arm. "Oh, dear, he does seem arrogant."

Regina nodded. "I know."

"And he's already mentioned the land," Nicole replied.

"Of course," Regina answered miserably. "I cannot go riding with him. He's certain to propose." She watched Daffin's back. He was several paces ahead, slowly walking next to the duke with Grandmama on his other side.

A splendid Christmas feast filled the large table in the duke's grand dining hall. Roast duck, suckling pig, goose, watercress soup, mince pie, gingerbread, and all sorts of spiced puddings filled the air with warm, delectable fragrance. Timothy and Matthew, the footmen, pushed the duke's chair to the head of the table and everyone took their seats. Regina, sitting across from Daffin, glanced up at him as another footman placed her napkin on her lap. The hint of a smile still played around his lips, and his brows shot up as he glanced pointedly between her and Dryden, who sat beside her.

"This is a lovely feast," Lord Dryden began. "Nearly as lovely as the dinners at Dryden Hall. I daresay once I have a proper countess, the dinners shall be even more resplendent."

"Oh, are you looking for a countess?" Daffin asked, blinking innocently and raising the wineglass to his lips.

Regina tried to kick him under the table, but the expanse was far too wide. Blasted huge fancy table. Instead, she settled for glaring at him over the rim of her own wineglass. Today's dinner certainly called for more wine.

"Yes, indeed," the earl thundered. Regina winced. She had also forgotten how very *loud* the man could be. "I'm looking for the perfect countess and I think I may have found her."

He turned to Regina and forced another smile. He looked positively pained.

Regina looked away and downed more wine. She couldn't help but smile when she considered how quickly the earl would probably grab his hat and coat and head home if he knew what she and Daffin had done last night.

"I know some lovely ladies in London," Nicole offered quickly from her seat beside Daffin.

The duke frowned at Nicole while Lady Harriet fanned herself rapidly with her handkerchief and held her wineglass aloft to be filled again.

As the dishes were passed around, Regina concentrated on keeping her head down. The less she said to the earl, the better.

After everyone's plate was filled, Nicole turned to Daffin. "Earlier we were talking about things we find unpleasant. For example, I know a girl who laughs like a donkey. Can't bear to listen to it."

Grandmama gave Nicole a look indicating she believed she'd lost her mind.

"What do you find particularly unacceptable, Daffin?" Nicole added, ignoring Lady Harriet's pointed stare.

Daffin arched a brow. "I've always found men who are violent to women and children unacceptable."

"Egad!" Lord Dryden exclaimed. "I thought we were discussing frivolous things like donkey laughs and puppies."

"Puppies? Who doesn't like puppies?" Daffin frowned.

"Lord Dryden said he doesn't care for dogs," Regina interjected. "I, however, adore them."

"That's interesting. I've never known of your penchant for dogs before today, my lady," Daffin said, a smile tugging at the corner of his lips.

"Oh, yes," Regina replied. "Dogs, dogs, dogs. I love dogs."

"And do you *have* a dog, Lady Regina?" Daffin asked, glancing about as if the canine in question might appear.

"Not at the moment," she told him through clenched teeth, a fake smile still plastered to her face.

"What was that?" Lord Dryden asked, cupping a hand behind his ear. "I'm a bit hard of hearing."

"Nothing," Regina replied in a singsong voice.

"Yes, well," Lord Dryden continued. "I daresay I've never encountered any men who were violent to women or children." He puffed up his chest as if proud of that pronouncement. "A gentleman would never be exposed to such ruffians. Those of us who are *well-bred* don't have that problem."

Regina glanced at Daffin. His jaw was tight.

"I assure you, my lord," Daffin said, "even the *well-bred* do indeed have that problem. I've been called to many a house in Mayfair where violence has taken place."

"I find that difficult to believe," Lord Dryden replied, setting down his fork and knife. He gave Daffin a withering stare.

"It's true," Mark added from his place beside Nicole. "I've seen it myself."

"Well, then, I'm glad *I've* never been exposed to such atrocities." Dryden picked up his utensils again.

"Someone has to," Daffin replied, his jaw still clenched.

"Indeed." Lord Dryden shook his head and turned back to the table at large, clearly prepared to change the subject. "I thought of something else I cannot countenance."

"What's that, my lord?" Nicole asked brightly, taking a bite of roasted goose.

"People who fancy themselves above their betters." He gave Daffin another pointed stare.

Regina squeezed her fork so tightly her fingers turned white. Daffin glared at the earl. She could tell he probably would like nothing better than to punch the man for that rude comment.

"I don't know," Mark interjected. "I, for one, have always found it difficult to countenance those who believe they are better."

They left the dinner table after two exhausting hours, most of them spent listening to Lord Dryden talk about how good he was at hunting, fishing, riding, and anything else he attempted. His endless stories about the vastness of his estate and the loveliness of his land and the largess in his pockets were equally fascinating to no one.

By the time dinner was over, Grandmama looked half-drunk. Mark was in a foul mood. Nicole seemed exhausted, Regina was cranky, and Daffin was angry. Only the duke appeared to be pleased with their guest.

Their little party strolled back toward the salon, while Regina tried to think of a reason why she could not go riding with Dryden. They'd all agreed not to discuss the danger she was in in front of the earl. They didn't want to start gossip. It would hardly be proper for Regina to say, "I cannot go riding with you, my lord, because a man who shot at me may be lurking in the copse of trees beyond the stables." If Lord Dryden had seen the story in the paper, he didn't mention it, thank heavens.

Just outside the dining room doorway, Dryden stopped, took Regina's hand, and pointed straight up.

She glanced up to see the bough of mistletoe she'd procured for her rendezvous with Daffin hanging from the rafter. "Who put that there?" she asked before she had a chance to stop and think.

She glanced at Nicole, who shook her head, a horrified look on her face.

Mark looked equally horrified, as did Grandmama, who shook her head and said in a strangled voice, "I believe one of the footmen did, dear."

Lord Dryden made a grand show of leaning down to kiss Regina, while the rest of them (save for the duke) watched in dismay.

As soon as his lips got close enough, his eyes closed. Regina pecked him quickly on the cheek, lifted her skirts and took off toward the salon. Dryden opened his eyes and blinked.

Daffin caught up with her and whispered, "Well played."

Regina glanced back at Lord Dryden, who looked both surprised and affronted, but quickly righted himself and followed the rest of them to the salon.

"I fear I must plead a bout of extreme tiredness," Regina announced, stretching and yawning for more effect.

"Nonsense." The duke gave his niece a stern stare. "You must visit more with Lord Dryden, here. He offered to take you riding."

Nicole cleared her throat. "I understand what Regina means. I fancy a nap as well. Regina, won't you be a dear and help me to my room?"

The duke wasn't about to argue with the pregnant marchioness. He nodded, and Regina and Nicole said their goodbyes to everyone in the room.

"I do hope you'll allow me to call upon you again, Lady Regina," Lord Dryden said as Regina wished him a merry Christmas for the last time.

"I'm afraid that's impossible, my lord," Regina replied. "We intend to leave for London soon."

"Not a problem at all." Lord Dryden smirked. "I'm planning to go to London after I return from Plymouth. I'll see you there."

That night, after Uncle Edward and Grandmama retired for the evening, Regina, Daffin, Nicole, and Mark met in the green salon to discuss how they would handle the next steps in the investigation.

Mark and Nicole were already in the room when Regina came down the stairs to find Daffin waiting for her outside the salon's double doors. The man made her toes curl just looking at him.

"How are you this evening, my lady?" he asked, bowing to her.

"Tired. Listening to Dryden will do that. Not to mention I didn't get much rest last night."

"That's funny. Neither did I." His grin was roguish.

"What did you think of Lord Dryden?" she asked.

"I think I cannot imagine you married to that blowhard." He offered his arm and escorted her into the salon.

After they entered the room, Regina and Daffin took seats next to Mark and Nicole near the fireplace.

"I didn't see anything on my outing today," Daffin began once they were settled. "The woods were empty and there were no new tracks, other than my own."

"Thank you for looking, Daffin, on Christmas Day nonetheless," Nicole said.

"Yes, well, scouring the area hasn't worked." Daffin shook his head. "It could be anyone. He knows we're looking for him. He's managed to sneak in and out of our midst."

"I don't want Regina to return to London until we find him," Mark said. "If he's eluding us out here, there's no way we can keep her safe in the crowds of the city."

"I agree," Daffin replied. "It would be good if we could lure whoever it is out into the open by making him think Regina is going out."

Mark narrowed his eyes. "Perhaps we can send out the coach without her in it."

"He's too clever for that," Nicole replied. "He's watching closely. He'd see whether she entered the coach. Regina must be there."

"Absolutely not," Daffin said. He glanced at Regina. "I refuse to put you in danger."

Regina cleared her throat. "Please let me ride out. I want to catch this man as badly as you do."

All three heads swiveled to stare at her.

"No," Nicole nearly shouted.

"No," Daffin insisted.

"Why not?" Regina asked, warming to her topic. "We can go for a short jaunt into the village just to see if we can lure him out. What harm is there?"

"There could be a great deal of harm," Daffin replied.

Regina glanced up at him. "But you'll be there to protect me, and Mark can place himself wherever we go ahead of time for added protection."

"No," Nicole replied. "I refuse to allow you to put yourself in danger, Regina."

Regina leaned forward and grasped her cousin's hands. She stared her in the eye. "Nicole, you taught me to be brave. I don't want to live hiding away in fear. Let me do this. Please."

"I don't like it." Mark glanced at Daffin. "But it may be

the only way, and Regina makes a good point. We'll both be there to protect her."

"You cannot be truly considering this madness," Nicole said to her husband.

"Please, Nicole. I have to do this," Regina said.

Both ladies were tearful. Nicole leaned over and hugged Regina. "I love you, Regina. Are you certain?"

"Yes. I'm looking forward to it, actually. It makes me feel as if I'm taking my future into my own hands. You of all people know how good that feels."

Nicole turned to Daffin. "Are you all right with it?"

Daffin expelled his breath. He scrubbed the back of his neck. "On one condition . . . I want to be the one in the coach with her."

# CHAPTER TWENTY-NINE

The next day, the duke's coach pulled to a stop behind another coach in front of the little village bookshop. Regina's belly was a riotous mass of nerves, but she'd never felt more alive. Whoever this lunatic was, she refused to cower from him.

"Stay with me," Daffin warned. Regina nodded. On the way to the village, Daffin had turned from the flirtatious Bow Street Runner to a consummate professional. His eyes were trained on every object at once. He spoke to her in short, clipped tones, his words clear and precise. She could tell by the look in his eyes, by the hard edge to his voice, that he was afraid for her, but he intended to keep her safe.

The coachman let down the steps. Daffin alighted first, then turned to help Regina. They walked toward the shop, doing their best to pretend they were merely a couple out for a stroll and some shopping on St. Stephen's Day. A man knocked Daffin's arm as he hurried past. Daffin nearly pulled his pistol on him.

"Sorry, sir," the man said, tipping his hat and moving on.

Daffin and Regina exchanged tense glances.

Daffin held the shop door for Regina to precede him inside. She made a show of casually looking about the small shop. It smelled like books and mold and dust. She'd been here the other day and had a long chat with Mr. Tillworthy, the proprietor. Today, Mr. Tillworthy was engaged in a conversation with another customer and hadn't seemed to notice that the Duke of Colchester's coach had arrived in front of his place of business. When Mr. Tillworthy talked about books, he became quite single-minded.

Daffin kept his own hat low over his eyes and folded his hands behind his back, perusing the store as if he hadn't a care in the world, but Regina knew his senses were fully attuned to the two other people in the store, and he paid close attention to the front door.

It was possible, of course, that the man after Regina wouldn't risk exposing himself today. Perhaps the jaunt to the village would result in nothing. But Daffin and Mark had been certain it would coax him from his lair.

After several minutes passed, Daffin strolled to where Regina stood before a shelf, pretending to browse. His hands remained folded behind his back. He faced the opposite direction from her. "Don't look," he whispered.

Regina caught her breath. "What is it?"

"There is a man across the street. He appears to be casually milling about, but I've seen him glance in here several times. He also appears to be watching our coach."

Regina's heart pounded, but she forced herself to continue

perusing the book she'd chosen from the shelf. "Should we remain here?"

Daffin's mouth was tight. "I'm hesitant to put you in harm's way by going outside, but it may help if you move closer to the front windows. I'll be able to see if his interest picks up."

Regina nodded. She spent another few moments looking at the book, while Daffin strolled off as if continuing his own shopping. She lifted her skirts and took her time inching toward the front of the store so her actions seemed natural.

By the time she reached a stack of books on a table near the front window, Daffin had positioned himself on the other side of the door.

The customer speaking to Mr. Tillworthy became louder. The two men were engaged in a heated discussion about politics.

Keeping her chin tucked down, Regina surreptitiously glanced out the window. The man across the street leaned against the brick wall of a storefront. His hat was pulled low, but she could see why Daffin questioned whether he was watching them. His eyes darted between their coach and the shop. It was impossible to tell his age, but he was of medium build and height and wore the clothes of a decent, but far from wealthy, man. It was the regular garb of anyone in the village.

She sucked in a breath. If the man across the street was indeed the one who wanted to hurt her, Regina refused to allow him to get away. Daffin and Mark wanted to nab him as much as she did, but they were also preoccupied by their concern for her safety.

She turned to the windows. The man didn't move. After many moments had passed, she strolled toward Daffin. "Can you tell anything?"

The storekeeper's discussion with the patron continued in a raucous vein.

"I cannot," Daffin said. "If he is watching you, he's doing a damn fine job of pretending as if he isn't."

Regina bit her lip. How could they tell if the man was the one they were after? "Should I go outside? Perhaps to the next store?"

"I'm not certain that's a good idea. I have no way of telling Grim that's our plan. We should go home. That man may follow us."

Mark was stationed across the street. He'd left much earlier than they had, in a rough-hewn wagon kept on the estate for moving hay. He'd worn the clothing of one of the stable hands so no one would recognize him. He was waiting in the shadows between two buildings across the road at an angle from the bookstore. Regina had glanced outside to try to get a glimpse of him, but she hadn't seen him, which was probably precisely the way Mark wanted it.

"But what if he doesn't follow us?" Regina asked. She hated to think of their hard work going to waste.

"We must be patient. We don't want to risk your safety," Daffin replied, his voice stern.

Regina nodded. It was disappointing to think of them leaving empty-handed today, but Daffin was the security expert. She needed to listen to him. "Very well, let's go home."

The two of them slipped out of the bookstore moments later. Regina turned her head toward the shop windows on her side of the street to continue her ruse of shopping, as Daffin escorted her toward the coach. He kept his hand on the small of her back. She didn't glance in the man's direction. Their work would be wasted if he suspected they knew he was watching them.

"Lady Regina!" a man's voice called from behind them.

Daffin swiveled to see a young man come bounding toward them. Daffin reached for his pistol. "Do you know him?" he asked Regina.

She squinted. "I don't think so."

"Lady Regina," another voice called. Regina turned in the opposite direction to see another man step out of a nearby alley straight into their path. Daffin turned, too.

"Excuse me," the man said, just as the first man came from behind and tripped Daffin.

Regina whirled to see what had happened. Daffin was lying on his back in a cloud of dust, the two men standing over him with pistols drawn. Two other men had materialized to point pistols at the coachman and footmen. She opened her mouth to scream, but a dirty hand clapped over it from behind. Before she could wrestle away, she was grabbed roughly around the waist, tossed over a fifth man's shoulder, and bundled off into the coach that had been sitting in front of theirs.

Fear clutched at her insides. Where was Mark? She could only guess he was being held at gunpoint, too. Oh, dear God, what had happened?

She managed to scramble up from the floor of the coach to look out at Daffin, who was still in the dirt, his hands lifted in surrender.

"No!" As the strangled sob left her lips, a crushing blow exploded at the back of her head, and her world went black.

# CHAPTER THIRTY

The duke's coach thundered to a stop in front of the manor house. Daffin jumped from the interior and raced to the front door, Grimaldi closely on his heels. Nicole had obviously been waiting and watching because the door flew open and she and Lady Harriet came running out.

Nicole's eyes were wide with fear. "Where is Regina?"

When she saw the bloody abrasions on the men's faces and the state of their ripped, dirty clothing, Nicole crumpled. Grimaldi caught her and scooped her up into his arms, carrying her into the green salon.

The others followed.

Once Nicole was settled on the settee, her face pale, her hands shaking, Lady Harriet ventured, "Regina?" The older woman's voice was weak, her handkerchief tightly pressed to her lips.

"Please sit," Daffin said to Lady Harriet.

Her eyes filled with tears, but she lowered herself to the settee. The men quickly recounted the story for them.

"After they took Regina, they ran off," Daffin said. "Scattered like roaches. There were at least seven of them by our count. Two each with their guns drawn on me, Grim, and the coachman in addition to the one who grabbed Regina."

Grimaldi's jaw tightened. "We suspected he was a professional, but we had no idea we were working against more than one man. They took us completely by surprise, outnumbering us." His nostrils flared. He was beyond enraged.

Tears ran down Nicole's face. Grimaldi pulled a handkerchief from his pocket and handed it to his wife.

"I'm sorry, darling. It was far different from what we thought," he said. "This was an organized group."

Daffin gave a grim nod. "I had no idea what we were up against." He wanted to slam his fist into the nearest wall. He would have if he hadn't been in the presence of ladies.

"What will they do with her?" Nicole sobbed. "You don't think they've . . . murdered her already? I will die if anything happens to her."

"We can only hope they will want to negotiate," Grimaldi replied.

"Negotiate for what? They shot at her once before," Nicole replied.

"Yes, but if murder was their intent, they could have killed her on the street today," Daffin replied.

"Oh, God. I cannot bear it." Nicole shook her head. Tears streamed down her pale face.

"Negotiate?" Lady Harriet asked, her brow furrowed.

"Probably for a ransom," Grimaldi intoned, a growl in his voice.

"None of us can think of any reason anyone would want to hurt Regina. A ransom must be what they're after," Daffin added.

"Oh, dear." Lady Harriet pressed her handkerchief to her eyes.

"Poor Regina." Nicole's voice was high with worry. "I cannot imagine how frightened she must be."

Lady Harriet's eyes darted from one man to the other. "What do we do?"

Mark expelled a breath. "Unfortunately, the only thing we can do for the time being is wait for the kidnappers to make their demand."

"I'll get her back," Daffin growled. "If it's the last thing I do."

The demand came the next day. A piece of parchment had been nailed to a tree near the entrance to the lane. Extensive questioning of the servants revealed no one had seen who'd left it. No doubt the bastards had crept in under cover of night after Daffin had fallen into an exhausted slumber. One of the groundskeepers had found the note and brought it to the house. Strangely, it was addressed to Daffin.

While Mark and Nicole looked on, Daffin ripped open the letter and scanned the page.

> *Bring five thousand pounds to the Pantheon bazaar on Thursday at one o'clock in the afternoon. Leave it in a bag at the confectioner's booth on the far side of the arcade. Don't be late or Lady Regina dies.*

It was Monday, December twenty-seventh, which meant they'd have to be back in London by Thursday afternoon. It also meant the kidnappers intended to take Regina back to London.

It was probably better that way. Daffin and Grimaldi needed reinforcements. If they returned to London, they could call upon the other runners to help, as well as some of Grimaldi's spies.

"Let me see the letter," Nicole said. Daffin handed it to her and she examined it carefully. "It's definitely written in a man's hand, and there are no misspelled words."

"What does that mean?" Lady Harriet dabbed at her eyes with her handkerchief.

"It means whoever wrote this has some education, or at least access to someone who has," Daffin replied.

Daffin scanned the page again. At the bottom of the letter, there was what looked like a flourish of ink. A mistake of the quill perhaps . . . or . . . He tilted the page slightly. It could be a *Q*. A large *Q*. That initial sent prickles along the back of his neck.

Mark cursed under his breath. "Five thousand pounds."

"It's nothing. I'd give all the money we have to get Regina back safely," Lady Harriet said.

"I want to go with you," Nicole said to her husband. "You'll need more people to help, and you and an army couldn't keep me away."

Grimaldi opened his mouth to protest. "But darling—"

"Nicole's right about one thing," Daffin said. "This time, we shall need a team of our own."

# CHAPTER THIRTY-ONE
*London, December 28*

Daffin glanced around. The salon in Grimaldi's town house was filled with investigators and spies. In addition to himself, Nicole, and Grimaldi, and a few of the runners, there were Rafe and Cade Cavendish, and their wives Daphne and Danielle. There was also Delilah Montebank, Daphne Cavendish's teenaged cousin, and, for reasons he didn't bother to inquire about, a painfully verbose parrot.

Daffin had been filled with rage for two days now. It had been two days since he'd watched helplessly from the dirt while Regina had been snatched by that man and thrown into the coach. He'd been unable to stop them. Grimaldi had been unable to stop them. There had been something at play that day in the village. Not only was the culprit not alone, but he had known their plan. He'd been ready for them. Daffin's blood boiled as he thought about it. He had a suspicion. Now that they were all gathered together, forming their plan to rescue Regina, he intended to let the others know.

"What do we know about this person?" Rafe began. The viscount's eyes narrowed as he glanced around the room with the experienced gaze of a professional spy.

"People," Daffin corrected. "We're convinced it's a group. The man who tripped me on the street was working with several other chaps, including the man who grabbed Regina."

"But what about $Q$?" Cade asked. "Who do we think that is?"

Nicole sat on the settee, her features pinched and pale. "Believe me, I've scoured my memories. I cannot think of anyone whose name, first or last, begins with $Q$. At least no one who would want to harm Regina, whether an individual or a group."

Danielle Cavendish paced the floor. "Why would Regina be a target? There are scores of rich debutantes in London. Why her?"

Daffin watched her for a moment before pinching the bridge of his nose and forcing his gaze away. Danielle reminded Daffin of Regina. They had the same coloring, dark hair and blue eyes. But Danielle Cavendish was shorter. She had been a French spy for many years before she turned to work with Grimaldi. She'd met her husband, Cade, while working on a case with Grim.

"Five thousand pounds is a lot of money," Daffin replied, pacing in the opposite direction from Danielle. "I'm not certain how many families could pay it. She mentioned to me once that she was worth quite a purse. Others must have known."

Daffin was on edge, beyond on edge. As soon as he found out who this $Q$ was, he would rip the bastard apart. If the monster had harmed one hair on Regina's head, there was nowhere the man could hide in this town, country, or world. Daffin would find him and make him pay.

"This is a nightmare." Nicole gently rubbed her belly. "None of it makes any sense."

"Makes any sense," called Delilah's parrot. The bird had a penchant for repeating whatever people said. It was getting on Daffin's final nerve.

"What I want to know is how, whoever these people are, they know Regina's every move," Rafe said.

"Precisely," Daffin interjected. "That's what bothers me most, too."

Rafe shifted from his position by the fireplace and rubbed a thoughtful hand along his jaw. "Whoever left that note in the stables got quite close without a trace. That is odd."

"Without a trace," called the parrot.

"The tracks that led away from the stables were definitely a man's boots. There was only one set of them," Daffin replied, "but I'm still convinced he's not acting alone."

"He was alone at that time, however." Rafe shook his head. "No doubt he realized he'd be less conspicuous sneaking into the stables by himself."

"Stables by himself," the parrot called.

Danielle paused in her pacing and perched on the arm of the settee near Nicole. "Or the tracks were a ruse."

"What?" Everyone's head snapped to look at the half-French woman.

"What?" called the parrot in a similarly shocked tone.

Danielle continued, "I worked on a case once where the culprit was someone inside the house, but he'd actually taken the time to leave tracks leading away in the mud. Turns out he'd circled back across the grass after removing his boots. Quite clever, actually."

Daffin scratched his chin and shot her a thoughtful look. "You may be on to something, Danielle. Grim and I have begun to suspect something similar."

"But that would mean . . ." Daphne trailed off.

"That someone in the house is working with them," Nicole finished, her face pale and drawn.

"Working with them," the parrot screeched.

"Shh," Delilah said to the parrot.

"Exactly," Danielle said with a firm nod.

Grimaldi swiveled on his heel. "Oakleaf, you said you brought extra servants with you from the town house when you went to Surrey. Is that right?"

Daffin nodded. "Yes. In addition to the two coachmen and the two groomsmen, there were two footmen."

"Timothy and Matthew," Nicole added.

"Six servants total?" Grimaldi asked.

"Yes," Daffin replied with a dawning mixture of realization and alarm.

"It has to be one of them," Cade said. "Whoever it was fed information to the kidnappers in London *and* in Surrey."

Nicole pressed a hand over her mouth. "Someone in this house?" She lowered her voice. "I feel sick. Who could it be?"

"Who could it be?" the parrot reiterated.

"My guess would be one of the groomsmen or coachmen. They were with you every time you went out, weren't they?" Grimaldi asked.

Nicole nodded.

"We don't want to accuse an innocent person," Grimaldi pointed out.

"We must watch them," Daffin said.

"We need to find a way to eavesdrop on them," Danielle added. "We must listen to their conversations."

"Listen to their conversations," the parrot echoed.

Daphne shot the bird a lethal glare. "Delilah, please—perhaps you can take Miss Adeline to another room."

Delilah nodded and stood to leave. She shook a finger at the parrot. "You see, Miss Adeline? I told you that you would get me banished eventually. You must learn to be silent."

"Learn to be silent," the parrot cawed.

"If only we could overhear them," Nicole added.

"Overhear them," the parrot repeated, stepping daintily onto Delilah's hand.

"If you want to overhear them, you should use Miss Adeline," Delilah said, stopping at the door. "He'll repeat anything anyone says."

# CHAPTER THIRTY-TWO

Daffin excused himself from the salon full of people and made his way to Grimaldi's empty study. He poured himself a brandy and stood staring blindly out the window, the glass in his hand all but forgotten. He'd made a mistake, a costly one. He would never forgive himself if anything happened to Regina. He had barely slept since she'd been taken. He had feelings for her, damn it. Deep ones, and he missed her desperately. He wanted to punch his fist through a wall when he thought about the danger he'd put her in.

"There you are." The voice behind him shook him from his reverie. He turned to see Nicole step into the study. "A penny for your thoughts," she said with a sad smile, as though she already knew what he was thinking.

"How are Lady Harriet and the duke?"

"They're fine," Nicole replied. Lady Harriet had traveled back with them from Surrey. The duke had come, too. At the moment he was in one of the guest rooms, resting. Regina's kidnapping had caused him to suffer a relapse of his lung condition, and his health was as precarious as ever. "And you're not answering my question."

"My thoughts?" Daffin expelled a long breath. "I'm thinking this is the worst mistake of my career."

She wandered over to stand next to him and patted his shoulder. "You know her, Daffin. You're too close."

"Yes. I know her, and I intend to get her back." His voice was nearly a growl.

Nicole nodded solemnly, her hand falling to her side. "She wouldn't blame you. She knew there was danger involved."

He bit the inside of his cheek. "She trusted me to keep her safe."

"Yes, but she saw what happened," Nicole countered. "You were outnumbered."

He shook his head and glanced at her. "I keep thinking there's still something odd about all of this."

"Like what?" Nicole asked.

"I don't know. It doesn't make any sense, but at the moment all I care about is getting Regina back safely."

"Yes," Nicole replied. "We can worry about the kidnappers' motives later."

"Their motives are important. Learning why they want her will help us discern why they're doing what they're doing, and possibly who they are," Daffin said.

Nicole nodded. She'd been trained by Daffin himself. They both knew she understood why it was important to learn the kidnappers' motives. "I'm just so worried about Regina I can't think straight."

"Don't worry," he said, staring unseeing out the window. "I'm going to get her back, and then I'm going to make the bastard who took her pay."

# CHAPTER THIRTY-THREE

Regina's eyes fluttered open. Panic flooded her. She had a raging headache and was lying on a dirty mattress on the floor in a darkened room. The same room she'd been in for what felt like days. From the bustle that reached her ears from outside the window, she'd guessed they were in London, and a busy part of the city at that. Her wrists were bound tightly in front of her and her ankles were also tied so she couldn't move from the mattress. The rope chafed her delicate skin, making it bleed.

She glanced down at herself. She was still wearing only her shift, but the last time she'd awoken, she'd recognized her clothing, the gown and pelisse she'd worn to the village, thrown in a corner.

The room smelled of mildew and dust, as if it hadn't been used in an age. The only furnishing was the mattress on the floor and a dirty, torn blanket that had been tossed over her.

She had no way of knowing how long she'd been here. The only person she'd seen was the man who'd grabbed her and tossed her into the coach while his cohorts had waylaid Daffin and Mark. He returned at odd times with a glass of cloudy water that he forced her to drink. It made her brain foggy and she quickly fell back to sleep.

Her family must be sick with worry. She was putting the people she loved in danger, because she knew without a doubt that as she lay here uselessly, they were forming a plot to save her. Unless they all believed she was dead. Why wasn't she? She suspected the only reason was because whoever had kidnapped her wanted something. What? Money? She'd tried to get him to talk to her once, but he had stuffed a dirty rag in her mouth and tied it behind her head. When Cousin John died, Nicole and Daffin had trained her in the skills of investigation. She remembered the right questions to ask, if only she could persuade her abductor to speak to her.

She was going to have to save herself. Her friends would be coming to save her, but she needed to escape and get back to them before she put them in such danger. She could just imagine Nicole pleading with Mark to allow her to help save Regina. She couldn't let her pregnant cousin do such a thing. Regina had to save herself, and she could only guess there wasn't much time.

She glanced around the dark room. Night had fallen. She had no idea what day of the week it was. The man left her alone mostly, other than bouts of stopping in to give her more water laced with drugs. Despite her foggy head, she had to gather the wits she had left to attempt to escape the next time he came.

Hours seemed to pass before the door finally wrenched open and the man who'd abducted her stuck in his head.

"Ahh, you're awake, my lady. Time for more laudanum."

She waited for him to come and remove the rag tied behind her head over her mouth before she struggled to sit up. The last time he'd come, he'd given her some bread and jam and untied her so she could use the bedpan he'd provided for her personal needs.

"Please untie my wrists," she said as soon as the gag was out of her mouth.

"Why would I do that?" he said.

This time she got a better look at him. He was older than she expected. He looked to be at least fifty. He was of medium height and build. Dark hair, dark eyes, a moustache. She did not recognize him.

"My wrists are sore," she said, trying to appeal to any bit of empathy he might own.

Instead, he threw back his head and laughed. "You pampered aristocrats. You think the entire world should cater to you."

Regina snapped her mouth shut. "Who are you?" She'd never been so bold with him, but she wanted to know, and the laudanum had finally worn off.

"Name's Quinton. That's all you need to know."

Regina stuck the name in her memory. She didn't recognize it.

"Not that it would mean anything to you . . . but your friend the Bow Street Runner might remember me," he continued.

"Daffin?" She shook her head.

Quinton smirked. "Ah, on a first-name basis."

"Daffin is my . . . friend."

"You have horrible taste in friends."

"How do you know Daffin?" She watched as Quinton

made his way over to the window and stared at the street below.

"Let's just say I've run into Oakleaf before. Criminals and lawmen tend to be at odds, you know."

"Why have you been trying to hurt me?"

"I haven't been trying to hurt you," he answered.

"Then why did you shoot at me?"

He laughed. "I was shooting at Oakleaf. Hit 'im too, I reckon."

"What? Why?"

"For fun, of course. I hit him, didn't I?" He chuckled to himself. "He's been a damned nuisance." Quinton scratched at his dirty chin. "When I learned Oakleaf was involved, I doubled my fee."

"Fee?" Her mouth dropped open. "You're doing this for money?"

Quinton turned toward her and took a bow. "Why else would I do it? It's my profession, my lady. One I've become quite good at over the years. In fact, I've dealt with Oakleaf more than once when he didn't even know it was me. You see, Oakleaf and I are two sides of the same coin. I do favors for aristocrats who pay me indecently large sums of money, and so does he."

She scowled at him. "Daffin investigates crime and brings criminals to justice."

"And I do the opposite. We're not so unalike."

Regina didn't know why Quinton was talking to her now when he hadn't before. Possibly because she'd been unconscious then, but she needed to ask him all she could while he was willing to speak. "You're not alike at all," she spat.

"I think we are, my lady." He sauntered toward her.

"Oakleaf merely likes to believe he's better than me. We both perform tasks for bounties. Mine just happen to be . . ."

"Illegal and immoral?" Regina offered.

Quinton tossed back his head and laughed. "There is a fine line between good and evil. The right purse makes all the difference. I daresay Oakleaf would turn to crime himself if the price was right. We're cut from the same cloth."

"No you're not. Daffin would never do any of the things you've done. He's a good man. You're . . . scum."

Quinton's face twisted into a scowl of rage. "Spoken exactly like someone who grew up with a silver spoon in her mouth and has never wanted for money a day in her life. Oakleaf might have fine friends, but he had to find his own fortune in this world, just like me. Especially with his upbringing."

"What do you mean?" Her heart pounded. What did this awful man know about Daffin's past?

"You don't know? I thought you were *friends*." His laugh was filled with scorn.

She straightened her spine. "It doesn't matter what his upbringing was. He's a good man."

"Well, well, well, why do I suspect you fancy the good runner? Now that's interesting, indeed. Apparently Oakleaf can get a high-class bit of trim these days."

Regina clenched her teeth. Whoever this man was, he was evil and he knew Daffin and someone—who?—had paid him to hurt her. Regina had to keep him talking, keep asking him questions so she could tell Daffin the details after she escaped.

"Daffin Oakleaf is a good man."

Quinton's smile faded. "No he's not. He's a liar and a fake.

His name isn't even Oakleaf. Did he tell you that? How long have you known him? I've known him since he was a child."

Regina sucked in her breath. It couldn't be true. Daffin's name wasn't fake. But even if it was, it didn't speak to his character. How had this horrible man known him since he was a child? She didn't have time to think about all of that at the moment, however. "They'll never pay you for me, if that's what you're thinking," she shot back.

Twisted humor spread across Quinton's lips. "Should I kill you now, then?"

Regina swallowed hard. She lifted her chin. "Is that what you've been paid to do? Kill me?"

Quinton's smile revealed yellowed teeth. "If I were merely planning to kill you, you'd be dead by now, my lady. No. I'm merely buying time for your friends to leave me alone until my benefactress arrives."

"Benefactress? You mean the person who's paid you to hurt me?"

Quinton shrugged. "Benefactress sounds so much nicer, doesn't it?"

"Who would want to hurt me? I've done nothing."

His laugh made her skin crawl. "We all make enemies, my lady. You've made a powerful and rich one, which is the worst sort."

Quinton laughed again. "Don't worry. Your friends think they can outwit me, but I've been in the game longer than any of them. I consider this the ultimate challenge, beating a gang of spies at their own work." He narrowed his eyes and stared at the floor. "I could have been a spy. I could have worked for the government. They're not smarter than I am, and I'm about to prove it."

"What are you talking about?"

He lifted his head again and stalked toward her. "This entire time, I've been toying with your friends."

"Toying with them how?" Regina asked, scooting away from him as best she could.

Quinton snorted in disgust and turned toward the door. "You're all so predictable. Your friends think they're going to fool me, but I already know precisely what they're planning. I've told those idiots I want five thousand pounds, and of course they think they'll be able to catch me when I pick it up. I'm supposed to meet them at the bazaar tomorrow." He waggled his eyebrows. "I think I'll go myself, just to see them squirm."

Regina pressed her back against the wall. A fear unlike any she'd known slowly spread through her veins. "How do you know what they're planning?"

"*That* is my little secret. They will fail, however, because they're fools."

"Are you going to trade me for the money?" Regina could barely hear past the rushing of blood in her ears.

"Of course not, Lady Regina. I've been paid to kill you. The ransom is merely going to be an added bonus. I'm only keeping you alive long enough to collect it."

# CHAPTER THIRTY-FOUR

"I honestly cannot believe we're relying on a *bird* to spy for us," Daffin muttered as he and Grimaldi waited in the study for Daphne and Delilah to return. They'd moved the blasted parrot from space to space today, and had had absolutely no luck overhearing anything out of the ordinary that the coachmen or groomsmen said. The bird had spent hours in the mews this afternoon. Now it was nighttime. They were scheduled to meet the kidnapper at the bazaar on the morrow.

They'd moved the bird to the corridor near the servants' dining room below stairs, under the premise that the housekeeper was keeping an eye on the thing. They'd enlisted her help, of course. They were waiting for the parrot to listen in on Matthew and Timothy, the footmen who had traveled with them to Surrey. None of the servants took the bird's presence seriously.

Delilah came scurrying into the study, the parrot perched

on her shoulder. "I believe we've got it," she said, a proud smile on her gamin face.

Daffin shot out of his chair. "What? What happened?"

"What happened?" the bird croaked.

Daffin glared at the bird.

Delilah lifted her chin. "Miss Adeline said the following things as soon as I fetched him from the servants' corridor."

She glanced at her cousin Daphne, who flipped open a notebook where she'd obviously scribbled down what the bird had said, and handed the notebook to Delilah.

Delilah cleared her throat and began to read. "'Last payment tomorrow. Meet at the bazaar.'"

"Who said those things?" Daffin asked.

"Timothy did," Daphne said. "I confirmed it with Matthew after the fact. We believe Matthew is completely innocent in all of this. Timothy was attempting to enlist him."

"Why do you think it was Timothy and not Matthew?" Daffin asked, taking his seat again.

"Because," Grimaldi replied, leaning against the back of the settee. "I remember when I questioned the servants last summer after John's death. Timothy had a penchant for drinking. He'd stolen wine from John upon occasion. Said he needed money for his sick mother and younger sister. At the time I felt sorry for him and gave him some money. It turned out he wasn't pleased with his wages. He stood to gain more from whoever this character is."

"Did the bird say anything else?" Daffin asked.

"Yes." Delilah nodded. "Miss Adeline distinctly said, 'Knowles.'"

Daffin rubbed his jaw. Knowles. Quinton Knowles. That son of a bitch. Daffin had known that name since he was eleven years old.

# CHAPTER THIRTY-FIVE

Regina waited until she heard a heavy door open and close on a lower floor, likely a front door. Quinton had tried to drug her again, but she'd managed to hold the liquid in her mouth until he left the room, then she spat it on the floor. She'd heard him moving about the house for a while. She had no idea what he was doing, but he'd finally left. She'd waited at least an extra quarter hour to ensure he wasn't coming back.

She used her teeth to gnaw at the ropes that bound her wrists. When that didn't work, she managed to stand and hop to the candle Quinton had left burning on a stool by the door. She pulled her hands as far apart as she could and stuck the knot in the fire, waiting for its fibers to burn away, hoping it would fall off before it scorched her skin.

She suffered a minor burn, which she doused with the cup of water Quinton had left for her. Knowing she'd need her strength, she quickly choked down the dry, stale bread spread with jam that rested on a plate near her mattress. While she ate, she used her free hand to untie and pull off the ropes at her ankles. When she was finally free, she rushed to the door and tried it.

Locked.

She hurried to the nearest window and glanced outside. It had snowed over the last few days, the ground and rooftops covered in white. The window had a layer of ice on it. She peered down. She was on the second floor. It was a steep drop. She'd kill herself that way. Turning in a circle, she rushed to the only other window in the room. She glanced outside and breathed a sigh of relief. The roof on the porch of the adjoining house jutted out several feet below. She could make it.

She jiggled the window, hoping against hope that it would be open.

Locked. Drat.

The image of her time in the dining room at Mark and Nicole's house with Daffin came roaring into her mind. *"A skilled criminal can knock out a pane of glass with his hand if he knows what he's doing."* Daffin had demonstrated, but the windows in Mark and Nicole's town house had not been poorly made. Regina could only hope the windows in this dank house were flimsy. She knocked on the top of the lower pane with the heel of her hand.

Nothing.

Was it frozen in place? Swallowing her rising panic, she knocked again, angling her hand this time and using more force. The pane popped free, sliding down and out of the frame. Regina caught it quickly with both hands and lowered it to the wall below the window. Cold air rushed in to nip her bare skin. She shuddered but stuck her head out the window and breathed in fresh air for the first time in days. Even freezing air was welcome after the dankness of the room she'd been held in.

Woozy from both the drugs and several days' inactivity, she prayed she would be able to navigate slipping through the window and jumping to the rooftop below without falling to her death. She held her breath and waited for a lone coach to pass. Otherwise, the street seemed deserted. She didn't dare try to alert the neighbors. The area looked disreputable. For all she knew, the neighbors were aware Quinton kept people locked in this house and approved of it. She wasn't about to trust her safety to a stranger. Not when everything was riding on her getting home to keep her family from more danger.

She didn't dare get dressed before trying to climb about on rooftops. The clothing might impede her escape. Instead, she decided to drop her clothing out of the window and dress once she'd made it safely to the ground. She could only hope it was a decision she would not regret. She hurried to the pile of her clothing on the floor, gathered it into her arms, returned to the window, and leaned out as far as she could. Then she dropped it all in an ignominious heap into the snow below.

No turning back now. She took a deep breath and hoisted up her shift. She lifted a foot and stuck out her leg from the window. The cold air sliced across her bare skin. She lifted the other foot. Balancing on the windowpane on her derriere, she managed to turn backward onto her belly and dangle, her feet floating free in the freezing night.

A single glance down tightened her throat with panic. The drop to the rooftop seemed much more daunting now that she was dangling from a second-story window. Summoning all the courage she could muster, she shimmied out until only her hands gripped the windowpane, clutching for dear life. She closed her eyes briefly.

Regina's feet were probably only a yard away from the top of the roof. She couldn't hold on much longer. Now was probably not the best time to wonder if the neighbors' roof was old and rotted. Would it hold? Or would she go crashing through it and land in a heap on their doorstep?

It didn't matter. There was no way she could pull herself back up to the window. She had to take the chance.

She counted to three, closed her eyes again, and let go of the window frame. Her shift whooshed up around her thighs and she fell to the rooftop, banging her knee against it. But the rooftop held. It held. She said a silent prayer of thanksgiving as she crouched there, steadying herself on the balls of her feet, listening for any noise. There was only the haunting call of an owl in a nearby tree. She expelled her breath, trying to ignore the ice and snow burning her bare soles. She peered over the edge to see how awful the rest of the drop would be.

Thank heaven for small favors. A nice, fat hedge covered in fluffy snow sat underneath the rooftop to the side of the front door. Normally, the hedge would be nothing but sticks in winter, but the pile of snow made it look almost inviting. Regardless, it was the only choice she had. She pulled her shift as far down as it would go and lowered herself off the side of the roof, her fingertips clinging to the gutter just as they had the window. Her feet skimmed the snow on the top of the hedge when she let go.

What happened next was . . . uncomfortable. Very well, it was downright painful. But moments later, when she landed on the ground—having rolled there off the hedge—and assessed the damage, she was happy to find only bleeding scratches versus broken bones. She could live with bleeding scratches.

Now to keep from freezing to death.

She scrambled to her feet and located the pile of her clothing a few yards away. She grabbed up the gown first and tossed it over her head, pulling it down to cover herself. There was no way she could button it properly without help, but at the moment that was the least of her worries. Next, she pulled the pelisse over her already shaking shoulders. Her teeth were chattering. She didn't bother with her stays, or stockings. They were too much trouble under the circumstances. Instead, she rolled them into a ball and stuffed them into the hedge. She smiled to herself. Whoever found them come spring would be in for a surprise.

She grabbed her boots and shoved them on her feet. Then she took off in the direction she'd seen the last carriage go, limping from the damage she'd done to her knee. The road had to lead somewhere, hopefully somewhere she recognized.

Nearly an hour later, she found herself back at the same intersection where she'd begun. Tears stung her eyes. She'd merely gone in a circle, and she didn't recognize anything. She was hopelessly lost. The laudanum lingering in her body affected her more than she'd known. Her thinking wasn't straight. She stood there, contemplating what she should do next. A hackney coach came rumbling down the street. A mixture of relief and sudden wooziness nearly crumpled her to the ground. She waved down the conveyance. She had no money in her pockets, but she would ask for help and pray he was kind. It was her last hope.

The man pulled the coach to a stop next to her. "Are ye all right, missus?"

"No," she said, opening the door and using the last bit of

strength she possessed to pull herself up and collapse onto the dirty floor of the conveyance. "Take me to the Marquess of Coleford's house on Upper Brook Street. *Please.*"

"The Marquess of Coleford? Are ye certain that's wot ye want, missus?" the man called to her. The poor driver sounded extremely skeptical that the bedraggled woman in the back of his coach had business with the Marquess of Coleford.

"Yes," she managed to breathe before passing out.

# CHAPTER THIRTY-SIX

The butler rushed into the salon where Daffin sat with Mark, Nicole, Lady Harriet, and the duke. The five thousand pounds the duke had gathered sat in the middle of the settee in a brown leather satchel, ready for the next day's exchange for Regina's life.

"My lord," Abbott said, his face pale. "There is a hackney driver at the door and he insists he has a young lady in his conveyance who demanded to be brought here."

Daffin jumped from his seat and took off toward the front door at a run. Grimaldi and Nicole followed him. Daffin didn't stop to question the hackney driver. Ignoring the cold wind that seared through his clothing, he grabbed a lantern from the porch and hastened to the hackney coach that sat on the road in front of the house.

As soon as he reached the conveyance, he ripped open the door and stuck in the lantern. His heart stopped. Regina lay in a heap on the floor, unconscious and shivering. Grimaldi had made it to the coach too, and Daffin shoved the lantern into his friend's hand. He scooped Regina into his arms and turned for the house. She blinked up at him and a hint of relief shone in her eyes before she fell back into unconsciousness.

Daffin stalked into the foyer, Regina nestled against his chest. "Which bedchamber?" he asked a shocked-looking Nicole, who had remained at the door.

"Follow me." Nicole scurried up the stairs, Daffin behind her, carrying Regina.

Nicole hurried down the long corridor and stopped at a doorway in the middle of the hallway. She pushed open the door, hurried to the bed and pulled back the covers. Daffin followed her and gingerly laid Regina on the soft, clean sheets. Lady Harriet and a bevy of housemaids came scurrying into the room to see to Regina, and Daffin was forced to leave for propriety's sake. He made it to the hallway, before leaning back against the wall and sliding down to sit with his arms on his knees. A relief unlike any he'd ever known flooded him.

Minutes later, he looked up to see Grimaldi standing above him. The general leaned down and grasped his shoulder in a gesture of support.

"She's back," Daffin said, the words barely making it through his dry, rough throat. Tears burned the backs of his eyes. "Oh God, Grim. She's safe."

Regina pushed herself up against the pillows in her bedchamber. She'd been home for over two days, but the events were still a blur. She vaguely recalled blinking up at a lantern held into the interior of the hackney and Daffin staring down at her incredulously. She remembered the feel of his warm chest as he scooped her into his arms. She had the vaguest memory of finally feeling safe again and recalling his welcome scent, before she slipped back into the blackness.

The next time she'd awoken, she was clean and wearing a new, fresh-smelling night rail, propped up in her bed at Mark's house. A stream of maids had come in to check on her as well as Nicole and Mark and Grandmama. They were treating her as if she were an invalid. The rope burns on her wrists and ankles had been treated with balm and were healing nicely. The fire burns on her palms were barely even sore anymore. The scratches and scrapes she'd got from her dive into the hedge had turned to scabs. The only thing that still bothered her was her knee. Nicole insisted she keep it propped upon a pillow at all times.

Otherwise, Regina felt fine, but Mark and Nicole insisted she rest. Their guilt had turned them into a pair of mother hens. That, along with Grandmama's constant check-ins, made Regina think she might go mad. She was perfectly healthy. She had to get out of this bed. Out of this room. She'd begun to feel as if she were trapped again.

Nicole had been in to see her a half-dozen times, gushing over her bravery and coddling her as if she were a child. Her cousin had the staff of housemaids at Regina's beck and call, and tea and cakes and anything she desired were sent up regularly. But Regina longed to push off the covers and get out of bed.

She was just about to do so when a knock at the door stopped her.

"Come in," she called, expecting to see Nicole's worried face peep around the door again.

"Are you decent?" came a deep male voice.

It was Daffin.

Butterflies flew through Regina's belly. She smiled to herself and bit her lip. "I'm always decent," she called back.

He slipped into the room, leaving the door half open behind him. He looked as if he hadn't slept in a fortnight. Several days' growth of beard covered his face, and he appeared thinner. "I know it's completely improper for me to come in here, but given that I haven't been allowed to talk to you until now, I decided to take a gamble."

Daffin walked to the bed and took a seat in the chair Nicole had set there for her and Grandmama's regular visits.

Regina pushed a lock of hair behind her ear. It was so good to see him again. She'd missed him, she realized. Had missed him terribly. But the look of guilt on his face made her wary. "If you've come to apologize, you needn't."

"I am sorry." He hung his head. He looked so guilty, her heart tugged.

"There's nothing to be sorry about, Daffin."

He lifted his head and met her gaze. "That's kind of you, but you're wrong. We should have protected you better. *I* should have protected you better."

Her breath caught in her throat. Her heart thudded painfully. "You had no idea there was a team at work. He hired those people to help him. He told me."

Daffin shook his head. "That doesn't matter."

Regina smoothed her dressing gown. "What? You think you should have guessed? You're intelligent, Daffin, but you're not omniscient."

"Let me be guilty, love, please," he whispered, leaning forward and brushing her hair away from her cheek.

Regina sucked in her breath.

He self-consciously withdrew his hand. "Do you want to talk about what happened?"

"If you think it will help to find him. I heard Timothy, the footman, was working with him."

"I carted that blighter off to jail. He confessed to everything."

"Good. I never want to see him again."

"Neither do I."

Regina lowered her voice to a whisper. "I haven't told Nicole everything, Daffin. Not the things he said . . . about you."

"Me?" Daffin moved forward to sit on the edge of the chair. "What did he say?"

She traced a fingertip along the bedspread. "He said you weren't who I thought you were."

Daffin glanced away.

"He said your name isn't Oakleaf."

Daffin remained quiet for several seconds before dropping his gaze to the floor and saying quietly, "It's true."

Regina narrowed her gaze on him. "Who are you, Daffin?"

Daffin leaned forward, bracing his hands on his knees. He expelled a breath. "Oakleaf isn't the name I was born with. I changed it after school."

"Why?"

"Because I wanted nothing to do with my father."

She shook her head. "His name was Quinton, Daffin, and he knows you. He said as much."

"Yes. He knows me. And I know him." Daffin's jaw turned to rock. "His name is Quinton Knowles."

Regina frowned, but nodded. "How do you know him?"

"He is the man who killed my mother."

# CHAPTER THIRTY-SEVEN

Regina took a deep breath. After everything they'd been through, it was time for Daffin to open up to her. She refused to let him change the subject this time. "Tell me, Daffin. Tell me the truth about your mother's murder."

His eyes were jade-hard. "It is a complicated story."

She settled back against the pillows and pulled the blanket to her chin. "I just happen to have plenty of time."

He leaned forward in the chair, scrubbed a hand across his face, and let out a long, deep breath. Regina studied his face. She knew telling the story would cost him something. His mother's murder had shaped the life of this gorgeous, enigmatic man. How had it happened?

He faced her. "My mother was a beautiful woman. She had many admirers."

"I can imagine." Regina watched his profile. The tiny lines by his eyes indicated his pain. Was he ashamed because his mother had taken lovers? Many married women in the *ton* did.

"I found her body at the bottom of the staircase in our house," Daffin said abruptly. Though his tone was flat, matter-of-fact, the stiffness of his spine and shoulders spoke of deep agony.

Regina sucked in her breath. Dear God. He'd been the one to find his mother's dead body? She couldn't imagine anything worse. "On Christmas Eve?" she whispered, tears filling her eyes.

"No. On Christmas Day." He glanced at her and away again, his lashes leaving shadows on his cheeks as he stared at the fire in the grate. "I'd raced down the steps to get the Christmas cookies our cook usually left for me on Christmas morning."

The tears spilled down Regina's cheeks. "I'm sorry, Daffin."

Daffin's eyes clouded. "The constable came. He barely even scanned the scene before declaring my mother's death an accident. But I knew it wasn't."

Regina wiped away her tears with the backs of her hands. "How did you know?"

"The way her body was angled at the bottom of the stairs. It made no sense that she'd fallen. She wouldn't have landed that way. And she had marks on her neck that the constable entirely ignored."

Regina could only imagine how that moment had made Daffin want to become an investigator one day. "What happened to you after that?"

"My father sent me off to boarding school. I didn't return to London to live again until I was a grown man."

Regina searched his profile. "You didn't see your father on holidays? School breaks?"

"No." His voice was clipped. "I wasn't welcome in my father's home."

"That's awful," Regina said. No wonder he thought his father was hideous. "And when you were grown . . . you managed to prove your mother had been killed and find her murderer?"

Daffin's features were stony in the firelight, but his hands clenched and unclenched in his lap. "I hunted him for years, beginning when I was a teen. I worked with the night watch. I waited outside the homes of great men to get sponsorship. I talked to constables, asked them questions, investigated every detail, every possible angle. I earned a reputation at it. Later, certain men of means came looking for me to help them solve crimes. When I was old enough, I went to Fielding, asked him if I could join Runners. He told me he'd been looking for *me*. He asked me to be a part of the team."

"And doing all that you eventually found your mother's murderer?"

"Yes." Daffin shook his head as if banishing the painful memories he'd uncovered, and turned back to face her. "I was able to prove he was in the house that day from a scrap of paper with a *Q* on it he'd left behind near my mother's body. Arrogant bastard. I wrung a confession out of him. Took all I had not to wring his neck. He rotted in gaol for years."

Regina dabbed at her eyes with a handkerchief she'd retrieved from the bedside table drawer. "How did he get out?"

Daffin shook his head. "I wish I knew. After half a dozen years, I was told he was killed by another prisoner. I went to his burial and spat on his grave."

"I don't blame you," she said. "I would have done the

same. But if he died in prison, how could Quinton Knowles be the one?"

Daffin's expression softened as he reached to touch her cheek. He let his fingertips trace its curve, and she shuddered at the tenderness in the wake of such a brutal account of his past. "I've seen the worst of people doing what I do, Regina. I suspect he staged his own death, and money changed hands somewhere."

Regina nodded, even as her heart thundered in her chest at the lingering touch of his hand. "I can . . . only imagine." She took a deep breath. "But *why* did Knowles kill your mother? Did you ever find out?"

"For the same reason he kidnapped you. Someone paid him."

Regina sucked in her breath. "Who?"

"My father."

# CHAPTER THIRTY-EIGHT

Daffin shut the door to Regina's bedchamber behind him and paused, momentarily unable to acknowledge Nicole's presence beside him as he struggled with myriad realizations. She seemed to sense his need to gather himself and didn't try to engage him while he lingered outside Regina's door, one hand covering his eyes.

He'd admitted the truth to Regina about his father hiring his mother's murderer. He'd never divulged it to anyone before. Never told a soul. He'd been ashamed. For more than one reason. But he and Regina had a special connection. It was undeniable. The days when he'd wondered if he'd ever get the chance to see her again had been hell. The moment he'd laid eyes on her in the hired hackney a few nights ago, he couldn't breathe he'd been so filled with relief. He never wanted to feel that sort of fear again.

Nicole finally cleared her throat. "She doesn't blame you, you know?"

Daffin rubbed a hand across his forehead as they walked together down the corridor toward the staircase. "I know. But she should."

"No she shouldn't."

He clenched his fingers into a fist. "I am going to rip that son of a bitch apart when I find him."

Nicole patted his arm. "Settle down. Your anger won't help. Come with me to the study. We're going to discuss the next plan."

They stopped at the head of the staircase.

"I'll be there in a bit," he told her.

Nicole's eyes sparkled with mischief. "I must say I was disappointed you didn't try to steal a kiss while you were in there with Regina."

"Pardon?" He arched a brow.

"She especially likes your handcuffs. She's mentioned them more than once." Nicole winked at him.

Daffin's mouth fell open as he watched her trail off down the stairs.

An hour after Daffin had left her room, Regina finally couldn't stand another moment of bed rest. She climbed from the mattress, wrapped her dressing gown tightly around her, and sneaked down the stairs to the study. Nicole had informed her they intended to plan how to track down Quinton Knowles, and Regina wanted to be a part of it.

Her dressing gown's collar pressed to her throat, she tiptoed to the study doors.

She was just about to knock when Mark called, "Come in, Regina."

She smiled. "How did you know I was here?"

"You're hiding outside a room full of spies, I daresay we all knew you were there," Mark called back.

Smiling, Regina stepped into the room and scanned its occupants. In addition to Nicole and Mark, all four of the Cavendishes were present. Daffin was there, too. They each gave her a smile or a nod as she entered, ignoring her unconventional attire.

"I am a part of this investigation," she announced, her cheeks hot, "and I refuse to sit in bed one moment more."

Nicole made her way over to her. "Of course. You've certainly earned your place here. Come. Sit. Help us."

Regina settled herself on the sofa on the far side of the room, next to Nicole.

"Regina is the only person among us who has recently spoken with Knowles," Nicole said. "I daresay she has a great deal to share."

"Yes, Regina," Daphne Cavendish said. "Tell us."

Regina took a deep breath. Smoothing her dressing gown, she moved her gaze around the room. She met Daffin's eyes and he gave her an encouraging smile. "Knowles loves the challenge of being up against all of you. He wanted the chance to match wits with the best spies in the country."

"He's about to get his chance tenfold," Mark ground out.

"He's escaped us twice. We're not dealing with a novice here," Danielle added.

Daffin shifted on his chair by the fireplace and folded his arms over his chest. "He's had the upper hand because we didn't realize how sophisticated he was. Now we do."

"Regina says he's been hired by someone," Nicole pointed out. "Who? Who would want to hurt her?"

"He wouldn't say," Regina replied. "He only referred to a benefactress."

"A woman? But who?" Nicole shook her head.

"Someone with money," Daffin replied. "Knowles doesn't do anything cheap."

"And someone who wanted me dead," Regina added. "He only kept me alive to get even more money from Uncle Edward."

"Greedy bastard," Daffin growled.

"He knows we know now, however," Mark added. "He's made a mess of things, but he'll come back for Regina to get his purse. If whoever hired Knowles learns he had his chance and lost it because of his greed, he will have hell to pay."

"I agree," Daffin replied. "Until we catch him and find out whom he's working for, Regina remains in danger."

Nicole squeezed Regina's hand. "I won't let you out of my sight. I'm so sorry you were kidnapped."

Regina gave her friend a wan smile.

"There's no use in recriminations," Danielle Cavendish said. "All that matters now is finding Knowles."

"Agreed," Mark said.

Daffin turned to Regina. "We need you to take us to where you were held. We'll drive around the city until we find it. I have the direction from the hackney driver of where he picked you up. It's our only clue at this point."

Regina nodded. She wasn't at all certain she could remember where she'd come from, but she would do her best. "Of course."

"We need you to tell us everything you remember about where you were kept, Regina," Mark said.

Regina scoured her memory. "He gave me laudanum.

Everything was hazy. When I left, it was dark. I stumbled away looking for a street I recognized. I was still groggy."

"I know, but think hard," Mark pressed. "Do you remember anything? Anything at all?"

Regina did her best to concentrate. She'd been trying to remember the particulars of her escape for days. The details were lost in a fog of cold and fear. "I remember a lamppost and a milliner's shop."

"Anything else?" Daffin moved to a chair that faced her, his elbows braced on his knees.

Regina rubbed her hands across her face and groaned. "I remember while I was in the locked room, I heard a loud clanging noise. Over and over. As if someone were striking iron. Like a blacksmith."

"There is a blacksmith on the corner of Earlham and Mercer in Seven Dials," Cade Cavendish offered, leaning on a nearby wall. "Didn't the hackney driver say he picked her up near there?"

"Yes," Daffin replied, his nostrils flaring.

Regina nodded. "If we can find the street I was on, perhaps I can find the window I crawled out of."

Daffin reached out and squeezed her hand. His gaze caught and held hers. "It's settled. We'll leave in the morning at first light."

# CHAPTER THIRTY-NINE

Later that afternoon, Daffin entered Grimaldi's study. "What did you find out?"

Grimaldi nodded at him to sit. "I've had my best men researching Quinton Knowles. You're not going to like what I learned. Apparently, he's been out of prison for years."

Daffin expelled a breath. "But how? I was there the day they buried him in a cheap coffin outside of town."

"You know as well as I do that Newgate is rife with prison guards out to make a few extra pounds."

Daffin scratched the back of his neck. "I was afraid you were going to say that."

"You never saw his body, did you?" Grim asked.

"No. And I was young and naïve enough back then not to ask. God, I'm a fool. All these years, I believed he was dead."

"You're not a fool, Oakleaf. You merely believed in a system that let you down . . . more than once."

Daffin rubbed his hands over his eyes. "You found out who I am, didn't you?"

Grimaldi smiled a little. "It's nothing to be ashamed of."

Daffin laughed a humorless laugh. "Easy for the grandson of a duke to say."

"Ah, but you're the grandson of a duke, too, now aren't you? The illegitimate eldest son of the Duke of Portland."

"Yes." Daffin clenched his jaw. "I'm a bastard."

"This changes nothing, Oakleaf. You're still the best runner Fielding's got. You're a damn fine man and a damn fine friend."

Daffin hung his head. It humbled him to hear those words from his friend's mouth. Would Regina feel the same when she found out? He didn't have time to contemplate it. All that mattered was finding the son of a bitch who'd tried to hurt her and whoever had paid the bastard, and putting them both in prison where they belonged. This time Daffin would make certain Knowles never got out. "I want the name of the guard who took Knowles's bloody money to let him out."

Grimaldi cracked a smile. "I thought you might want it. I've got my best men on the case."

A slow smile spread across Daffin's face. "First, I'm going to find Knowles. Then I'm going to find the guard and send him to gaol, too. Now, who do you think is behind this?"

"Regina helped put John's killers away last summer. Do you think they might have paid Knowles to exact revenge?"

"Perhaps," Daffin replied, "but why only Regina? The rest of us helped put them away too."

"I agree. There's something still not right."

Daffin leaned back in his seat. "I'm through guessing. My plan is to find Knowles and drag the name out of him."

\* \* \*

Delilah Montebank and her parrot meandered over to where the Duke of Colchester sat in the center of the salon.

"Good afternoon, your grace," she said, executing an adorable, if wobbly, curtsy.

The duke looked up at her in surprise. "Good afternoon," he intoned.

"I am Lady Delilah, and this is my parrot, Miss Adeline."

"She looks like a fine parrot," the duke said.

"Oh, Miss Adeline *is* a fine parrot," Delilah agreed, "but unfortunately named, because he is a boy."

"Very fine parrot," squawked the bird.

"I see," the duke replied, doing his best to squelch his smile. "At times, unfortunate names are unavoidable."

"How so?" Delilah asked.

"How so?" echoed the parrot.

The duke cleared his throat. "For instance, one of my middle names is Hercules."

"I see. That is unfortunate," Delilah replied. "I'm so pleased to find someone who finally understands."

The duke nodded. "I am Edward Alistair Hercules Montague Coleford, the fifth Duke of Colchester."

"I am ever so pleased to meet you, your grace." Delilah executed another imperfect curtsy. "How do you find being a duke? I've always believed it must be an awful chore."

The duke chuckled. "Why do you think so?"

"My best friend Thomas is a duke, and he's forever having to do something boring."

"Who is your best friend?"

"Thomas Hobbs, the Duke of Huntley."

"And does he find being a duke an awful chore?"

"Awful chore," said the bird.

Delilah tilted her head. "I've never asked him. I've merely assumed. But Thomas is good at things like handling catastrophes and being in charge of things. I, however, am not. Miss Adeline does not care for him, though."

"Does not care," Miss Adeline squawked.

The duke cocked his head to the side. "Why doesn't Miss Adeline care for his grace?"

Delilah let out a loud, long sigh. "Because Miss Adeline is terribly jealous of Thomas."

"Jealous," the bird confirmed.

"That is unfortunate. I should like very much to formally thank Miss Adeline," the duke said. "I understand he was instrumental in helping us to flush out a traitor in our midst."

"Traitor in our midst," the bird cawed.

Delilah gave the duke a bright smile. "I knew Miss Adeline's repeating things would be good for something one day. I've been trying to find a way to sneak him into my lessons with Miss Baxter. I thought perhaps he could memorize the answers to my quizzes."

"Who is Miss Baxter?" Colchester asked.

"My tutor," Delilah replied. "She is doing her best to teach me how to be proper."

"And how are your studies coming?" the duke asked.

"Dreadfully slow," Delilah admitted.

The duke smothered another smile. "Why is that?

"Because I say what is on the tip of my tongue and not what is proper. It's as if my brain refuses to wait and say the proper thing. Lately we have been practicing *p-a-t-i-e-n-c-e* and *d-e-c-o-r-u-m*."

"Patience and decorum?" The duke frowned. "Why did you spell them?"

The parrot opened his mouth to speak but Delilah gave him a look that silenced him.

"Because I hate those words." Delilah shuddered. "I refuse to say them aloud."

"My apologies for uttering them, my lady," the duke replied.

"It's quite all right, your grace. You couldn't possibly have known my aversion to them. I fear I may never be good at either of them, however, so I have chosen to eschew them from my vocabulary. Meanwhile, I have retained the word *eschew* as you have just observed. It makes no sense, but there you have it."

"You know what I think, Lady Delilah?" the duke said.

Delilah leaned forward. "What?"

"I think it's quite possible for you to grow to be a lovely young woman without either patience or much decorum. Again, with all due apologies for uttering those words."

Delilah blinked at him. "Do you, truly?"

"I do."

"I desperately hope you're right, your grace. My mother despairs of me ever making an advantageous match. She says I am *u-n-c-o-n-v-e-n-t-i-o-n-a-l*. I suppose owning a parrot has not helped."

"Has not helped," squawked the bird.

The duke nodded. "I think you shall have every reason to believe you can make an advantageous match. *U-n-c-o-n-v-e-n-t-i-o-n-a-l* or not."

Delilah gave him a bright smile. "Thank you very much, your grace. I am pleased we met." She turned away.

"Lady Delilah," the duke said, causing her to turn back momentarily.

"Yes?"

"I find I must ask. Why doesn't Miss Baxter allow Miss Adeline in her lessons? Is it because he repeats things?"

"Oh, no," came Lady Delilah's prompt reply. "It's because he bites."

# CHAPTER FORTY

After they'd decided to hunt down Knowles and whoever he might be working with at dawn, Regina reluctantly trailed her way back to her room, not wanting to leave Daffin's company in the study. She had dinner in her room and Genevieve helped her change into a fresh night rail and dressing gown. She spent the better part of an hour pacing her room. She couldn't sleep, knowing they'd be leaving at sunrise to find the man who'd kidnapped her for some reason she still didn't understand. Knowles had told her she had made a powerful enemy. But who? And why? The man was obviously mad. Perhaps he didn't even have a benefactress.

There was another reason Regina couldn't sleep. The man she was falling in love with was only a few doors down the corridor. Daffin was in one of the guest rooms. Mark had insisted he spend the night at the town house so they all could leave as soon as the sun rose. Regina straightened her shoulders and lifted her chin. This was it. She might not have another such opportunity.

She wrapped her dressing gown tightly around her and, steeling her resolve, marched to her door. She had pulled it open to step into the corridor when Daffin's large frame filled the doorway.

His shoulder against the frame, he was barefoot and had a sinful grin on his face. "May I come in?"

A slow smile spread across her lips before she silently grabbed him by the lapel and pulled him into her bedchamber. "Why are you here?" she asked, closing the door solidly behind him.

"I realized how much I missed you while you were gone."

"Did you?" She trailed her hands up around his neck.

"Yes, that, and . . . Nicole mentioned you might be interested in my handcuffs?" He pulled them from behind his back and dangled them in front of her face on one finger.

Regina's eyes widened. "Ooh, you have no idea how much."

He backed her up to the bed and lowered her to it, tossing the handcuffs onto the mattress. When he moved atop her, she rose up to meet his lips. They kissed for long minutes, their bodies straining together through their clothing, yet neither could be bothered to shed a single garment until they drank their fill of each other.

At last Daffin lifted his head and stared down at her, his heavy-lidded gaze searching hers. Whatever he was looking for in her eyes, he found, for a warm smile softened his features. He scrambled to his knees to wrestle off his coat, then he unwound his cravat and ripped off his vest. With a jolt of delight, she noted his slightly shaking hands. Finally, he reached back, grabbed the neck of his shirt, and whisked it over his head, leaving his blond hair rumpled. He looked unruly and dangerous as his hands slid to the fall of his breeches.

Regina pushed herself up on her knees to help him undo the buttons. Their fingers tangled. When the breeches hung open, she put her hands on his hips and helped push them down until they were bundled at his feet. She gasped, sitting back to take in the sight of him. His body was perfection. His scarred shoulder, his flat abdomen, his long, lean legs . . . and his manhood that jutted out, thick and strong. All for her.

"Is that your final scar?" she asked, pointing to his thigh.

"It's a scar," he replied. "I'm not yet certain it's the final one."

She shook her head while he moved to the edge of the bed to pull off his breeches. Then she leaned forward and nibbled at his neck as he had hers earlier.

"If you keep doing that, love, I won't be able to rid myself of these."

"I'm not going to stop," she teased.

He ripped the breeches from his feet and tossed them aside, then fully, finally naked, he flipped her onto her back again and crawled up her body, slow, playfully predatory, at last letting his hips settle against hers. All that separated his flesh from hers was the thin muslin of her nightclothes.

"What about my clothes?" she asked, biting her lip.

"Your clothes?" He glanced down at them as if considering, then met her gaze again with a mischievous glint in his eyes. "The truth is I want to rip them off you."

"Do it," she breathed. "I challenge you."

The sensual smile on his face told her he would. He untied her dressing gown and pushed it over her shoulders, then used both hands to grasp the neckline of her night rail. In one solid movement, he ripped the garment in two. "I hope you didn't particularly like that one," he whispered against her ear.

Regina giggled. "I can only guess what Genevieve is going to think in the morning."

At last she was as naked as he and it was his turn to stare at her body. His gaze began at her face and traveled slowly down, reverently taking in each part of her.

She waited for him to look his fill before she said, "I want you." She reached her arms around his shoulders and tried to pull him against her.

He kissed the space where her neck and shoulder met. "I want to make this good for you."

She crossed her wrists together and offered them to him. "Aren't you going to use your handcuffs, Mr. Oakleaf?"

His eyes widened before he schooled his expression and kissed her. "Regina, you're a virgin. I thought we might do it the, ahem, more customary way first."

She pushed herself up on her palms, her breasts jutting out toward him, shamefully, delightedly naked and free and offering herself into his hands. "Daffin, nothing has ever been customary between us. I want our lovemaking to be the same. I've been fantasizing about your handcuffs since July."

He gave a disbelieving laugh, studied her for a moment with his eyes shining, then seemed to make a decision, and deftly grabbed the handcuffs from where they lay on the mattress while he kissed her. She offered her arms again, and he clapped a metal ring over her wrist. "Does it hurt?" he said, knowing she still had sores from the ropes Knowles had used.

"A little," she replied. "But in a *very* good way." She grinned at him and offered her other wrist.

"You trust me this much?" he asked in awe, his eyes searching hers.

"Of course I do."

He clamped the other side of the handcuff down and locked it into place.

She cleared her throat and affected a stern expression. "Tell me. What do I have to do for mercy?" she asked him with a sly smile.

Daffin closed his eyes. His deepest fantasies were coming true. He'd been wrong about her from the beginning. Well, since she'd propositioned him at Bow Street. She wasn't conventional. She wasn't the same as the other ladies of the *ton*. She was Regina. Unique and original and perfect for him.

"Put your hands above your head," he ordered, straddling her hips.

She complied, raising her handcuffed wrists high above her and resting her arms on the mattress. "Now what?" she breathed.

"Now?" He arched a brow. "Now I'm going to make you beg me."

He lowered his head to her breast and sucked her nipple into his mouth. Regina gasped. He tugged at it with his lips and bit it softly with his teeth. Her hips thrashed against the mattress.

He didn't waste any time, his intent unerring as his hands slid straight down her body and between her legs. "I'm going to watch your face when you come." He slowly slid one long finger inside her and out again while her hips twisted help-lessly beneath his caress.

"I want to touch you." She strained against the handcuffs. She was filled with the secret thrill of being helpless, and yet knowing, from the way his hungry gaze followed the yearning rise of her body against his touch, that she was truly the one who wielded the power.

"No. I want to taste *you*."

He lowered himself until his mouth was hovering above her mound. He lingered there for a moment, his warm exhalations brushing her tender skin, until she felt ready to scream. Then, without warning, his tongue dipped down to lick between her wet folds. She cried out and his other hand came up to clap over her mouth. "You must be quiet."

"Yes, Mr. Oakleaf," she obediently replied through his fingers, shivering with lust.

His strong hands grasped her hips and he licked her again and again. She clenched her jaw to keep from crying out. She dug her restrained hands into the pillows above her head, gripping harder with every pass of his wicked tongue over her most intimate flesh. His finger returned to slowly slide in and out of her, going deeper and deeper. Then he used the tip of his tongue to circle her in tiny swirls that beckoned her body to arch against his mouth and seek each tiny, searing stroke, until her every muscle strained to reach him. His mouth was relentless and suddenly her body was no longer her own, as pleasure seized her limbs and crashed over her again and again in massive, soul-tumbling waves.

Her body was still shuddering with delightful zings of pleasure when Daffin moved back up, raining kisses along her belly and breasts until his face hovered above hers again. "Do you want me to take off the handcuffs?"

She shook her head. "No."

He settled himself between her legs, his hot length probing between her thighs.

She snapped out of her state of delight. "Daffin?"

"Yes, love?"

"Will it . . . hurt?" Her voice held a note of vulnerability that tugged at his heart.

"No," he whispered in her ear.

"How do you know?"

He smiled against her ear. "Because I already breached your maidenhead with my finger several minutes ago."

"You did?" She blinked at him. "But I didn't feel anything but pleasure."

He braced himself on one elbow and looked down at her. "That, my love, is because you chose wisely for your first lover." His grin was downright arrogant.

She smiled back at him. "By all means, then, proceed."

Daffin braced his hands on either side of her head, shifted himself into place, and slid into her hot, wet warmth. Once he was in to the hilt, he groaned. He'd never felt anything as perfect as Regina's body clamping around him. She fit him as if she'd been made for him.

He pressed his forehead to hers and forced himself to count to ten. Then he opened his eyes and looked down at her. The effort to keep from moving inside of her was about to cause his premature death, and the fact that her hands were still cuffed above her head made him harder than he'd ever been, but he leaned down and traced her cheekbone with his finger, kissed the sides of her eyes and the tip of her nose. "You're perfect. Do you know that?"

"I think the same about you," she breathed.

He braced his arms on either side of her head again and pulled nearly all the way out of her. She gasped. "Daffin!"

He lowered his mouth to hers to silence her while he sank slowly back inside.

His hips continued their torturous movements, in and out, while her hips thrashed beneath him and her head moved fitfully on the sheets. She strained against her handcuffs, obviously wanting to touch him.

He pulled all the way out and circled his hips against her. "No!" she protested.

"No what?" he prompted breathlessly, still circling his hips, teasing her, tempting her.

"I want you. Come back."

"Beg me," he ordered.

"Please, Daffin," she breathed. "I want you. I need you."

He slid back inside her then, and she gasped when he filled her. He did it again and again, pulling out of her and making her beg him not to stop. By the time he plunged into her for what was no doubt the dozenth time, they were both panting and nearly mad with lust and the need for release.

He reached down to touch the sensitive nub between her folds with the tip of his finger. "Tell me you want me," he growled in her ear.

"I want you," she cried. "I need you."

"Beg me." He nipped her ear.

"Please."

His finger circled her flesh again and again. She was so close. So very close. Right on the edge.

And then he stopped.

"No," she cried. His mouth swallowed the word.

"What do you want?" His grin tortured her.

"Don't stop. Your finger . . . please don't stop." She tried to bring her hands down to pull him toward her, but he clamped a hand against her arm, holding her cuffed wrists above her head.

"This?" He circled her again with his finger. "You want this?"

"Yes," she moaned. "Don't stop. Please don't stop."

He circled her again and her hips picked up the rhythm once more. She was going to come. She was going to—

He pulled his finger away.

"Please. Don't stop. Please, Daffin."

His mouth covered hers and his finger returned to circle her nub, again and again, while she arched her hips, helpless against the movement of his hand. "Please," she begged. "Don't stop."

He quickened the intimate caress without stopping this time, and the crushing weight of her climax made her scream his name into his mouth.

He pushed her legs apart roughly with his knee and slid into her, thrusting until his own climax followed hers. As it peaked, he pulled out and spilled his seed on her belly, crushing himself against her, groaning her name into her ear.

She was incredible, beautiful, made for him.

He'd never known such pleasure—of the body, and strangely, of the heart.

# CHAPTER FORTY-ONE

Handcuffs, Regina learned, could be used in a variety of pleasurable ways, and Daffin was only *too* willing to teach them to her. They spent hours naked and tangled in each other's arms, and much of it Regina spent begging Daffin for release.

Whatever she'd expected lovemaking to be, she had never guessed at the intense physical and emotional connection she found with Daffin in the darkness. The things he did to her body—she never wanted him to stop touching her. Over and over, he brought her to the peak of passion and held her aloft until she begged him to let her go, and when he did, he did it unselfishly, holding nothing back to ensure she experienced the maximum pleasure.

It was still dark outside when he pulled her into his arms and kissed her temple. "Love," he whispered, "I must go."

"Must you?" Regina replied in a pouty voice.

She felt his smile against her ear. "The sun will be up

soon. People will be looking for us. I doubt you want them to find me here."

She wasn't entirely certain she didn't, but she wasn't about to say that to Daffin.

"Very well," she agreed. "But kiss me one last time."

"For the memories?" he asked.

He'd meant it to be a jest, but when he dipped his head to kiss her, Regina couldn't help but be struck by the fact that this might be the only night they would ever spend together. All she would have were memories. If they found Knowles today as they hoped, she might never even *see* Daffin again, let alone spend the night in the same house with him. The thought made her throat ache.

He kissed her thoroughly, and then rolled to the side of the bed and sat up.

She pulled the blanket to cover her chest and sat up behind him. "Promise me you'll be careful today, Daffin."

He turned to look at her over his shoulder as he tugged on his breeches, a grin on his face. "I'm always careful, love."

*Love.* He was using the word as a term of endearment. Meanwhile, she was all but certain she was truly feeling that emotion for him. Falling in love wasn't something she'd thought of when she'd been trying to lure him into bed. Oh, God. What had she done to herself?

Daffin made it back to his room without being seen, thank God. He even managed to change his clothing, a quick ablution, and to run a brush through his hair. He didn't have long before he needed to be in the foyer to meet Grimaldi for their planned outing to Seven Dials.

The night with Regina had been the stuff of dreams. In his wildest imagination, he wouldn't have thought their lovemaking would be like that. He hadn't wanted it to end. Regina was special. She was beautiful, and intelligent, and funny, and brave. She was everything he'd believed her to be last July in Surrey, and more. And he was falling in love with her. It wasn't anything he'd expected, but it was true. The nights he'd spent knowing she was in the clutches of a madman had tortured him. He didn't want to ever leave her side again. He would have to tell her that he was a bastard, eventually, but he hoped—no, had to believe—she would still accept him the way Grimaldi had. He couldn't stand it if she ever came to regret their night together.

The thought of not seeing her again made his chest tight. He didn't like it one bit. Daffin shook his head. The sun was beginning to peek in the window. He was running late. He'd think about his future with Regina later.

First, he had a killer to catch.

# CHAPTER FORTY-TWO

Regina washed and dressed quickly. She chose a simple blue cotton day dress and planned to wear a white pelisse and thick wool stockings. It was freezing outside, and a glance out the window told her the dawn would bring dark gray skies. She had to help Daffin and Mark today. They were relying on her to find the window from which she'd crawled a few nights ago. There was no guarantee Knowles would still be there, but perhaps there would be clues to his whereabouts. She only hoped they would find enough to track him down. She didn't want her time with Daffin to come to an end, but she did want her family to rest easily. She wanted to be able to put her head on the pillow tonight knowing they were all finally safe.

A soft knock at the door interrupted her thoughts. She stuffed the ripped dressing gown into a drawer and called, "Come in."

The door opened and Nicole's bright head peeked in. She

wore her night rail and dressing gown. She slid into the room and padded to Regina's bed.

"Good morning," she said, stretching and yawning. "I came to hug you and wish you the best of luck." She gave Regina a serious look. "I truly hate to see you put yourself in danger again, but I realize you must go."

Regina nodded. "I must. I'm the only one who's been there."

"I know, and you're brave and daring for doing it, but I don't have to enjoy it. Please don't take any risks, and come back safely. I'll be worried sick until you've all returned."

"Don't worry." Regina hugged her cousin. "I learned my lesson about taking risks."

Nicole turned toward the door.

"Nicole," Regina called.

Her cousin turned back to her. "Yes?"

"I . . . may I ask you a question?" Regina bit her lip. She wasn't at all certain she should mention her feelings for Daffin to Nicole, but she desperately needed advice.

"Of course." Nicole moved back toward her and took a seat on the edge of the bed.

Regina pressed her hands to her cheeks. "There's something I must tell you."

Nicole searched her face. "What is it?"

"Daffin and I spent the night together."

Nicole's smile was enormous. "I was hoping you would." She shot Regina a satisfied smirk. "Was it everything you thought it would be?"

"It was . . . magical," Regina breathed.

"Please tell me he used his handcuffs." Nicole waggled her eyebrows.

"I am a lady. I would never admit to such a thing." Regina

burst into laughter. "But yes, he did, and yes, it was magnificent."

"Ooh." Nicole bounced a little on the mattress. "I need to ask Mark if he has a pair."

"But as wonderful as it was," Regina continued, "I'm not certain what to do now."

"What do you mean?" Nicole asked, blinking.

"I mean I'm not at all sure Daffin wants more."

A sad look crossed Nicole's face. "And you want something more?"

Regina bit her lip and slowly nodded. "Yes . . . I do. Oh, Nicole. I think I . . . I may . . . be in love with him."

Nicole grasped her hand. "Oh, Regina, I'm so happy for you."

"But how can I convince him we should be something more?"

Nicole squeezed Regina's hand. "Love doesn't have to be convinced, my friend. My advice? Follow your heart. Always."

"But even if Daffin feels the same, we're sure to face Grandmama's and Uncle Edward's reprobation."

Nicole sighed. "That remains to be seen."

Grandmama came bustling into the room. "Oh, I'm so glad I caught you before you left. I was worried I'd missed you." She scurried to Regina and planted a kiss on her cheek.

Regina and Nicole traded a look.

"Thank you, Grandmama," Regina said.

"Now, be brave but be careful," Grandmama said. "You've always been such a headstrong girl. Please come home safe."

Regina cleared her throat. "Grandmama? Speaking of my being headstrong . . ."

"I'll leave you two," Nicole offered, standing and sailing from the room before Lady Harriet had a chance to object.

"What is it, dear?" Grandmama asked, smoothing her hand against Regina's cheek.

Regina took a deep breath. "What if I told you I love someone who's not of my class?"

Grandmama pressed her hands together with obvious glee. "Oh, my dear, I'd given up hope you would ever fall in love. Does this man love you?"

"I hope he does."

Grandmama's smile widened. "Does he want to marry you?"

Regina shrugged helplessly. "I hope he does."

A knowing light came into her grandmother's blue eyes. "Then grab him with both hands and don't let go." She patted Regina's hand and turned toward the door. "I'll see you when you return."

"Wait. Grandmama? Don't you want to know who it is?" Regina asked with a laugh.

Lady Harriet paused at the door and turned back with a sly smile. "It's Mr. Oakleaf, darling. I'm old, not blind. And I'm certain my great-grandchildren are going to be gorgeous!"

Her grandmother winked at her and trotted off.

# CHAPTER FORTY-THREE

Mark's coach rolled to a stop near the intersection of Earlham and Mercer in the early morning light. Mist still rose from the ground, and the freezing temperatures made Regina burrow her hands more deeply into her fur muff. She glanced out the window, trying to fight off the panic rising in her chest that threatened to choke her.

The last time she'd been here she'd been nearly paralyzed with fear, convinced that Knowles would find her at any moment and drag her back into her bedchamber cell.

"Take a deep breath," Daffin said, his strong, warm hand at her elbow.

"Is it that obvious I'm frightened?"

"Yes, but you have nothing to be frightened of," Daffin said.

Mark sat across from her, his gaze trained out the window for any sign of movement. There were some newspaper boys and other vendors setting up shop for the day on the street corners, but the roads were mostly barren, the residents apparently still sleeping off their amusements from the previous evening.

Daffin jumped from the coach and turned to help Regina down. The moment her boots touched the frozen earth, the memories of the night she'd escaped came rushing back. She forced herself to take a deep breath. *Be brave. Be strong.*

She glanced around. The last time she'd been here it had been dark, but the smell of the place triggered her recollection, newspapers and fish combined with some type of offal she didn't want to contemplate.

She shook her head and forced herself to look around, hoping she could find her way back if she could only spot the same landmarks she'd seen that night. If only her head hadn't been so foggy with laudanum at the time.

"Take your time, Regina," Daffin said, his voice comforting from behind her. He hadn't let on anything while in the coach with Mark. He certainly didn't treat her as if they'd spent the night together. She might believe she'd imagined the whole thing if it hadn't been for the softening of his eyes when he glanced at her.

Not that she blamed him for remaining aloof. He could hardly act differently in front of Mark. She would also pretend nothing had happened between them, but the entire time she'd ridden next to Daffin in the coach, she'd been preoccupied by his nearness, his scent. She'd wanted to reach out and kiss him, grab his arm and drag it around her. She wanted his protection, his stability, his strength, his warmth. She wanted all of him. She knew he still thought the difference in their stations was too much, but she didn't care. She'd give up all of it to have him.

"Do you see anything familiar?" Mark asked, shaking her from her thoughts.

Regina glanced around again, shivering from the cold. It all looked alike, the rows of dirty façades on the sad little town houses, the trash piled about, the dingy windows, the grayness.

A glint of red caught her eye.

"Wait. I remember that." She pulled a hand from her muff and pointed.

"What?" Daffin asked, swiveling to follow the line of her finger.

"That. That red door," she said. "I remember hurrying past it, thinking what a bright color it was."

"Which direction were you coming from?" Mark asked as the three of them crossed the street toward the house with the red door.

Regina bit her lip and thought about it for a moment. She'd seen the door as she'd hurried past, and it had been on her left. She must have been going west. "That way," she said, pointing again. "I was coming from that way and headed that way." She pointed in the opposite direction.

"Let's go," Daffin said.

They took off in the direction she'd indicated.

"Yes," Regina said, warming up and becoming more excited as they picked up their pace. "I remember that street lamp there, too, because of the doll at the bottom. I thought how strange it was to see a doll on the side of the street."

As they neared the lamp, she glanced down at the broken, discarded doll at its base. It had reminded her of the dolls she'd abandoned as a child. "This way," Regina said, lifting her skirts and stepping even more quickly.

The two men followed her.

"How far had you walked by the time you saw the doll?" Mark asked.

"Not far," Regina replied. "It was only perhaps half a dozen houses from where I'd been kept."

She continued to nearly run until she came to the set of houses where she was certain she'd been held. She dropped her skirts and put her hands on her hips, contemplating them. They looked exactly alike. "It's hard to tell. There was a great deal of snow that night."

The snow had mostly melted. She couldn't trace her way back by picking out which hedge she'd fallen into . . . or could she?

"My stays!" she exclaimed.

"Pardon?" Daffin gave her a look that said he thought he *must* have heard her incorrectly.

"My stays and stockings. I didn't bother putting them back on. Instead, I stuffed them into the hedge of the house next to the one where I was kept."

"Are you quite serious?" Mark asked.

"I'm entirely serious. I stuffed them in the hedge on the side facing the house."

The two men spread out to examine every hedge. All the houses had similar hedges so that didn't narrow the search.

Regina searched, too. She was bending around the side of the hedge of the third house in the row when Daffin called out, "I found them!" He held the stockings and stays aloft, a wide smile on his face.

Regina was too happy they'd found the house to be embarrassed over the fact that her undergarments were being waved in the air.

"That's it!" she called, racing to join Daffin, with Mark on her heels.

"If they were in that hedge," she said, "then I came out of *that* window." She turned to the house next door and pointed up. The glass in the window she indicated was gone. A dirty blanket had been stuffed into the empty frame, ostensibly to keep out the cold air.

"That's it," she said, swallowing hard. "That's the room."

The two men tried to convince Regina to return to the coach, but she refused. Partly because she didn't want to miss a minute of this, and partly because she felt safer at Daffin's side. The three of them made their way to the front door of the house in which Regina had been kept.

Daffin rapped on the door. Once. Twice.

Several minutes passed before it swung open.

A frail-looking old woman with a shawl wrapped around her thin shoulders stood in the doorway, blinking at them.

"Who owns this house?" Daffin demanded.

"My son does, sir." The woman wrapped the shawl more tightly around her shoulders. "And who might ye be?"

"Oakleaf. Daffin Oakleaf. I work for Bow Street."

The old woman's eyes widened with respect and admiration. "Oh, I read about ye in the paper."

"What is your son's name?" Daffin asked, ignoring her remark.

The old woman shifted on her feet. "Michael Mitchell."

"Does anyone else live here? Or stay here?" Daffin demanded.

"Michael's got the odd friend who stops by from time to time." The old woman shrugged. "I've been gone until yesterday for the Christmastide holiday. Spent time with my sister in Devon."

"Is your son here?" Mark asked.

"Yes." The old woman nodded. "But he's asleep."

"Go get him," Mark demanded. "We'll wait."

When Michael Mitchell arrived at the door minutes later, he looked none too pleased to have been awakened at such an early hour. "Wot in the 'ell do ye want? And it better be good, I tell ye."

"Do you know a man named Quinton Knowles?" Daffin asked. "And you'd better tell the truth. I've got no time for games."

Regina could tell from the surprised and guilty look on Mitchell's face that he *did* know Knowles. She nearly closed her eyes in relief.

"Wot ye want 'im fer?" Mitchell asked, narrowing his eyes on their little party.

His mother lumped him on the back of his head. "Tell the chap wot ye know, Michael," she said. "He's a real live Bow Street Runner, he is."

Michael appeared to be less impressed than fearful of that news, unlike his mother.

"We're looking for Quinton Knowles, and if you know where he is, you'd better tell me immediately," Daffin warned.

"Wot's in it fer me?" Mitchell asked, poking out his cheek with his tongue.

"Two pounds," Mark stated.

Michael Mitchell's eyes lit up. So did his mother's.

"Where's the money, first?" Mitchell asked, obviously still suspicious.

Mark opened his coat, pulled out his purse, and extracted two pounds. "Right here."

Mitchell held out his grubby hand.

"Not until you tell us where Knowles is and we find him," Daffin replied.

Mitchell scowled. "How do I know ye'll give me the money?"

"You don't," Mark replied. "You just have to trust me. Or I can allow my friend here to beat Knowles's whereabouts out of you."

Daffin narrowed his eyes on the younger man. "Believe me. I'd like nothing more."

"Fine," Mitchell said. "He's staying at a boarding'ouse not two streets from 'ere. Mrs. Penworthy's. But if ye tell him I were the one who told ye, my life won't be worth a ha'penny."

Mark withdrew one pound and tossed it to him. "I'll be back with the rest after we locate Knowles."

They retraced their steps to the coach and climbed inside.

"When we get there, Regina, you must stay in the coach," Mark warned. "Nicole will have my hide if you're harmed."

Regina nodded. She didn't want to put Mark and Daffin in danger again. "Very well."

Daffin gave the coachman instructions to the boarding-house two streets over, and soon their coach came to a stop in front of the ramshackle address.

"Let's hope it's our lucky day," Mark said.

"If he's not here, I'm going back to find Mitchell," Daffin said, flexing his fist.

"No you're not. But I understand the sentiment," Regina replied with a smile. "Be careful."

"I will be," Daffin replied, winking at her.

Daffin led the way to the front door. After they briefly consulted with Mrs. Penworthy and gave her two pounds for her trouble, the middle-aged woman led the way up a dark staircase to a door in the middle of the corridor.

Pistol drawn, Daffin put his ear to the door. Snores filled

the room on the other side. Daffin grinned. Never failed. The best time to catch criminals was always when they were sleeping. He didn't bother to knock. He exchanged a glance and a nod with Grimaldi before kicking in the door.

Quinton Knowles was sound asleep, alone in a small bed that took up most of the room. He didn't even move when the door splintered and the two men crashed through it.

Daffin and Grimaldi both shook their heads. Daffin strolled to the edge of the bed, cocked his pistol, and pointed it at Knowles. "Good morning," he said, kicking the mattress.

Knowles scrambled up and pushed his back against the wall, his hands in the air. He visibly swallowed. "Oakleaf?"

Daffin smiled grimly. "Please give me a reason to pull this trigger."

Knowles was breathing heavily. "Damn you, Oakleaf."

"Who hired you to kidnap Lady Regina?" Daffin asked through clenched teeth.

"I'll rot in hell before I tell you," the older man said, his eyes flashing defiance.

Daffin grabbed him by the collar and lifted him halfway up the wall, where he pressed his forearm tightly against Knowles's throat. "Who. Hired. You?"

"Who do you think?" Knowles choked, tugging haplessly at Daffin's arm.

Daffin stared him directly in the eye. "Some piece of scum, no doubt, but I want a *name*."

Fear flashed in Knowles's eyes. "A name won't spare my life, will it?" he managed to choke out.

Daffin pressed harder.

Despite the lack of oxygen, Knowles managed an ugly smirk. "Ha. You're going to kill me, aren't you? You *are* a killer. Just like me. I tried to tell the fair Lady Regina you and me are cut from the same cloth, but she wouldn't listen. More's the pity, poor woman. I do believe she's half in love with you, though God knows why."

Daffin ground his teeth. "You and I are *not* cut from the same cloth, Knowles."

"If you kill me, we are." Knowles grabbed anew at Daffin's arm, his complexion darkening from red to near-purple.

Daffin loosened his grip only slightly. "Give me a name and I'll spare your life."

"You promise?" Knowles asked, voice raspy and hope shining in his eyes.

"Yes," Daffin ground out. He loosened his hold enough for the man to speak normally.

Knowles spent a few moments bent over coughing before facing Daffin again. "I do believe you're telling the truth, Oakleaf, or should I say *Portland*?"

Daffin slammed him against the wall again. "Damn you. Give me a name!"

"Millingham," Knowles choked out. "Lady Rosalind Millingham."

"Who?" Grimaldi, who had been standing close by in case Knowles tried to make a run for it, broke his silence.

Daffin let Knowles drop to the mattress, where the man clutched at his throat and coughed. "Why did she hire you?" Daffin demanded. He didn't recognize the name, either.

Knowles took a moment to right his breathing before glaring at the two men. "Apparently, Lady Rosalind fancied Lady Regina's would-be fiancé, the Earl of Dryden."

"What the hell are you talking about?" Daffin shook his head.

Knowles's grin revealed rotted teeth. "Lady Rosalind has

been pining for the earl for five seasons. Meanwhile Dryden was only interested in Lady Regina and the land he stood to gain from their marriage."

"That makes no sense," Daffin ground out. "Killing Regina wouldn't ensure Dryden married Lady Rosalind."

Knowles shrugged. "Perhaps my lady was willing to take the chance. She told me more than once that Lady Regina and her damned land were the only thing keeping them apart. She'd been sitting on the shelf for five seasons waiting for him to realize Lady Regina wouldn't ever accept him. The earl was her best suitor, turns out, and apparently, the Duke of Colchester had recently given Dryden a reason to hope a marriage to Lady Regina might take place after all."

"That's insane." Daffin wanted to choke Knowles to death after all. He wanted to kill both Knowles and Lady Rosalind. He forced himself to step back, while red-hot rage consumed him.

"When did she hire you?" Grimaldi demanded.

"Over a month ago. I decided to wait till after Christmastide to swipe Lady Regina. Thought I'd have some fun with you all in the meantime. You're no better than I am, Portland. Don't you forget it."

"My name isn't Portland," Daffin ground out.

Knowles shook his head. "Never understood why you refused to claim such a rich and powerful father. Proves what an idiot you are."

"Who's the idiot?" Daffin kicked the bed hard enough to slam it against the wall. "I was never going to kill you, and you just confessed to everything. You're going to gaol, and I'm going to personally ensure you never get out again. When you die, I'll set a match to your bones myself."

"You can burn in hell, Oakleaf." Knowles spat at him.

Daffin grabbed him, spun him around, and slapped handcuffs on his wrists. "No. That's your job. You'll never hurt a woman I love again."

Grimaldi grabbed Knowles and pushed him in front of him toward the door.

"Maybe not," Knowles said, "but I still have some protection."

"What sort of protection?" Daffin asked, narrowing his eyes.

"H. J. Hancock." Knowles smirked over his shoulder.

Daffin narrowed his eyes on him. "The reporter? At the paper?"

"One and the same. He's been asking around about you for months. Searching into your past. Looking for every bit of information he can find. One of my compatriots has a letter from me addressed to Hancock."

It took every ounce of strength Daffin possessed not to punch Knowles so hard his neck snapped. "Why?"

"The letter contains all the details of who you really are, Portland," Knowles replied. "Unless I contact my mate by sundown, he's got instructions to send Hancock the letter. He'll get it in time to make the paper tomorrow morning. Everyone will know what a whore your mother was and what a nameless bastard you are. Unless, of course, you're willing to set me free."

# CHAPTER FORTY-FOUR

The next morning, Daffin's coach rolled to a stop in front of Lord Millingham's town house in Mayfair. He and Grimaldi were shown into a beige salon where they waited the better part of an hour before Lady Rosalind's father deigned to join them.

"Mr. Oakleaf," Lord Millingham said as he entered the room. "I'm sorry I'm late. I was just reading about you in the paper." He tossed the front page of the paper down on the table in front of Daffin.

The headline glared at him. FAMOUS RUNNER IS DUKE OF PORTLAND'S SON.

"To what do I owe the pleasure of having a *bastard* in my home?" Millingham asked with a false smile.

"Careful," Grimaldi growled.

Daffin grabbed the paper. He'd been prepared for this. Knowles hadn't been bluffing. He scanned the article quickly. As predicted, it was written by H. J. Hancock himself. It revealed that Daffin Oakleaf, the dashing Bow Street Runner, was actually Daffin Portland, the Duke of Portland's illegitimate son. The duke had sired him via his mistress. She was born Sally Oakleaf, but as a famous courtesan to members of the *ton,* had changed her name to Marie Dubois. It was all there. And it was all true.

Daffin had made his choice. He would have to live with the consequences. He'd give up his reputation before negotiating with a piece of scum like Quinton Knowles.

"Lord Coleford," Millingham said to Grimaldi, "perhaps you'd like to explain the reason for your visit."

"We're here to speak with your daughter, Lady Rosalind," Grimaldi replied. "We have reason to believe she was involved with a recent attack on Lady Regina Haversham."

"My Rosalind?" The viscount's eyes widened. "What on earth are you talking about?"

Daffin and Grim exchanged a glance. As they suspected, Lord Millingham knew something.

"Yes, Millingham, and we wonder where she got the amount of money involved in paying the criminal who carried out the attack."

Millingham puffed out his chest. "You can't possibly think *I* had anything to do with it."

"May we speak with Lady Rosalind?" Grimaldi asked, his voice tight.

"I believe she's still abed," Millingham replied.

Grimaldi gave him a false smile. "We'll wait."

Millingham looked perturbed at their resilience but he hastened from the room and came back not half an hour later with his daughter in tow. Lady Rosalind was tall with blond hair, crystal-blue eyes, and a calculating smile.

"Lord Coleford, Mr. Oakleaf," she said as she walked

solemnly into the room. "My father says you'd like to have a word with me." She blinked at them innocently.

"Do you know a Mr. Quinton Knowles?" Daffin asked.

Her gaze turned to the floor and she shook her head. "No. I don't believe I've ever heard that name."

"He claims you paid him a thousand pounds to have Lady Regina Haversham murdered."

Lady Rosalind gasped. Daffin had to admit she was a fair actress. "Whatever in the world do you mean? I don't know what you're talking about. I barely know Lady Regina."

"You see, my daughter doesn't even know who this Knowles character is," Lord Millingham replied. "Let alone have access to that amount of money."

"Yes," Daffin ground out. "It's quite a mystery how Lady Rosalind might access that amount of money . . . without help." He eyed the viscount up and down.

Grimaldi stood. He addressed his remarks to Lady Rosalind. "According to Mr. Knowles, you were hoping for a proposal from Lord Dryden and knew he and Regina were soon to become engaged."

"Are Lord Dryden and Lady Regina engaged?" Lady Rosalind asked, fear and anger flashing across her features.

"Not yet," Grimaldi replied.

"Not ever," Daffin muttered.

"What's that?" Lady Rosalind asked.

"Nothing," Daffin replied.

Lady Rosalind tossed her head. "Lady Regina seems nice enough, but I sincerely doubt Lord Dryden intends to marry *her*. She's a bit, shall we say, long in the tooth, for a marriage proposal. Besides, Dryden's told me more than once that the land was more attractive than the lady." She laughed.

Daffin jumped to his feet. "Lady Regina is a better woman

than you'll ever be. Dryden would be a lucky man to have her."

Millingham pushed his daughter behind him. "How dare you speak to my Rosalind that way? How dare you come in here spouting accusations from a common criminal without any proof? I assume you've got no proof or you would have produced it by now. Show me immediately or leave. I refuse to have you under my roof for another moment, Mr. Oakleaf, or should I say . . . Dubois?"

Daffin lunged for the viscount, but Grimaldi got there first, pushing Daffin away.

"Please leave," Millingham ordered, lifting his nose in the air.

Daffin straightened his coat and watched the viscount through narrowed eyes. "Rest assured, my lord, when we get proof, we will be back for Lady Rosalind."

Grimaldi made Daffin leave the room first. They made it out to the coach where Daffin punched the side of the conveyance. "Damn it, Grim. She's going to get away with it."

"I'm afraid you're right. You know as well as I do that in our world a lady's word against a known criminal's is taken as truth."

Daffin shook his head. "At least Knowles is locked away in the bowels of Newgate."

"Yes, for the exact opposite reason. He was accused by Regina, a lady." Regina had been able to identify Knowles easily yesterday afternoon and the magistrate at Bow Street sent him away with nary a second glance. "This is precisely why we need a police force."

Daffin nodded. "You're right."

"It's doubtful we'll ever find proof that Lady Rosalind paid Knowles," Grim said, entering the coach.

"I know," Daffin replied, climbing in behind him. "But I told her we'll be back because I want her to look over her shoulder the rest of her life."

Grim leaned back against the squabs. "Where to?"

"Your town house. I have an important question to ask your uncle."

Daffin spent the ride to Grim's house in silence. He'd made his decision. Hearing vile Lady Rosalind say those horrible things about Regina, he'd realized. He couldn't allow Regina to marry Dryden. Dryden wasn't right for her. Dryden didn't love her. Daffin did. He'd guessed at the depths of his feelings for her when she'd been kidnapped, but now he knew for certain. He loved Regina desperately. He didn't want to spend another day of his life without her. He had to try, at least. First, he needed her uncle's approval.

They stepped into Grimaldi's foyer together.

"Do you want me there with you?" Grim asked.

"No." Daffin shook his head. He didn't want to put his friend in a difficult position. "What I have to say is for the duke's ears and the duke's ears alone."

"Understood." Grim clapped him on the shoulder. "Good luck, Oakleaf."

Daffin nodded and turned to the butler. "I'm here to see the Duke of Colchester."

Abbott showed him into the salon, the same room where Regina had treated him for a pistol wound. Today he was here on a much different errand. Daffin had no more secrets. It was all there in the *Times,* printed in black-and-white for the entire town to see. The duke might well reject Daffin for his past, but Grimaldi's reaction had given him hope. There was only one way to find out what her uncle and grandmother thought.

Not a quarter hour later, the duke was wheeled into the room by two footmen who quickly left.

Daffin stood and bowed. "Your grace."

"Mr. Oakleaf," the duke intoned. "I read about you in the paper this morning."

"I'm sorry to hear that." Daffin tugged at his cravat.

"I knew the Duke of Portland," the duke continued, his tone dour. "I cannot say I liked him."

"Neither did I." Of course the *ton* still didn't know what Portland had done. Portland had never admitted hiring Knowles to kill Daffin's mother. But Portland was dead. Daffin could only hope the afterlife had delivered the reckoning the man deserved.

Daffin shifted to the other boot. "I'm here, your grace, to ask you something important."

The duke lifted his chin. "What's that?"

"May I have your blessing to marry Lady Regina?"

The duke lowered his chin to his chest. His white eyebrows dipped low over his eyes. "Mr. Oakleaf," he said, "you've done many commendable things for this family. We owe you an immeasurable debt of gratitude, but . . ." The duke paused.

"But that gratitude does not extend to your niece's hand in marriage?" Daffin finished for him.

"I'm afraid it does not." The duke did not meet Daffin's eyes.

"You'd prefer someone like the Earl of Dryden for Regina?" Daffin asked, his nostrils flaring.

"I would prefer someone of Regina's same class. Yes."

Shame burned his chest. "Not the bastard son of a *duke*?"

"Please don't make this difficult, Mr. Oakleaf. You're a

highly respected member of Bow Street, and I have great admiration for you."

"As long as I remain on Bow Street, where I belong."

The duke shifted uncomfortably in his seat, but remained silent.

Daffin turned and paced away a few steps. Humiliation burned in his chest. "Does Lady Harriet feel the same way?"

The duke nodded. "I don't see how she couldn't. We both only want the best for our Regina."

"I see." Daffin stopped and shook his head. *Enough.* "Thank you for your time, your grace."

He stalked from the room, bile rising in his throat. He hadn't asked Regina for her hand first because he'd guessed how his meeting with the duke would go. Members of the aristocracy were happy to have his help when they needed him, but they wanted him to conveniently go away when he'd served his purpose.

Soft sobs coming from the salon across the foyer caught Daffin's attention. The door was slightly ajar. He stuck in his head to see who was crying.

Regina sat on the settee in the center of the room, the front page of the morning paper spread across the table in front of her.

"Regina," he breathed, entering the room and crossing over the expensive rug to sit next to her.

"Daffin," she sobbed, pointing to the paper. "Is this true?"

God. It felt as if his heart were being ripped from his chest. "Yes," he said. "It's true. All of it. I'm a bastard, Regina." He paused and drew a deep breath. "Why are you crying?" Was it because she'd spent the night with a bastard? He couldn't bear it if she regretted being with him.

She swiped at her tears. "I'm crying because I'm sad for you, Daffin. I'm sad because your father was so awful and your mother made bad choices that you had to bear the brunt of your whole life."

Daffin clenched his fists and looked away, some unnamed emotion tightening his throat. He'd been worried she wouldn't accept him for who he truly was. But she was crying not out of shame, but sympathy. She loved him. She truly loved him. And he loved her too, which was why he would die before he would allow *his* shame and scandal to ruin her. Regina didn't deserve any of this. "Don't cry, darling." He cradled her head against his chest.

She allowed his comfort for a few moments before pulling away from him. "Why didn't you tell me about your family? Why did I have to read about it in the paper?"

"I'm sorry." He hung his head. "I was ashamed. My mother was a courtesan. I loved her, of course, but as an adult, when I investigated her murder, I came to understand what she had been."

Regina nodded. "There's something else I don't understand. If your father wanted her dead, why didn't he have her killed when she was pregnant?"

Daffin took a deep breath. "My father paid for her death, but he wasn't the one who wanted her dead. His wife did. The Duchess of Portland couldn't stand the fact that my mother and I lived so close. She saw us from time to time. It angered her. She ordered my father to get rid of both of us."

Regina caught her breath. "No."

Daffin nodded grimly. "He hired Knowles to do the job."

"Yet he didn't have you killed."

"No." Daffin clenched his jaw. His tone was harsh. "Instead, he sent me far away to school." A humorless smile twisted his lips. "I suppose he thought that was the least he could do. I'm certain you'll understand why I fail to give him credit for his generosity."

"Did the duchess know you were still alive?"

"I made certain she knew. After I became a Bow Street Runner, I went to visit her. We had a nice, long talk, the duchess and I. I'll never forget the look on her face when I walked into the room. It was as if she'd seen a ghost. I told her I'd send her to gaol for my mother's murder if she ever tried to harm anyone I loved again. The truth was, I didn't have enough proof to send her away, but she didn't know that. She believed me, and she steered clear of me until her death two years ago."

"The current Duke of Portland is your younger brother?" Regina asked.

"Yes, but I doubt he even realized I existed until today. I'm certain my father and his wife wanted it that way."

"I'm sorry, Daffin. So sorry."

"I am too, but it doesn't change the fact that I'm who I am . . . the illegitimate son of a duke and a courtesan."

"I don't care if you're a bastard, Daffin. I've never cared about your lineage."

He pulled her into his arms and hugged her, knowing this was the last time he would ever be able to touch her. "Oh, Regina. You might not care today or tomorrow or even next week, but eventually, when your friends stop accepting you into their homes, when the life you've always known is ripped away from you, you would blame me. You'd have to. It would hurt you, and I would give up my own life before I would hurt you." He pulled away from her and softly rubbed his knuckles along her cheek, giving himself a moment to memorize the fine details of her features before he stood to leave. "I'm sorry, Regina." It nearly crushed him, but he forced himself to turn and strode toward the door. With every step, he told himself not to look back. He didn't want to remember her with tears streaming down her pretty face.

"Daffin, wait," she called.

He paused at the door and bowed his head. "Regina. We cannot be together. You're a lady and I'm a bastard. Marry someone of your class. You belong with them."

There was a rustle of fabric, and then her soft voice at his ear. "But I don't want them." She had come to stand behind him.

"One day, you'll realize this was for the best," he murmured.

At the sound of her choked sob, he opened the door and stalked out, never looking back at the heartache he'd wrought, not even breathing until he'd reached the street outside. Only then did he allow himself to whisper the truth. "I'll never forget you."

# CHAPTER FORTY-FIVE

It was her birthday, a day that was supposed to be happy. A day she should have been excited about. Regina had managed to make it to the age of thirty unmarried, yet no longer burdened by her virginity. She should have been joyful. She'd got exactly what she wanted. Instead, she'd been wandering around the house all day, heartsick over Daffin.

"You don't want to go riding in the park?" Nicole asked from her perch on the sofa across the salon.

Regina shook her head.

"You don't want any of the scones Cook baked for your birthday?" Nicole asked next.

Regina shook her head.

"You don't want to go shopping?" Nicole offered.

Regina shook her head.

Nicole sighed and dropped her hands into her lap. "It's your birthday, Regina. Please tell me, what would you like to do?"

"Is renouncing my title a choice?" Regina muttered.

"I don't think so," Nicole said, shaking her head. "I'm sorry."

"I'm sorry, too. I've hated my title my entire life, and now it's keeping me from the man I love."

Nicole sighed. "Daffin is being an idiot."

Regina whirled around and swiped angrily at the seemingly endless flow of tears on her cheeks. "He thinks I'm too good for him, and I'm not. We're equals in all other ways."

"Did I mention he's an idiot?"

The doors to the salon opened and two footmen wheeled in the duke. Lady Harriet padded in by his side.

"Mark tells us you're not enjoying your birthday, Regina," the duke said.

Regina's only reply was a drawn-out sigh.

"She's heartsick, Edward. She needs some time," Lady Harriet replied, laying a quelling hand on her nephew's shoulder.

"Heartsick?" Uncle Edward asked, blinking. "What for? Did Dryden do something?"

Nicole snorted. "Dryden is hardly the reason Regina is moping."

"If not over Dryden, then who?" the duke asked, still looking confused.

"Oh, Edward. How dense can you be? She's heartsick over Mr. Oakleaf," Grandmama said with a sigh. "And I, for one, was so certain he loved her back."

"What's this?" The duke's thick white brows pushed together over his rheumy eyes. "Mr. Oakleaf, you say?"

"Yes, Edward," Grandmama replied. "Regina's been madly in love with Mr. Oakleaf for months. Haven't you noticed?"

"But he's a Bow Street Runner," the duke replied. "And that story in the paper . . ."

"None of which matters one whit to a woman in love," Grandmama replied.

"Oh, dear," the duke said, tugging at his bottom lip. "I fear I may have made a mistake, then. A grave one."

Regina snapped up her head. "What, Uncle Edward?"

The duke continued to pluck at his lip. "Mr. Oakleaf came to visit the day after he caught that Knowles fellow. He asked for your hand in marriage."

"What?" Regina leaped to her feet and glared at her uncle.

"Yes, he did." Uncle Edward nodded. "I turned him down. I'd just discovered he was a bastard, after all."

"Oh, Edward, how could you!" Grandmama said. "Regina has been looking for love all these years and she finally found it. I don't care if she married one of the footmen at this point. I want a great-grandbaby!"

"I had no idea," Uncle Edward said. "Egad. I am sorry. Truly."

"Oh, Uncle, why?" Regina said. She paced back and forth in front of the fireplace, rubbing her hands up and down her chilly arms.

Uncle Edward sighed. "Because I'm a sick old man who knows nothing about the ins and outs of love. I'm not used to this sort of modern approach to marriage, dear. My marriage was arranged for me and it was happy."

"Yes, but I never loved the Earl of Dryden. I didn't even like him," Regina replied.

The duke shrugged. "I didn't love your aunt when we first married, and she certainly didn't love me."

"Oh, Edward, how unprogressive of you." Grandmama shook her head.

Regina spun on her heel and faced Nicole. "You know what this means, don't you? Daffin does love me after all. He only left because Uncle Edward wouldn't accept him."

"Yes, precisely." Nicole clapped her hands. "It also means I must go find Mark immediately to send him off to find Daffin and tell him what an idiot he's being."

Regina frowned. "Why can't *I* go tell Daffin what an idiot he's being?"

Nicole shook her head. "Oh, no, dear. That's not how these things work. Our set has a long tradition of men meeting in pubs to tell each other what they need to hear. You mustn't ruin it."

# CHAPTER FORTY-SIX

The snow had been falling for hours, but the Curious Goat Inn was warm and filled with its regular rowdy, midday patrons. Daffin sat at a table alone. He was two mugs of ale into the day, his chin braced on his palm, feeling nothing but sorry for himself.

Since walking away from Regina over a sennight ago, he'd done his best to throw himself back into his work, but his new cases didn't excite him like they once had. All he could think about was Regina's smile, Regina's laugh, the coy things she'd said to him, the way her hair shone like blue silk in the sun. He scrubbed a hand across his face. He missed her. And not just her, but Mark and Nicole. His time with them had finally made him feel like . . . he belonged to a family. He'd enjoyed it. Damn it, when the hell had *that* happened?

"Look alive, man, you seem as if your puppy died."

Daffin glanced up to see Grimaldi, the Cavendish twins, and Thomas Hobbs, the young Duke of Huntley, circling him. Huntley had been keeping company with the Cavendish twins of late, having been introduced to them by his brother-in-law, Owen Monroe.

"Worse than my puppy dying," Daffin muttered.

"You're drowning your sorrows over Regina, aren't you?" Grimaldi asked.

"How *did* you know?" Daffin shot back. He was in no mood to hear any sage advice, nor take any ribbing from his friends. They'd do well to leave him in peace.

"I've been there. I know the look of a man in love," Grimaldi replied. "Now, I suggest you stop drinking cheap ale and go declare your love for Regina."

Daffin glared at him. "I can't declare my love for Regina."

"Why not?" Grimaldi shot back. "Don't tell me you don't love her."

"I love her, all right. But I cannot declare myself because I happen to be a bloody bastard and she's a duke's niece. Or are you the only person in London who didn't get a good look at the article in the paper?"

"Oh, I saw it." Grimaldi grabbed a chair and eased down beside Daffin, followed by the other men. "Read every last word of it. Problem is, I don't give a toss."

"What?" Hope unfurled in Daffin's chest.

Grimaldi leaned back in his chair and crossed his arms over his chest. "I don't care if you're a bastard, but I do care if you're an idiot, and you're being a complete idiot at the moment. You and Regina are clearly meant for each other. I've never seen either of you happier than when you're together."

Daffin scowled at him. "But she's a lady."

Grimaldi fought a smile. "I realize she's a lady, and you're my friend. You're forgetting two quite important things. First,

I never cared about the aristocracy until it was thrust upon me. And second, Regina obviously doesn't care about having an aristocratic husband or she would have taken one long ago. She's had her pick over the years, believe me."

"But I'm a bastard." Daffin lowered his voice.

Rafe laughed. "You're in good company. We've all been bastards a time or two."

Grimaldi shrugged. "Please. Half the men in this town are bastards. Who cares? You're Daffin Oakleaf, the Bow Street Runner, as far as I'm concerned. I will continue to treat you as I always have."

"But it means Regina will be scorned," Daffin insisted. "She won't be allowed at Society events."

Grimaldi rolled his eyes. "She doesn't attend them now. She deserves to be with someone she truly loves. You're a good man, Oakleaf. You make Regina happy. That's all that matters to me and, most importantly, it's all that matters to Regina."

Daffin glanced around at the others again. Surely they would help him make Grim see reason. "She won't be accepted into fine households. She'll be treated as an outcast."

"Nonsense. I'm a marquess, and you'll both be quite welcome in my house," Grimaldi said.

"And I'm a viscount," Rafe added, "and you're welcome in mine."

"I'm merely a lowly knight, but you're welcome in mine," Cade said.

"I'm a duke, and you're welcome in mine," Hobbs said, with a resolute nod.

Daffin stared at all of them. "Truly?"

The men nodded their agreement.

Daffin gulped. Did he really have a chance to win back Regina? "Do you think Regina feels the same way? What if her feelings have changed?"

Grimaldi groaned. "Her feelings haven't changed. She's been moping around the house like a lovesick fool. She adores you."

Daffin took a last, fortifying swig of ale. "There's one thing I haven't told you yet."

"What's that?" Grim looked positively bored.

"Your uncle refused me already," Daffin said, feeling smug this time. "I asked for her hand and he refused me. He told me Lady Harriet felt the same."

"Yes, well, there's one thing *I* haven't told *you* yet." Grim looked similarly smug.

"What's that?" Daffin asked.

"Lady Harriet and Nicole have been berating Uncle Edward all morning for allowing you to get away, and he's more than given his assent. Especially after Regina laid into him."

"Really?" Daffin asked, looking at his friends in awe. His heart pounded in his chest, while joy unfurled in his middle.

"Yes, really," Grim replied. "Now get up, leave here, and go do the right thing by asking my cousin to marry you, damn it!"

Pulling his hat from the table and clapping it on his head, Daffin leaped from his chair and raced for the door.

The other men glanced around at each other, raised their mugs, and clinked them together, trading smiles and laughs.

"Another success," Rafe shouted, lifting his mug high in the air.

Thomas Hobbs shook his head. "You chaps always know the right thing to say. Why is that?"

"I suppose it's because we've got a great deal of experience between us," Grimaldi replied.

"I'm glad to hear it," Hobbs said, "for I shall need your help when the time comes for me to take a wife."

"Why's that?" Cade asked, clapping the younger man on the back.

Hobbs shook his head. "The girl I want to marry one day is entirely convinced we're nothing more than best friends."

"Not to worry," Grimaldi replied. "When the time comes, we can *definitely* help you with that."

# CHAPTER FORTY-SEVEN

Daffin sped toward the park, trying his damnedest not to skid on the snow and ice. He'd just come from Grimaldi's town house, where he'd been informed by a smiling Lady Harriet that Regina and Nicole had taken their maids and gone to the park to build a snowwoman.

Daffin was rounding a curve in a footpath when he came upon Regina and Nicole and a fully formed snowwoman. The maids lingered nearby.

He skidded to a stop. "Regina!"

The two ladies swiveled to face him. Nicole's face wore a bright smile. Regina's eyes flared, a range of emotions playing across her pretty face.

"May I . . ." He cleared his throat and started again. "May I have a moment of your time?"

"We'll, just . . . see you at home," Nicole said, ushering the maids ahead of her down the snowy path toward the town house.

When she and Daffin were alone, Regina turned back to the snowwoman to place black licorice above the eyes. "What are you doing here, Daffin?"

"I've come to give you something," he replied, doing his best to sound casual while his heart was dancing a jig. "And to ask you a question."

She paused in her work.

Daffin took his time, strolling slowly around the back of the snowwoman and peeking his face around the side of its head.

She eyed him carefully, the hint of a smile popping to her lips.

He strolled out from behind her creation and stood facing Regina. "Happy Birthday, Regina." He pulled a small green velvet box from his coat pocket and presented it to her.

"What's that?" she asked, glancing at the box.

"A gift. For you. Open it and find out."

She tossed the rest of the licorice into the snow, grabbed the box, and flipped it open to reveal a large oval sapphire ring set amidst smaller diamonds.

Daffin lowered himself to one knee, crunching through the snow on the ground.

"You'll get your breeches wet," she warned, tears in her eyes.

"I don't care."

"It's gorgeous," she said, covering her mouth with her mitten.

"It reminded me of your eyes," he said. "Say yes?"

"You want to marry me?" she breathed.

"I do." Daffin jumped to his feet and wrapped his gloved hands over her shoulders. "If you'll have me, that is."

She nodded tearily. "But why, why do you want to marry me?"

"For the best reason," he continued.

"What's that?" The tears rolled in quick succession down her cheeks.

He lifted her chin with one finger. "Because I cannot live without you."

She dashed away the tears with her mitten.

"I can only hope you feel the same about me," Daffin continued.

"I do." She nodded, cradling the ring box to her chest. "I will marry you. I don't care about your past. I'm only sorry you had to go through all of that. But if you hadn't I wouldn't have you here to love, to be my husband."

Daffin pulled her into his arms. "I don't deserve you, Regina, but I promise I'll spend the rest of my life trying to make you happy."

"I will be, Daffin. As long as I'm with you." She gave him a tearful smile.

He returned her smile. "Will you be happy married to a Bow Street Runner?"

"I'll be nothing but proud." She cupped his face between her mittened hands. "I don't want you to stop being a runner. I don't think I'll ever stop worrying about you, but someone needs to chase down the bad people out there, people like the Duchess of Portland and Quinton Knowles. You're a gifted investigator, Daffin. The streets of London need you."

Daffin picked her up and spun her in his arms. "I love you, Regina Haversham, with all my heart."

"And I love you, Daffin Oakleaf, with all of mine."

He set her down and they strolled back toward Grimaldi's town house, arm in arm.

Daffin gave a sudden laugh. "You know what?" he asked, kicking his boots through the fresh snow.

"What?" Regina leaned down to roll a ball of snow between her mittens.

"For the first time since I was a child, I'm actually looking forward to Christmas next year."

"I'm glad to hear it." She tossed the snowball away, stood on her tiptoes, and wrapped her arms around his neck. "Because I adore Christmas and every Christmas from now on will be even better because we're together. Now kiss me."

Thank you for reading *Kiss Me at Christmas*.
For some reason I'm still not sure of, this book
was one of the most difficult I've ever written,
but now that it's written, I have to say
I've fallen in love with Regina and Daffin's story,
and I hope you have, too.

I'd love to keep in touch.

- Visit my website for information about upcoming books,
  excerpts, and to sign up for my email newsletter: www
  .ValerieBowmanBooks.com or at www
  .ValerieBowmanBooks.com/subscribe.
- Join me on Facebook: http://Facebook.com
  /ValerieBowmanAuthor.
- Follow me on Twitter at @ValerieGBowman, https://
  twitter.com/ValerieGBowman.
- Reviews help other readers find books. I appreciate all
  reviews whether positive or negative. Thank you so much
  for considering it!

*Coming soon. . .*

Don't miss the next novel of
delightful noble romance by

# VALERIE BOWMAN

## No Other Duke But You

*Available in May 2019
from St. Martin's Paperbacks*